Slices of Life

**Center Point
Large Print**

**This Large Print Book carries the
Seal of Approval of N.A.V.H.**

Slices of Life

Judy Baer

CENTER POINT PUBLISHING
THORNDIKE, MAINE

This Center Point Large Print edition
is published in the year 2008 by arrangement with
GuidepostsBooks.

The text of this Large Print edition is unabridged. In other
aspects, this book may vary from the original edition.
Printed in the United States of America.
Set in 16-point Times New Roman type.

ISBN: 978-1-60285-153-5

Library of Congress Cataloging-in-Publication Data

Baer, Judy.
    Slices of life / Judy Baer.--Center Point large print ed.
      p. cm.
    ISBN 978-1-60285-153-5 (lib. bdg. : alk. paper)
    1. Class reunions--Fiction. 2. Bed and breakfast accommodations--Fiction.
    3. City and town life--Fiction. 4. Pennsylvania--Fiction. 5. Sisters--Fiction. 6. Large type books
    7. Domestic fiction. I. Title.

PS3552.A33S58 2008
813'.54--dc22

2007049873

🍇 Acknowledgments

For Jennifer and Jay Abrahamson—I love you guys!
—Judy Baer

Chapter 🍇 One

Life's tragedy is that we get old
too soon and wise too late.
—Benjamin Franklin

"Hi Clarissa, what do you have for me today?"
The screen door banged shut behind Jane
Howard as she entered the Good Apple Bakery.
Clarissa Cottrell's best marketing tool was to open her
bakery door wide and allow the delicious aromas to
escape through the screen door into the street. Her
customers, led by their noses, could rarely resist stopping in for muffins, cookies or doughnuts.

Jane paused in front of the display case and felt her
mouth water.

"How many guests do you have up there at Grace
Chapel Inn?" Clarissa asked. "My yeast doughnuts are
mighty good today, but there are only five left."

"I never worry about the number of guests, you
know that. Everything I buy here gets eaten by
someone." Jane patted her flat belly. "Usually me."

"Wouldn't know it to look at you."

Neither, Jane thought, would anyone think that
Clarissa ever tasted her own wares. She was tall and
very thin. She worked off any of her products that she
might have had time to eat.

"Seems to me you need some fattening up. How
about a chocolate éclair with lots of filling and a

nice big glass of milk?" Clarissa offered.

Jane remembered her sister Louise's telling stories about Clarissa's parents, from whom she had inherited the bakery. They had done the same thing for Louise when she was a child. The Cottrells knew that once someone got even a bite of their baked goods, she would be back for more.

Jane chuckled to herself. So many people wanted to fatten her up since she had returned to Acorn Hill from California. If she let them, the friendly people of Acorn Hill, Pennsylvania, would have her weighing three hundred pounds.

"I'll take the biscotti, some of each kind, lemon, chocolate . . ."

"I'll give you all I've got then. That makes a dozen." Clarissa grabbed a sheet of thin white paper from the box on the counter and started filling a white paper bag printed with the bakery's slogan: "If You Love It, We Baked It at the Good Apple." Clarissa counted aloud to fourteen.

"That's more than a baker's dozen," Jane reminded her. "You're giving away your product. Is that good for business?"

"You come back, don't you?"

"Every day."

"There you go, then." Clarissa handed Jane the bag and winked. "I'll put it on your tab. I expect Louise to be in any day to pay your bill."

"You're a lifesaver, Clarissa." Jane sat down on one of the spindly wrought iron chairs by a matching table. Clarissa always said that she did not want people to get too comfortable and linger too long at the bakery; the Coffee Shop was for that kind of business. Her policy paid off when the Coffee Shop became her very best customer. The shop made its own pies, but every slice of bread, every muffin, cookie and doughnut served there was baked at the Good Apple. Symbiosis was how much of Acorn Hill worked and thrived.

"You've made my work at the inn so much easier." Jane bit into the éclair that Clarissa insisted she have and delighted in its vanilla flavor. "Since your breads, sweet rolls and scones are without equal, I can concentrate on making the specialties I use for our teas and for the guests' breakfasts."

"And to tinker with those candies of yours," Clarissa added. "How is Madeleine and Daughters faring these days?" Madeleine and Daughters was Jane's brainchild, a small candy company that used only Jane's recipes and those of her mother.

"Since I partnered with Exquisite Chocolatiers in Philadelphia, life has been much easier. They're producing my signature chocolates, marketing them as 'Pennsylvania's own' and are doing quite well with the tourist trade. I'm proprietary about my recipes, but I must say, they do them as well or better than I."

"That's saying a lot," Clarissa said. Jane's culinary expertise was well known in the area, and her occasional afternoon teas at the inn often had waiting lists.

"They're keeping me busy, always wanting more

imaginative candies. They import their chocolate from Belgium and have distributors all over the nation. 'The Best of the Best' is their motto, and I believe it's true. I've been working on a new recipe that uses coconut milk, macadamia nuts and an essence of ginger, a 'tropical treat' of some sort. The candy has been a nice boost to our income, which, as you can imagine, we always welcome."

"Like pouring money down the drain," Clarissa said obliquely, referring to Jane's rambling Victorian home. "Too bad the upkeep on these big old houses is so expensive, but I'm grateful you and your sisters decided to convert your family home into an inn. It's a landmark here in Acorn Hill." Then Clarissa chuckled. "Doesn't hurt my pocketbook either."

The wrinkles that marked Clarissa's features as she laughed were a shock to Jane, who rarely paid attention to age. *How had Clarissa managed to grow so old-looking without my noticing?*

Before Jane had time to consider the question, the screen door burst open and two people hurried into the room. They were Jane's Aunt Ethel and Ethel's friend Lloyd Tynan. Lloyd's trademark bow tie was askew, and his thinning hair looked almost messy. These were true signs of agitation, for the mayor of Acorn Hill was never unpolished or undignified.

Ethel was trembling from head to toe. In her maroon, polyester pantsuit and dyed-red hair, she reminded Jane of a quivering bowl of plum jelly.

"Now, Honey Bunch," Lloyd clucked, "don't

believe everything you hear. There's lots of gossip going around about the big reunion, and we don't know that any of it is true."

Honey Bunch? Jane almost laughed but caught herself in time. Lloyd must really be in a pickle with Ethel to call her "Honey Bunch."

Jane's aunt lived in the small carriage house next to Grace Chapel Inn. She had been there since her husband Bob Buckley had passed away some years before. Always a bit of a busybody, Ethel often meddled in the affairs of the inn—if she was not riled up about something else going on in Acorn Hill, that is.

Lloyd, the mayor and Ethel's "beau," was nearly as excitable as Ethel was, and the two of them in concert were like rubbing matchsticks together. It was inevitable that some sparks would fly.

Ever since Daniel Howard, Ethel's brother and pastor of Grace Chapel, had invited her to live next door, Ethel had "adopted" the Howard girls as her maternal project. It was no wonder, Jane thought sometimes, that the three Buckley cousins always thanked them for "taking over Mom." Being mothered by Ethel must have been a full-time job for her children. Neither Jane nor her sisters really minded Ethel's involvement in their affairs. After all, she was a loving aunt, and her late husband, a man of great faith, had been very close to their parents. Until she and Lloyd became friends, Ethel must have been terribly lonely. She did, of course, have a good friend in Clara Horn, but since adopting a potbellied pig, Clara had been involved in her own form of nurturing and motherhood.

Today's uproar was, apparently, about the upcoming all-school reunion scheduled to take place in less than two weeks. Several small towns, including Acorn Hill, had agreed to join with Potterston in a countywide gathering that was, according to the excited residents, "the best thing that's happened since Ben Franklin flew that kite."

"What's the matter?" Jane asked. "You two don't look very happy."

"We were just over in Potterston to pick up the reunion book that was printed for the Acorn Hill graduates and heard in the café that . . ." Ethel jumped, a reaction to Lloyd's gently poking her with his elbow. He made a policy to be loyal to Acorn Hill businesses and never liked to be caught being unfaithful—even by drinking a cup of coffee on what Lloyd considered foreign territory.

"We just stopped for a cup of coffee, no food or anything, if you don't count that piece of pie we shared," he explained.

"And my, oh my, what inferior pie they have over there," Ethel commented. "Why, between the Coffee Shop and the Good Apple and, of course you, Jane, our people can outbake their people any day."

"With one hand tied behind our backs," Jane said, winking at Clarissa. Then she directed her aunt back on course. "And?"

"It seems that Orlando's Restaurant in Potterston

has the sole contract to serve food for the reunion. They presented a bid to the planners without being asked, and everyone assumed that no one else would *consider* trying to take on a big job like that, so they gave it to them. Why this wasn't common knowledge until now is beyond me."

In other words, Ethel felt left out of the loop. She had determined long ago that it was necessary for her to know everything that happened in Acorn Hill *as* it happened.

"And I hear the owner isn't even from Pennsylvania but somewhere in the Southwest. Why, they'll probably try to serve us tacos or something else foreign. Disgraceful." She turned to Jane. "Can't you *do* something?"

"Me?" Even Jane, who was familiar with Ethel's convoluted thinking, was surprised.

"You're Sylvia Songer's closest friend, and she's on the reunion committee. Why can't you do the catering?"

"For one thing, I haven't been asked. For another, I don't have a staff or the kind of kitchen it would require. And finally, Orlando's will do a fine job. It's too late anyway. There simply aren't that many days until the reunion begins."

"Where's your civic pride, Jane? Acorn Hill needs to put its best foot forward, and you are definitely one of those feet." Ethel grabbed Lloyd and managed to turn him toward the door. "We need to talk to Sylvia about this. Come, Lloyd, don't dally."

Jane and Clarissa stared at each other for a long moment before bursting into simultaneous laughter.

"Hoo, hoo, hoo," Clarissa chortled. "One of Acorn Hill's best feet."

"I've been called a lot of things," Jane said, wiping her eyes, "but that was the zaniest yet."

"That Ethel is on a real mission this time." Clarissa had known Ethel for years, and even she had been taken aback. "I had no idea she felt so strongly about our part in the reunion. I suppose Lloyd has been fanning the flames of civic pride."

"Well, forewarned is forearmed," Jane said philosophically. "Now this 'best foot' must go home and get some work done." She picked up the bag of biscotti.

Clarissa wiped her hands on her apron. "See you tomorrow?"

"Of course. I glanced at the reservation book before I left, and we have two new guests coming in."

"You're one of the reasons I keep on with this bakery, you know." Clarissa's face wrinkled once again as she smiled, her eyes bright. "I'd miss all the wonderful people who pass through these doors, and you most of all."

Jane walked around the counter and gave Clarissa a hug. "And I'd miss you, but I'm counting on your being here for a long time. You're an institution in this town. Don't you forget it."

As Jane went out the door, Clarissa shook her head sadly as she thought that even institutions have to close someday.

Jane's walk back to the inn was interrupted by a steady stream of Acorn Hill neighbors. She met Jose Morales on the corner across from Fred's Hardware. Joe, as he preferred to be called, was pushing a wheelbarrow full of yard tools, clippers, hand trowels, a hand rake and an assortment of products for fighting weeds, bugs and crabgrass.

"Off to work, I see."

Joe beamed at her. "*Sí*. I'm going to work in Ms. Reed's yard. Mr. Humbert is letting me take all these things from the hardware store, and I will pay him back when I earn the money from my yard jobs," Joe explained. Sunlight glinted off his black hair, and his teeth flashed white in his nut-brown face.

Joe had built up Fred Humbert's rental service for the mowers and snow blowers by offering his own services to run them. Fred now had a waiting list for rentals of his machines. Symbiosis again.

"How is the decorating progressing in your apartment?" Jane asked.

Joe lived in a tiny apartment that Fred had prepared for him above the hardware store. Joe had gone to Jane the week before to ask for help in making it seem homier.

"I've painted," he said proudly. "I like the colors you suggested. I like the red best." A perplexed expression flitted across his features. "But I don't know what to do next."

"I'll tell you what, Joe, I'll paint a picture for your wall. We'll find a few baskets and some dried flowers and a new bedspread and you'll have the coziest place in town."

"I must pay you. . . ."

"It's my gift, Joe." Then she saw the consternation on his face. Joe was proud, and tried to have obligations to no one. "Well, if you must pay me, then just come over and help me out at the inn some time."

"I could do that." Joe's head nodded in agreement. "Are you having any more teas?"

Since Jane had opened the inn for occasional afternoon teas, she called upon the town gardener to be a waiter at least three times a month. He had been working on his English while Jane brushed up on her Spanish, and they made an effective team when there were a dozen ladies waiting to be served in the parlor.

"Stop over and we'll look at the schedule. I'm sure I've got work for you and Justine and Josie as well." As she spoke, the subjects of her conversation appeared out of the door of the pharmacy across the street from them.

"Jane!" Josie cried, jumping up and down and waving both arms. "It's me!"

As if the adorable little girl could be missed.

Mother and daughter walked across the street hand-in-hand. Josie danced on tiptoe like the eight-year-old ballerina that she was. Both mother and daughter had masses of blond curls and eyes blue as cornflowers. "I got a candy bar. See?" She held it up. "Mr. Ned gave it to me."

"Tsk, tsk," Jane said in mock concern. "He's going

to run Chuck Parker's store out of business if he keeps giving away the merchandise."

Ned Arnold was the fill-in pharmacist who spent a good part of every month running the store so that the Parkers, who were reaching their retirement years, could travel. A handsome fellow, with prematurely gray hair, Ned stayed at the inn when he was in town and had practically become a part of the family. Often, he took his meals in the kitchen with Jane, Louise and Alice when no other guests were booked. They had even quit counting him when they referred to the number of guests they had.

"He put money in the till," Josie informed her. "He treated me."

"That was very nice." Jane knelt down and gave Josie a hug. They had become friends months before when Jane noticed Josie, in old skimpy clothes, riding a rickety bicycle in the Grace Chapel parking lot. Since then, Jane had often provided extra work opportunities at the inn for Josie's mother, a struggling single mom. Justine had proved to be a capable waitress for the inn's teas.

Jane's next encounter was with Viola Reed. Around sixty and heavy-set, Viola always made a fashion statement with her penchant for bright colors and dramatic scarves. Today she wore a vivid blue tunic and a scarf of red, yellow and green wrapped around her neck. Viola was among Louise's best friends. They shared a passionate love of books and learning. As the owner of the Nine Lives Bookstore, Viola took it as a personal affront if someone did not like to read.

"Your aunt's book on lowering cholesterol came in," Viola said. She peered into Jane's eyes. "Do you think it's for her? She hasn't mentioned having high cholesterol to me. I do know a few things about the subject, since it runs in my family. Or could it be for Lloyd. They've both put on a few pounds since you opened the inn. . . ."

"Aunt Ethel and Lloyd are in town somewhere. I saw them not long ago in the bakery. They were in a dither about the reunion."

"Well, the bakery is certainly the wrong place for someone with high cholesterol." Viola suddenly looked fierce. "This whole reunion thing is getting completely out of hand. I don't see why we couldn't have handled our reunion by ourselves. I just got a call from a bookstore in Potterston. They want to set up a booth and display popular books from the forties, fifties, sixties and so on. They have the idea that everyone will want to reminisce. They think that if we offer a selection of the most popular books of each decade, we could sell quite a few."

Jane thought it sounded like a great idea, but was wise enough not to say it aloud. She already knew what had set Viola on her high horse, the single word *popular.* It was Viola's theory—and she therefore felt it should be shared by everyone else in Acorn Hill—that good literature and popular literature were not necessarily the same. Good literature could be redeeming, yes. Educational, enlightening and edifying, certainly. Uplifting and informative, of course. But *popular?* Did that not imply frivolity? For Viola, popular fiction was defined as facile, inane, simplistic prose meant purely to entertain. Viola thought people entertained themselves much too much as it was. To rectify the situation, she had been giving readings at her store of the writings of authors on her approved list—most of them long dead.

"It would be a wonderful way to let others know about your shop," Jane pointed out. "Great advertising."

"It would be sinking rather low, don't you think?"

"Not everyone views the written word the same way, Viola. Look at Hope."

Viola snorted. Her eye twitched a little with the tic that always seemed to appear at the mention of Hope Collins' name. Hope, an avid reader, had said that she would buy all her books on-line if Viola did not bring in new releases and best sellers. She had even threatened to have June Carter, the owner, sell books at the Coffee Shop. Jane figured that Hope had doubled Viola's business, even if Viola insisted on displaying those "simplistic" books on all the lower shelves in the store.

"Think of it as a service to the people of our communities," Jane suggested, knowing Viola's soft spot. "I know how much you care about our community."

"When you put it that way . . ." Viola gave a gusty sigh and started off again, frowning. It was always perplexing to her when someone made a good argument for having an opinion opposed to her own.

Jane took the mail from the box at the end of the driveway and sauntered toward her nineteenth-century Victorian home. Though she had viewed its exterior countless times since its renovation, she never failed to be pleased by its appearance. The cocoa-colored exterior, highlighted with eggplant, green and creamy white, was striking. The house restoration had turned out better than she had imagined, and the place truly spoke "welcome" to its guests.

Wendell, the inn's house cat now that his former owner, Rev. Daniel Howard, had passed on, sat sphinx-like on the top step. A gray tabby with coal-black stripes, white paws and a black-tipped tail, Wendell still assumed that the house was his property and that he was allowing these interlopers to stay only because they had been feeding him rather well. Sometimes Jane had the uncomfortable feeling that the cat was right.

It had not been easy making the transition from the Blue Fish Grille in San Francisco to her childhood home and to living with her two older, still occasion-ally bossy, sisters. Alice, a nurse at the Potterston hos-pital, was kind and caring. Louise, a widow, was also good-hearted but her staid demeanor often made her seem aloof. A pianist, Louise was always in demand to teach students and to play for events. One of the biggest thrills for Louise these days was playing back-ground music for the inn's teas.

Jane sat on the top step and scratched Wendell's

head until he rumbled an appreciative purr. "Hey, big guy, what's going on inside? Have our guests left yet?"

He yawned and plopped onto his side for a belly rub.

The screen door opened and Ted and Millie Larken stepped onto the porch. They were carrying suitcases, and Millie had a sun hat anchored on her graying hair. Jane jumped to her feet. "Leaving already? You don't have to check out until noon, you know."

"I'm afraid we have to go, though both of us wish we could stay right here for another week. This is the sweetest, most relaxing place we've ever visited." Millie put down her luggage to adjust her hat.

"I'll agree with my wife," Ted, a retired executive from a large Philadelphia bank, added. "We've already made reservations for another visit next summer."

"Good. Then we don't have to say good-bye," Jane said with a smile. "Just see you later."

"What's this about a big reunion that's about to happen? I suppose Grace Chapel Inn will be busy then."

"It's the first time anyone has ever tried this sort of thing. There are a number of small towns like Acorn Hill in the county. This will enable all of us to share the same celebration. There will be class reunions, music, meals and entertainment."

"What a charming idea. In fact, everything about this place is charming." Then Millie frowned. "Except for that crabby man in the room next to ours."

"Mr. Enrich is certainly interesting," Jane said.

Jane had quickly discovered that people who passed through their doors were all fascinating in their own ways. Sometimes it took a little longer to dig through the outer shell of a person to find the kernel of good inside, but it was always worth it. Some had, of course, considerably harder shells than others.

"Before we leave, I have to tell you how attractive your clothes are." Millie eyed Jane's hand-painted, oversized T-shirt and leggings.

"Thanks. I decided to doctor up these things to make them a little more interesting." She turned her ankle so Millie could see the little cat whose tail roped around the bottom of one leg. "It's fun."

"It's talent," Millie corrected. "You should be selling things in boutiques. Have you considered it?"

Jane had, but had not found the time to pursue it. Being chef at the inn was a full-time job, and her painting and her jewelry design were on hold until after the reunion.

"I took a few of your cards," Millie continued. "I plan to tell my friends about you."

As Jane waved good-bye to the couple, it occurred to her that if every inn guest took a few cards—those for the inn itself, for Madeleine and Daughters candy and for her jewelry and art—and distributed them, she might be able to advertise under Ethel and Lloyd's radar.

Acorn Hill was a perfect small town with its quaint shops, picturesque churches and friendly people.

Lloyd, and therefore Ethel, wanted to keep it just that way. His campaign slogan and the motto by which Lloyd performed his duty as mayor was: "Acorn Hill has a life of its own away from the outside world, and that's the way we like it."

At first, Lloyd had worried that the inn might bring too much change to Acorn Hill but had come to realize that it brought even more charm to the town. It was just fine with Lloyd that the inn existed—he had eaten enough meals there with Ethel to pack on fifteen extra pounds—but he still did not want an influx of visitors ruining the ambiance of the town.

Jane reminded herself to order more business cards and brochures before the reunion.

Both Louise and Alice had gone off somewhere and the house was quiet. Over the year, her sisters had also become her good friends. Jane could not imagine not having them to consult, chat and laugh with every day. Still, Jane relished going into the library, sitting there alone among her father's books and feeling his spirit. She and Daniel had always shared a love of the Psalms, and it was in the library where they had had their theological discussions.

There was no time for reminiscences today, Jane reminded herself. She had dinner to fix for herself and her sisters. She slipped into an ankle-length apron she had sewn and wrapped it around her waist. Regular aprons were little protection from flour dust and splattering stains. She thought of her creation as a raincoat that protected her from food showers. After putting a pot of potatoes on to boil and starting a pan of eggs in cold water so that they wouldn't crack, she took a knife from the cupboard and marched down the back steps and into the garden with her eye on the huge-leafed rhubarb with its succulent red stalks growing there.

Rhubarb always reminded Jane of her mother Madeleine, whose recipe book was full of rhubarb recipes. It was through the personality-packed anno-tated pages of the recipe book that Jane had come to know her mother better.

Jane was dicing rhubarb, cooling the potatoes and preparing to shell boiled eggs when Sylvia Songer rapped on the back door and walked in.

"If I cooked as much as you do, I'd weigh a ton," Sylvia said. She went to the cupboard for two glasses, took them to the table and then removed the peach iced tea from the refrigerator.

"It's a good thing you're the seamstress and I'm the cook, then." Jane scraped the red crescents from the cutting board to a bowl and began rapping boiled eggs on the side of the sink to crack and peel them. She always worked on at least two projects at a time. "My pleasure comes from making food, not eating it. Speaking of food, how's the reunion progressing?"

Sylvia groaned, leaned forward and buried her face in her hands so that all Jane could see was the top of her head with its soft red hair. "Tell me again why I'm on this committee."

"You were trapped into it, if I remember, because of

your creativity and organizational abilities. Serves you right for being so unerringly capable." Jane rinsed the eggs, put them in another bowl and joined Sylvia at the table. "What's up now?"

"Something I thought we had under control until Ethel and Lloyd paid me a visit today. They believe that we shouldn't have accepted the first proposal we got for catering. Lloyd and Ethel think it was unfair not to give everyone an opportunity to bid."

"Pay no attention. With the reunion so near, there's nothing you can do about it now. Besides, they're so thrilled with the entire event that they'll be on to something else by tomorrow."

"The trouble is, I think they're right."

Jane's eyebrows raised practically into her hairline. "No kidding?"

"Orlando's is making noises about the job being too large for the amount of money they bid, which is, of course, their own doing. I think they've realized that with the influx of people for the reunion, they're going to be swamped at the restaurant itself and are trying to squirm out of some responsibility."

"They should have thought of that a little earlier." Jane had done plenty of catering and knew the enormous amount of work it could involve. "But they can't squirm far in only a few days."

"I'm blaming the inexperience of the new manager," Sylvia murmured. "Otherwise I'd feel like strangling him." She looked up hopefully. "Do you have any ideas?"

"Sylvia, there's no time left."

"Just pretend there is time, Jane," Sylvia pleaded.

"How much money do you have to work with if you relieve Orlando's from some of the responsibility? That usually tells the tale."

"If I find out, will you brainstorm with me?"

"With what little brain I have left."

Chapter 🍇 Two

Contentment makes poor men rich;
discontentment makes rich men poor.
—Benjamin Franklin

I'll need vitamins if I'm going to be in charge of a car wash!" Alice said as she entered the kitchen. Obviously agitated, she stopped short when she saw that they had a visitor. "Oh, hello, Sylvia."

"Hello, yourself."

Alice dropped into the chair. "I should have my head examined—and offer Pastor Kenneth the same service. Whatever made us think the reunion would be a good time for the ANGELs to earn money for their charity projects and the youth group's mission trip?"

"Because it's the perfect opportunity," Jane said. "There'll be more people in Acorn Hill during the reunion than there will be for the rest of the year. *That's* why you thought this would be a good time to have a fundraiser."

"Having a fundraiser is fine, but we should never

have let the *kids* pick the event. At least we should have told them to choose something tidy. All that water is going to make a mess."

"I have to admit that the committee was surprised at the choice," Sylvia said, adding with a smile, "but we decided that it would be clean fun."

Alice moaned at the joke. "There's only one redeeming thing about this car wash," she said, her voice muffled as she held her head in her hands. "The younger kids love the idea of it, and they love working with the high-schoolers. They'll do anything to make it happen."

"Everything will work out beautifully," Sylvia said. "The kids are also planning to sell caramel apples and lemonade, and they're bound to have a big success."

"Call me vain," Alice said, "but I'd hoped that when I saw my old friends and classmates, I'd be doing something a little more laudable than wearing a rain slicker and running a car wash."

"I think you look very fetching in your slicker," said Jane.

"Thank you. I feel *so* much better," said Alice with a rare touch of sarcasm in her voice.

Sylvia studied Jane across the table. "And how do you feel about the reunion, now that it's practically here?"

Jane and Alice exchanged a telling glance. "Mostly I'm excited," Jane said.

"Just 'mostly'?"

"Jane had an unpleasant experience in high school

with one of her classmates." Alice said. She paused and the others remained silent. "You know that our mother died when Jane was born."

Sylvia nodded.

"Regrettably, our father decided not to tell Jane all the circumstances of her birth when she was growing up. Our mother had complications during childbirth and didn't live long after. He felt that there was no need to connect sadness with the joy we felt at having a new baby in the family. Mother would have wanted it that way—or, at least, that's what he thought."

Jane took up the story. "I never asked too many questions about that time and never connected Mother's death with my own birth."

Sylvia waited.

Finally, Alice spoke again. "Shirley Taylor was always an odd girl. More than once one of Jane's friends commented on how jealous she was of Jane. We all chalked it up to immaturity."

"Then Shirley took it upon herself to tell me the circumstances of my birth and my mother's death. I suppose she'd heard it from her own parents."

Sylvia leaned forward. "How nasty!"

Jane looked down at her hands. "I could barely fathom it—if I hadn't been born, my mother might have still been alive. I was devastated."

"We had no idea how hurt Jane would be. Father later grieved over his choice not to tell her, but it was how he'd decided to handle it and he couldn't go back." Alice murmured.

"It would have been easier if I'd known from the time I was a child," Jane admitted. "Hearing the story that way for the first time was heartbreaking. It wasn't until I came back to Acorn Hill and helped my sisters open the inn that I was really able to put it in perspective." She smiled faintly.

"It was the cookbook," Alice said. Her eyes glowed. "The one with the truffle recipes in it."

"It was so full of Mother's handwritten thoughts, comments and ideas, that it was as if she came to life right before my eyes."

"And she gave you a gift, didn't she, Jane? Madeleine and Daughters, I mean," Sylvia said.

"So, so many gifts."

"And Shirley Taylor?" Sylvia asked. "Whatever happened to her?"

"I have no idea. I haven't thought of her in years."

"Of whom?" Louise said as she entered the kitchen, a stack of sheet music under one arm. She took the fourth chair and sighed with relief. "I thought I would never get done choosing music today. Pastor Kenneth wants everything to be especially familiar and welcoming with all the visitors we will be having." She poured herself a glass of tea and took a sip.

"Now, about whom were you talking when I came in?"

"Shirley Taylor."

Louise looked as if the name rang no bell with her. Then recognition showed on her face. "Oh, you have been looking at the reservation book. We have a

Shirley Taylor staying here during the reunion. The name sounded so familiar, but I could not place it."

The room grew so silent that they could hear Wendell snoring on the windowsill.

"There are a dozen or more Taylor families in this county. . . ." Louise paused and looked at Alice, then at Jane. "*That* Shirley Taylor? But why would she make reservations here, of all places?" Louise appeared stricken. "I am so sorry. I would never have taken her reservation if I had known who she was."

"It may not be the same person," Jane said soothingly. "And if it is, then it's time to air and settle what's hung between us all these years. We were just kids—young, thoughtless kids."

God has a way of working things out, Jane knew. She did not really want to see her again, but if *the* Shirley Taylor were coming to stay at the inn, then Jane had no doubt that He had had a hand in the reservation.

Late the next morning, Alice came up behind Jane and put her arm around her sister's shoulders. "What are you so busy with today?"

Jane leaned back in the chair and pushed a box of stationery aside to make room for Alice as she sat down. "Catching up on some letter writing. Trent Vescio, my old employer from the Blue Fish Grille, has written to me twice. I thought it was time to respond."

Alice peered at the quotation Jane had scrawled on the bottom of the page.

"Hide not your talents. They for use were made. What's a sundial in the shade?"

—Ben Franklin

"You and your love of Ben Franklin go back a long way," Alice observed.

"Did you know that his autobiography is considered by some to be the first really great work of American literature?"

"No."

"Or that as a teenager he was a troublemaker who thought he was ten times smarter than his parents?"

"No."

"And he *was!* It was true. Think of trying to raise a child like that."

"I had enough trouble raising you, and you aren't more than four or fives times smarter than I am."

"Very funny, Alice." Jane grinned at her sister.

Alice smiled and stood. "I'd better go upstairs and write a few things down myself. I'm so afraid I'll forget to do something over the busy weekend." She peered out the window. "Besides, I think you have company coming up the walk."

"Can Jane come out and play?" A childish voice piped the question to Louise, who was sweeping the porch.

Jane peeked out the window to see Louise stop sweeping and rest her arm on top of the broom. As usual, Louise was dressed in what her sisters called her "uniform," another variation on her trademark skirt and sweater combination. Her signature lace handkerchief peeked out of one pocket. Louise, who loved discipline and order, never made the radical clothing statements that Jane enjoyed. Louise could seem stern even though her heart was soft. Today Josie made a smile tweak the corners of her lips.

"Jane? Well, I don't know. She might not have all her chores done yet."

Josie's small shoulders drooped. "Oh." Then she perked up again. "I got my chores done really fast today. Maybe I could help her."

"What a generous offer," Louise said, smiling. They had all grown to love Josie, who, after meeting Jane, had promptly adopted all the sisters as her surrogate family. Jane often took Josie with her when she escaped to Fairy Pond to sketch. With Sylvia's help, she was also teaching Josie to sew buttons back onto her own clothes and had promised that someday they would work together on a quilt for Josie's doll. Alice had once taken Josie to an ANGELs meeting, and she had been adopted promptly as the group's mascot. Josie, with her tangle of blonde curls and cornflower eyes, was easy to love.

Jane came to the door. "Did I hear an offer of help out here?"

"Me! Me!" Josie danced on her toes.

"Okay, but it's something very difficult."

"I don't care. I'm big."

"You'll have to help me finish my grocery list and help me shop."

"That's not hard." Josie opened the screen door. "That's fun."

"I'm glad somebody thinks so," Jane murmured to Louise.

"You just have to do it too often," Louise commented. "Maybe one day you can train Josie to do it for you."

"Not a bad thought," Jane said. "Not bad at all."

Later Josie and Jane strolled the aisles of the General Store looking for the items on Jane's list. Rustic as it was, the store provided Jane with most of what she needed. She especially liked their produce from local farms.

Josie pushed her own miniature cart, which the store provided to entertain shoppers' children, while Jane filled her big one.

"Bananas. And apples and oranges, I think."

"Bread?" Josie stopped in front of the case. "And cookies?"

"We'll get that at Clarissa's. Why don't you find me some dishwasher soap?"

As Josie scampered off, Vera Humbert turned her cart down the aisle toward Jane. "You have a helper today, I see."

"If she were a little bigger, she'd be my right-hand girl," Jane said with a laugh. "Now she can't reach groceries on the top shelves." She eyed Vera's cart, which was piled high with everything from lasagna noodles and butter to cereal boxes and frozen vegetables. "Looks like you have plenty of cooking to do."

"I never realized we had so many relatives—especially who graduated from high school somewhere in this county. They're all coming back for a visit and expect to stay—and eat—at our house. I'm trying to get food prepared and in the freezer so I can have a break too. Fred is already threatening to put cots in the attic and basement for the overflow. You don't have any more space at the inn, do you?"

"Not unless Alice, Louise and I sleep in the same bed, which might stretch the sisterhood thing too far."

Vera laughed and nodded. "The reunion will be fun, though, won't it?" She turned so that Jane could see her sideways. "Do I look thin to you?"

"You've definitely lost a few pounds."

"Good." Vera's eyes twinkled. "Fred's old girlfriend is coming to the reunion, and I don't want him to think that he picked the wrong woman."

"No danger of that."

"I dug out a miniskirt for me and a polyester leisure suit for him. I thought we could dress up for our class social. Fortunately Fred said that he wouldn't wear the suit, so I didn't have to admit that my mini would only fit around one of my thighs." Vera shook her head. "I'd forgotten what a little thing I was." Vera was all wound up in the reunion mode. "Do you remember Bill Paige and Betty Loomis? They got married right out of high school. You know the ones—Acorn Hill's only flower children. They're coming back and I'm dying to see them now. Do you think they still have ponytails or do you think they've turned into corporate CEOs?"

"We'll know soon."

"If only poor Sylvia and Joseph Holzmann get the food problem straightened out." Vera clucked like a mother hen.

" 'Food problem?' "

"Didn't you hear? Just this morning Orlando's Restaurant in Potterston asked that the committee find some other place else to cater the class breakfasts and afternoon teas in Acorn Hill. They decided they'd taken on too much." Vera sighed. "We just aren't accustomed to the kind of crowds that this event promises." She looked sideways at Jane. "But you are."

Jane held up a hand. "I'm hoping no one remembers that. It would be nice to go to something and be on the eating end once in a while." No wonder Sylvia had been asking her for ideas. She must have suspected that this would happen.

"I'm sure, but people know what a treasure you are. It's likely that your name will come up."

Vera was one of Jane's best customers at the inn; her teachers' group held teas there regularly. Jane had also begun to create new pieces of jewelry with them in mind because they loved her bright, eccentric pins and bracelets. The last time they had come, Jane had painted and framed some miniatures, mostly of local birds and wildlife. Every one of them had sold. It felt good to Jane to be selling her art again—and having time to pursue it.

Vera eyed her cart and sighed. "I suppose I'd better get a move on. I still have to red-up the house today."

"Red-up" was Vera's quaint way of saying ready up the house for company.

Jane and Josie drove home with the groceries and put them away. Then Jane held out her hand to Josie. "Want to come to the Good Apple with me now? It's a nice day for a walk."

Josie's eyes glowed. "Yes. It smells really good in there."

When they arrived, Clarissa was sitting on a stool behind the counter. She had a cup of coffee and a cookie in front of her. Wearing a flowered house dress, white socks and nurse's shoes, with her hair tied back from her face and hidden under a hairnet, Clarissa did not seem the least bit surprised to see Jane and Josie. They were often a pair on the streets of Acorn Hill.

Jane went around to the back of the counter and helped herself to a cup of coffee as she often did when Clarissa was rolling cookie dough or frosting a cake and did not want to stop.

"Have a peanut butter cookie too." Clarissa waved in the direction of the display case. "I outdid myself this time, if I do say so myself." Then she looked at Josie, who was eyeing the brownies in the display case. "And I suppose you'd like one of those."

Josie's eyes were round as saucers when Clarissa put two fat brownies in a bag and handed them to her. "Why don't you take one of those home to your mother and eat the other yourself?"

They both laughed as Josie threw her arms around

Clarissa and then around Jane babbling thanks before she darted out the door toward home.

Then Jane dropped into the seat across from her old friend. "Taking a break, I see."

"It's that lull between my morning shoppers and three o'clock when everyone begins to realize they're out of bread or buns or need a dessert for dinner."

"And then you'll go home, fall into bed exhausted, get up at three tomorrow morning and start all over again," Jane added.

"Pretty much." Clarissa took a sip of her coffee. "I appreciate talking to you, Jane. At least you understand how hard it is to be in the food business."

Clarissa put her cup down and absentmindedly rubbed her hip, something Jane had never noticed her doing before.

"Is it getting harder to stand on your feet?" Jane inquired gently, remembering all the thick-soled shoes and rubber mats she had used during her own years in the restaurant kitchen.

Her thin face looking drawn, Clarissa smiled ruefully. "You caught me. My bones are creakier by the day, and I'm not sleeping as well as I used to, but you know me, I love this place. The Good Apple is all I've ever known. My parents had it before me. My husband and I raised our family while working at the bakery. My children played in the big yard out back where we kept a swing set and a sand box. What would I do without it?"

"The Good Apple isn't going anywhere, and you've

told me yourself that business is the best it's ever been."

Clarissa's expression flickered with unexpected sadness and a hint of confusion.

"True, my dear, but though I hate to admit it, *I'm* the one who's not quite what she used to be. But if I weren't baking for the Good Apple, I'd just perish. I don't even have a hobby other than baking."

"Oh, Clarissa, I know it's hard to believe, but you are so much more than just the bakery. Though the business has been a part of you for what seems like forever, it's not your identity."

Clarissa considered that for a moment before asking with amusement, "Then who am I?"

"Mother of three. A much loved grandmother—I've seen photos of those children hanging onto your hands like they never wanted to let go. Churchwoman. Community supporter. Pillar of the community." Jane stretched her hand across the table and put it over Clarissa's. "Friend."

Then Jane's voice softened. "I'm saying things to you that at one time I didn't believe about myself. There was a time when I forgot I was anything more than chief cook and bottle-washer. I know how it is to totally identify with work. I put so much of myself into mine that it became 'me.'"

A grin spread across Jane's face as she continued. "For a moment there, I was giving you the lecture that I always hated to hear from everyone who thought I was too focused and working too hard. But I have found there's much more to life than my work." She rolled her eyes. "God had to drag me all the way back to Acorn Hill to discover that." She waggled a finger at Clarissa. "Who knows what wonderful thing He has in store for you?"

"Thanks for understanding," Clarissa said softly. "My family thinks I'm being a silly old woman about it. I'm glad someone knows what I mean."

On the way back to the inn, Jane noticed their guest, Mr. Enrich, leaving the Nine Lives Bookstore. The man had a way of looking unapproachable and gloomy no matter what he was doing. When he walked, he hovered near the buildings, as if he were trying to make himself unnoticeable.

Instead of turning north on Chapel Road, Jane impulsively crossed the street and walked toward Nine Lives herself. The store always reminded her of an old English shop with its large baskets of flowers and swinging sign. She had often wondered why Viola had not named the shop something Dickensian in honor of one of her favorite authors, but clearly Viola had preferred to dedicate it to her feline friends.

Viola Reed was behind the counter talking on the telephone. She waved a welcome but was obviously engrossed in placing an order. Jane found Rev. Kenneth Thompson crouched on the floor in the back corner of the store where Viola kept her popular fiction and best sellers. Engaged in a losing battle with the readers of Acorn Hill to get them to "enlighten" their minds with "fine" literature, her desperate tactic of hiding "modern" books in the back corner had only made that the most popular part of the store.

"What are you doing back here?" Jane said, hunkering down beside the pastor. "Don't you know this is as close as Viola gets to having to an X-rated section in her store?"

"Just think, if Viola *wanted* people to buy these books, she'd only sell a few. By boosting the curiosity factor, she's got them flying off the shelves." He gestured toward the shelves. "People want to read for themselves what's so scandalous."

They looked at Viola's "shocking" titles, which included everything from *New York Times* best sellers and a coffee-table book of contemporary artists to a dictionary of slang.

The pastor stood with a groan. "There's going to come a day, however, when I'll scrunch down there to read the titles and won't be able to stand up again." He looked at Jane and smiled. They had become good friends since he arrived in Acorn Hill shortly after Jane's return home and he took over the pulpit that Jane's father had once filled.

"By the way, I'm glad you came in," he added. "I wanted to give you a 'heads up' about the reunion."

"I'm not really involved," Jane said. "That's Sylvia's department. I'm just the innkeeper."

"You did hear that Orlando's in Potterston thinks it—pardon the restaurant pun—bit off a little more than it can chew?"

"Yes . . ." Jane said cautiously.

"And that your aunt and the mayor have offered to solve the problem by involving you?"

"Oh no, they won't," Jane said firmly, recalling her promise to help Sylvia brainstorm. Thinking and cooking were two entirely different activities, and those lovable but irritating busybodies had not even consulted her. "Neither of them has any idea about what they're asking. I don't have a facility big enough to prepare large volumes of food. I have no staff, unless you count Alice and Louise, who are busy with the reunion themselves. They'll just have to find another solution to their problem."

"Uh huh," Rev. Thompson said in doubtful agreement.

When Jane arrived at the inn, all was quiet. She picked up Wendell, who was sleeping in a porch chair, scratched him under the chin, and carried him into the house. The sleepy cat was heavy and relaxed in her arms and a purr rumbled from deep within his chest. Jane buried her nose in his soft fur and thought she could smell a hint of Alice's perfume there. This was not a neglected animal, Jane thought with a smile as she carried him into the parlor and curled up with him in a big chair. Wendell yawned widely, burrowed into Jane's lap and promptly fell asleep again.

She picked up the Bible from the table next to her chair and began to skim its pages. She almost always settled on the Psalms. Her father had loved poetry and had quoted it occasionally, and often it had been the poetry of the Psalms. She had always treasured the fervor of the Psalms and the honesty of those who had written them. The verses dealt with the depths of despair, the pinnacles of praise. She read in Psalm 150:6,

"Let everything that has breath praise the Lord. Praise the Lord."

With Wendell heavy against her legs and the parlor warm with sunlight, she began to read aloud from Psalm 111.

"Praise the Lord.
I will extol the Lord with all my heart
in the council of the upright and in the assembly.
Great are the works of the Lord;
they are pondered by all who delight in them.
Glorious and majestic are his deeds,
and his righteousness endures forever.
He has caused his wonders to be remembered;
the Lord is gracious and compassionate.
He provides food for those who fear him. . . ."

"Then it would be smart for us to be fearful right now," a voice suddenly interrupted her.

Both Jane and Wendell jumped. Neither had heard Sylvia come into the inn or step into the parlor.

"You startled us," Jane protested mildly. Wendell

gave Sylvia a slit-eyed glare and went back to sleep.

"Sorry. I knocked and called but you didn't answer. I could hear you talking in here so I knew you were home. I just couldn't get your attention. I see why now."

"Have a seat. Do you want some iced tea or lemonade?"

"Nothing for me." Sylvia sank into a cushiony chair. "And what did you mean, 'It would be smart for us to be fearful'?"

"So you haven't heard about our catering upset," Sylvia said. "What I worried would happen, has."

"Oh, I get it. 'He provides food . . .'" Jane laughed.

"Looks like He'll have to. Orlando's certainly won't. They have asked us to find another vendor to serve the breakfasts. It appears they want someone to take over and do everything they don't want to do."

"I've been looking for someone like that myself," Jane said.

"If I live through this reunion, remind me never, ever, to volunteer for anything again. If I do, stop me, and if you can't stop me, have me committed. We'd drop Orlando's completely, but we need them. It's too late to find anyone else now. This reunion is a logistical nightmare."

Sylvia paused and took a breath before asking, "Is there *any* chance that you would consider saving my sanity by taking over the rest of the catering?"

"Sure. Right after I perform my own appendectomy on the kitchen table." Jane snorted at the ridiculousness of the idea. "We are only days from this thing starting, Sylvia. You don't want me, you want a miracle worker."

"You tell me one person who is better suited. You've run huge kitchens."

"Will everyone be happy with cereal and milk for breakfast?"

"Come on, Jane, consider it. We're desperate here."

"No way. Besides, I'm planning to enjoy the reunion myself."

"How can you enjoy it when you know that people are missing meals, that I'm having a nervous breakdown and that the entire committee will be humiliated?" Sylvia pleaded.

"It will be hard, but I'll manage," Jane responded cheerfully. She stood up and put the limp Wendell in her seat. "What I *will* do is make you a nice cup of tea."

"Ja-a-ane . . ." Sylvia almost wailed as she followed Jane into the kitchen.

"Look at the size of this room, Sylvia. It's nowhere near big enough to do what needs to be done for the reunion. I can't cook for the masses in here."

"Maybe someone could help you? A group effort?"

"I'm not sure you can find enough crazy people in Acorn Hill to make a group like that. Unless . . ."

Sylvia's head shot up. "Yes?"

"Oh, never mind." Jane gave a dismissive wave of her hand. "Just a silly idea."

"All ideas are welcome, Jane. Even the silly ones." Sylvia gave her a pleading look. "Please?"

"The only way I could see it happening is if I sub-contracted the food. The Good Apple is the only place that can bake in that kind of volume, but we could have a buffet breakfast of sweet rolls, muffins, bagels, pecan sticky buns and the like. Fruit bowls, fresh juices and yogurt—things that don't have to be cooked on the spot. We're serving out of tents after all."

Sylvia kept her mouth closed as Jane spun off into the topic she liked best.

"In the afternoon, a pie social would go over well. If June Carter and Hope Collins at the Coffee Shop would agree to make pies and prepare the fruit for breakfast, then Wilhelm Wood from Time for Tea could set up a tea buffet. The General Store could be in charge of ice cream for the à la mode and the town's church ladies could serve coffee and . . ."

"So you'll organize it then? We'll pay you well. We have more people registered than expected, and we would be generous to anyone who helped us out in our time of need."

"Wait just a . . ."

"I'll assemble the church ladies myself," Sylvia interrupted. "Pastor Ken can help me. It will be perfect. No one has had more experience serving food than church ladies have. We'll have the tables up and ready, and we'll do anything you ask. Just get us out of this mess."

Jane groaned inwardly, knowing full well what she was getting into. "Oh, all right."

I've lost my mind, Jane thought. *Well, perhaps for the next few days I'm better off without it.*

"Thank you, thank you, thank you." Sylvia flung her arms around Jane. "Now I can sleep tonight."

"You'll be able to," Jane said, "but I won't."

"You agreed to do *what?*" Louise asked over the dinner table.

"You don't have to say a word," Jane assured her sister with a smile. "Alice has already offered to take me somewhere to have my head examined. It won't be that difficult. I've already spoken to Wilhelm and June. Both are more than willing to pitch in. So is the General Store. The only one I haven't talked to yet is Clarissa. Pastor Ken called about a half hour ago and says the presidents of every church ladies group in town are working to gather helpers. He says it won't be a problem."

"I am amazed," Louise murmured. "Just when people will be so busy with their own families, they are willing to take this on. There are some remarkable people in Acorn Hill, that is all I can say."

"I'm not surprised," Alice said. "I think Acorn Hill was feeling a little overlooked in this entire reunion. You know how upset Lloyd and Ethel were at the thought that some of the catering business wasn't coming our way. Besides, it will be good income for the businesses that take part."

"I suppose, when you put it that way." Louise still did not look completely convinced. "Jane, you will be awfully busy. You do need to take care of yourself." Louise blushed slightly. "Am I sounding like I am your mother again?"

Jane reached for another piece of apricot walnut bread. "I know you care, but you don't have to worry. It's what I've done for years, Louise. It might be fun to get right out there and mix with people. I'm actually—and don't you dare tell Sylvia this—rather enjoying the idea." Then she frowned.

"What's wrong?" Alice asked, noticing immediately.

"The only one I'm worried about is Clarissa. We may have to keep the baked goods menu very simple."

"Nonsense," Louise proclaimed. "Clarissa can bake rings around anyone in Potterston."

"True, but she's not as young as she used to be."

"None of us is." Louise eyed Jane. "Except, perhaps, you."

"Is there a problem with Clarissa?" Alice asked.

"She's tired, that's all." Jane could picture Clarissa absently rubbing her hip when they had visited. "I wish she had some help. Bakery hours wear a person out."

"Could she train someone to step in occasionally?" Alice asked. Then she responded to her own question by saying, "But who?"

Chapter 🍇 Three

Wise men don't need advice.
Fools won't take it.
—Benjamin Franklin

The three sisters sat in the library after dinner. Soft lamplight filled the room, and a bowl of potpourri gave off a delicate lavender scent. Louise was working on the intricate piece of needlework that she planned to give to her daughter Cynthia for Christmas. Alice was sorting through a pile of magazines and papers, and Jane was paging through a biography of Benjamin Franklin.

Jane never tired of reading about Franklin. She had already laughed out loud several times at Ben's sage advice. She particularly liked, "If a man empties his purse into his head, no man can take it away from him. An investment in knowledge always pays the best interest."

Wendell, who was curled into a tight ball on a pillow on the floor, opened one eye each time she chuckled, as if to ask what this human was up to now.

Ben Franklin was a model of industriousness, and every time Jane thought about all that he had managed to accomplish in a lifetime, she felt that she could accomplish more on her own. She put down the book. There must be things to do that she had been over-looking. "Alice, are we caught up on everything for the reunion?"

"I doubt it, but I can't think of a thing we've missed. Louise, what do you think?"

Louise pondered the question. "I cannot think of anything right now. If we have missed something, then we will deal with it."

Jane glanced at the small clock on the bookshelf. "Our new guests are late checking in."

"Yes, and Mr. Enrich hasn't returned yet. That's odd." Alice's brow furrowed.

"We are not his keepers, Alice," Louise pointed out gently.

"I realize that, but there's something about him. . . ."

"You mean that he's the crabbiest guest we've ever had?" Jane asked. "That a smile or a 'thank you' might kill him?"

"That is not gracious," Louise said.

"Oh, Louie," Jane teased her sister with the nickname only she dared use. "Don't try to kid me. I saw you bite your lip when he told you the bed linens were 'rough.' "

"Well, I do try to keep the Egyptian cotton on the guest beds. We were so busy the night before that I used our ordinary sheets. I never dreamed anyone would notice." Louise was unaccustomed to being criticized.

"He told me he expected telephones and televisions in the rooms, and an Internet hook-up," Alice added. "Didn't he read the brochure I sent him?"

Jane chuckled. "He told me white chocolate and cranberries had no business being in scones. He suggested that if I found a good bagel shop, I could stop trying so hard."

"No!" Alice looked horrified.

"Don't worry about it, Alice, I've got a tough skin where finicky eaters are concerned. I'm good at what I do. If someone complains, I always chalk it up to differing tastes, not a personal affront. Besides, despite all his complaints, he keeps hanging around."

Mr. Enrich had initially planned to stay one night as he traveled through Acorn Hill. Then it became two, then three, and now this was his fourth night at the inn.

"He must not have a fixed schedule," Louise observed. "I thought he would have checked out by now."

"I did tell him that we had an open room until just before the reunion," Alice said. "Ned told me today he'd be going home very soon because the Parkers want him to come back and fill in at the pharmacy during the reunion so they can enjoy the event. The Parkers knew we'd be busy, so Ned will stay with them for those nights."

"Remember what we told ourselves when we were planning our purpose for the inn," Jane said. "We would welcome people with open arms and unconditional love. Just enough Martha and a lot of Mary," she said with a smile, referring to her favorite biblical hostesses.

"Jane's right," Alice concluded. "It's just harder to get your arms around some people than others. I've been compelled to pray for Mr. Enrich ever since he arrived."

"And I."

"Me too."

Louise and Jane had spoken at the same time. They stared at each other, startled.

"Well, this changes everything," Alice said.

"Indeed," Louise intoned.

Jane could not agree more.

"If God has all three of us praying for Mr. Enrich, then he is here for a reason," Louise said. "We must also pray that we are the tools that God needs."

"I think of all the people who passed the poor man who was robbed and lay beaten on the road from Jerusalem to Jericho," Alice said. "The thieves who beat him and left him for dead, the priest and the Levite who moved to the other side of the road. Even the innkeeper only tended him because he was being paid."

"But the Samaritan had the heart and the attitude of Christ, and he cared for him," Jane added.

They were all silent, thinking of the commitment they had made when they had opened the inn, but the quiet was soon shattered by the slam of the screen door, announcing that Mr. Enrich had arrived. The women glanced at each other.

"I'll go," Jane offered. "I heard him mention a couple days ago that his favorite pie was apple, so I made one today. We can treat him and have something to welcome our new guests too." Jane's custom of providing late-arriving guests with a hospitable dessert was one of the most appreciated niceties that the inn offered. It was a chance for them to sit down, meet the other guests and relax a bit while one of the sisters—usually Alice—checked them into the inn.

"Mr. Enrich?" Jane came upon the man in the hall and was startled by his appearance. His dark hair was disheveled and he looked haggard and drawn, as if he had aged since morning.

His brown eyes darted toward her, hostility in his expression. "What?"

She felt a stab of fear. Of him? No. It was fear *for* him. He seemed desperate. It was as though he were a drowning man and she had the means to rescue him.

"I . . . ah . . ." She was not even sure that she should continue after seeing that look in his eyes, but she could not seem to stop herself. "I baked you an apple pie. Would you like a slice? With vanilla ice cream?"

He paused as he processed her invitation. "You did? Made me a pie?"

"Yes. You said you liked apple best. We have two new guests coming in later, but why don't you join me and my sisters in the kitchen. We could have ours now."

He looked as though the invitation baffled him. Though he took a quick glance up the stairs toward his room, his gaze finally settled on Jane. "That would be . . . nice."

"Good. Do you like it heated? One scoop of ice cream or two?"

They gathered to eat around the big kitchen table. Alice brewed tea while Louise took napkins and cups from the cupboard. Mr. Enrich observed their busyness as though they were aliens.

When he took a taste of the pie, his eyes opened a little wider. "This is good."

"Thanks. I'd hoped it would be," Jane said serenely.

He said very little as they ate, but he did not have to. Louise regaled them with a story about one of her piano students that day, a young boy who had come with a note he claimed was from his mother, a college professor. Louise took the note from her pocket and passed it around. It read, "Randy couldn't practis this week cause he had the flew."

They all laughed at the work of the professor's "ghost writer."

Then Alice began talking about the book she had begun reading. It was about God's gifts and how much each individual has been given. She turned in her chair. "What do you think your special blessings are, Mr. Enrich?"

He started in his chair. "Me? Uh . . . maybe you're asking the wrong person. I've never been very religious. God's never done very much for me."

"Really." Jane put her elbows on the table and her palms beneath her chin. "How do you know?"

"Because, well . . . just look at me."

"You look perfectly fine to us," Louise said.

"Handsome, even," Jane said. Even as she said it she wondered why those particular words had slipped out of her mouth.

"You don't know me," he protested, but he did not sound angry or put out. "There are lots of things I've wanted, and none of them happened."

Three curious pairs of eyes stared at him, and he felt compelled to continue. "I wanted a wife and a family," he stammered, "but my wife left me and took our son. I rarely see him any more. Now that he's a teenager, he doesn't want to hang around with his dull old dad. I wanted my own business and that went belly-up a year ago. Does any of this sound like God's been working for me?" His laugh was bitter. "I don't think so."

"So God's been ignoring you?" Jane asked.

"Sure seems like it. If He exists at all, that is."

Alice's eyes grew moist. "He exists, all right. We all know Him personally."

His eyes narrowed. "Yeah, right . . . whatever."

"Don't let us make you uncomfortable Mr. Enrich. It's just that each of us has had the experience of God's generosity." Jane smiled a little. "And He didn't give me what I thought I wanted either."

At his doubtful expression, she continued. "I wanted a marriage that worked, a successful, well-known restaurant, money, a taste of fame . . ." She spread out a hand and gestured to the expanse of the room. "And here I am, in the house I grew up in, in a little town in Pennsylvania that very few people have even heard of—and happier than I've been in years."

"I don't get it."

"Neither did I. I still don't, sometimes. It's amazing how God can turn a life around and make something mundane or unremarkable into a gift."

"Why are you telling me this?" His eyes narrowed and he scowled.

"I have no idea," Jane admitted cheerfully. "My mouth seems to be in gear without my brain tonight. More pie?"

He begged off, but not before thanking her for the dessert. He then excused himself and retreated to his room.

The kitchen was quiet for a long time after he had left.

The doorbell rang just after Louise had threatened to give up on the new guests and go to bed. Jane never minded staying up for late-arriving guests because, years before, she had grown to like the late hours that she had kept at the restaurant. Of course, now no one let her sleep late the next morning. Alice, who was equally accustomed to unpredictable hours as a nurse, was also flexible.

"Just in time," Alice said as Jane jumped up to get the door.

Two faces were peering through the screen door when Jane entered the hall. "Welcome," she said to Nancy and Zack Colwin as she opened the screen door to let them enter.

Jane suspected they were older than they looked. At

least, she hoped that was true because the pair looked all of nineteen years old. The woman had thick, black hair that fell to mid-back, a ruddy complexion, rosy cheeks and a big smile that revealed slightly overlapping front teeth. She was robust and altogether pleasant looking.

Her husband was very thin. He wore khakis and a white-and-blue striped shirt. His light brown hair was cut in a boyish style and his smile was even wider than his wife's.

"Sorry we're late," said Nancy. "We took more time than we'd planned looking at restaurants in little towns along the way. We had no idea how many there are out here."

"Looking for something to eat?" Jane inquired, thinking of her pie.

"Not that, although we did have an excellent blue-plate special at a place called Henrietta's Diner somewhere. Do you remember the name of the town, Zack?"

"Not a clue." He looked around the foyer and peered up the stairway to the second floor. "This is a great place."

"Thank you." Jane gestured toward the dining room. "We have pie for a bedtime snack if you wish. You can eat while Alice is checking you in. Or if you aren't hungry . . ."

"I'm always hungry," Zack said, enthusiastically rubbing his flat stomach.

"You'd never know it to look at him," Nancy grumbled cheerfully. "The thing I envy most about my husband is his efficient metabolism. He burns off calories sitting still."

Louise, yawning behind her ever-present white hankie, introduced herself before going off to bed. After registering the new pair, Alice settled them at the dining-room table and gave them some tips about the inn and Acorn Hill while Jane dished up pie and ice cream in the kitchen.

"This is the best pie I've ever had," Zack said enthusiastically. He looked up from his plate before taking another bite. "Believe me, that's saying quite a lot."

"Zack's a sweets freak," Nancy explained. "Some people have a sweet tooth. Zack has an entire set of them. It's a good thing he does what he does for a living."

"And what's that?" Alice asked politely.

"He's a cook, baker, chef, whatever. Just an all around 'food guy.' "

"Really?" Jane sat straighter in her chair. "Tell us more."

"Nancy and I have been working for a lunch and supper place that is open from eleven in the morning to eleven at night. It's been good work and good pay, but it was recently sold. The new owners closed the place for two weeks to remodel and gave us vacation time. So Nancy and I have been driving around, looking at scenery and scouting out restaurants."

"Our favorite pastime," Nancy chimed in.

"Some people like movies and popcorn, you just like restaurants," Jane said. "It makes perfect sense to me."

"Someday Zack and I would like to have our own restaurant," Nancy said. She glanced warily at Zack before continuing. "But we have a few details yet to iron out. We can't seem to agree on exactly what we want."

"Not really," Zack corrected his wife. "I think we're sure of the direction we're going."

Nancy stiffened. "Maybe you are sure, Zack, but I'm not."

A slight tension seemed to dance in the air until Zack stood up and said, "We have lots of time to relax and discuss it here, Nancy. Are you ready to go upstairs?"

After she had said good night to the Colwins, Jane loaded their dishes into the dishwasher and set it on delay so that it would start after everyone had fallen asleep. She absently brushed a tiny crumb from the counter and turned out all but a small night-light in the dining room. She always left that on for late-night snackers who sometimes raided the cookie jar.

So, Nancy and Zack wanted to buy a restaurant—if they could settle on a single vision. Jane wished she could help them or give them some direction. Perhaps she could put them in touch with her old boss, Trent Vescio at the Blue Fish Grille. Maybe he could give them some ideas. But this was not California, and it was not easy to make restaurants succeed.

"Morning, Jane," Fred Humbert greeted her as she entered the hardware store. "What's new with you on this fine day?"

"Same old, same old," Jane replied. "I ran into Vera and she told me your daughters Polly and Jean are coming home."

"For the school reunion. Just like everyone else who's ever passed through the doors of Acorn Hill's school. Vera is beginning to panic. She doesn't know where'll she put all the company. I told Joe just this morning that if it got much worse, I'd have to rent out his room and let him sleep in the basement." Fred looked up. "Didn't I, Joe?"

"Sì." Joe, his dark eyes sparkling, nodded in agreement. "And we could put a mattress on the floor too. We wouldn't have to charge so much for it."

"You've made him into a regular entrepreneur, Fred," Jane said as Joe grinned and returned to his work, loading bins with various sized nails.

"He's done it himself." Fred's eyes glowed with gratitude. "I don't know how many times I've silently thanked you for introducing me to Joe. I thought I was helping him by giving him a room and a job, but he's given me much more. Business has never been better since he started his lawn and snow removal services out of this place. People are so happy with his work that they come in and walk out with more bags of peat, fertilizer and weed killer than ever before. One day I had two ladies in here arguing over whose house Joe should go to first."

Jane looked at Joe, who had modestly hung his head. "Good for you, Joe."

When he looked up to shake his head, there were tears in his eyes. "Not me. You, Miss Jane, Mr. Humbert—and especially God."

Jane did not have any doubt of that. She and Joe had met under such unlikely circumstances—he had become caught in her rosebushes—that only God could have made their friendship happen. They had all been blessed by it ever since.

"But back to business," Fred said. "What can I get for you?"

"Just one of those special picture hangers for plaster walls."

"I'll get it, Miss Jane." Joe smiled happily, and for some odd reason Mr. Enrich popped into Jane's mind. Why couldn't everyone be happy and smiling like Joe? Mr. Enrich was often as surly and irritable as Joe was sunny.

After making her purchase and saying her good-byes, Jane left the hardware store and headed for the Good Apple where she found Mayor Tynan and her aunt Ethel seated on iron chairs on either side of a small table. From the powdered sugar on Lloyd's tie, Jane deduced that he had had doughnuts with his coffee. Ethel, who had been claiming lately to be watching her figure, had remnants of a blueberry Danish on her plate. Apparently she was, in fact, only "watching" her figure, not doing anything about it.

"Come sit down," Ethel invited, "and tell us what you've been up to."

Tell us the latest gossip, Jane translated mentally. Out loud, she said, "Thanks, but I just came in to visit with Clarissa. . . ."

"She's out back. Someone came to pick up a huge order of buns and cookies for the Methodists. They must be having something special this evening."

Jane was surprised that her aunt did not know exactly what was going on, what time it started and who would attend. Were Ethel's information-gathering skills slipping?

"I thought you knew," Lloyd said. "Big meeting with Potterston Methodists tonight. They're kicking off a new fund-raising campaign for missions. I'm going to pledge something myself."

"By the way, Aunt Ethel, are any of my Buckley cousins coming for the reunion?"

Ethel looked crestfallen for a moment but rallied immediately. "No, I'm sad to say. None of them has any vacation time left at work, but they all plan to visit Acorn Hill as soon as their jobs allow." She beamed. "We're thinking about a little family reunion. You girls, of course, will be the first to know. My place is so small that I'm sure that they'll all want to stay with you at the inn."

"Naturally," Jane said, sighing inwardly. *Another party where I'll be in charge of meals.*

"Ethel's not feeling too bad about it though," Lloyd said proudly. "You're taking it rather well, aren't you?"

"I will get to see them," Ethel said logically. "And there will be so much happening now that I'd hate to miss . . . be tied down . . . *er,* not be available to help wherever I'm needed."

The truth had come out. Ethel was relieved that she would not miss a thing at the reunion.

"Any new guests at the inn?" she asked, eyes bright. A good share of Ethel's home entertainment was observing the activity at the inn, which for her was like a separate channel on her television. She was always tuned in to what was happening next door.

"A young couple checked in last night. We didn't visit much, but I'll bet you'll see them around today." Jane was careful not to divulge too much information about her guests lest Ethel take it and run with it—all over town.

"That's it?" Ethel was obviously disappointed.

"Believe it or not," Jane said, amused, "life at the inn isn't a laugh a minute or excitement all the time. I did experiment with a few recipes for tea cookies and made a pie yesterday. Oh, and I spent part of the afternoon sketching at Fairy Pond." The little pond tucked far off Chapel Road into a lush grove of trees was one of Jane's favorite retreats.

"*Harrumph.* I've always thought that was a silly name for a pond," Ethel said. "What were people thinking? That fairies actually lived there?"

"Maybe she's seen one, Ethel. It's a pretty magical place," Lloyd said.

Jane smiled. Fairy Pond had charmed Lloyd too. It

62

was a delightful, serene place, surrounded by a canopy of trees, vines and delicate ferns. Even the deer seemed tamer and the birds less timid around Fairy Pond. There she had done some of her best creative work—sketches and jewelry designs that took on the lacy, delicate feel of the place.

"Tsk, tsk," Ethel clucked disapprovingly.

There was nothing of the dreamer in Ethel.

Jane and Lloyd exchanged an amused glance. It was not often that the conservative mayor and the exotic resident artist of Acorn Hill shared the same imaginings.

Ethel dusted a bit of sugar off her bosom and looked at her watch. Jane noticed with some satisfaction that her aunt was giving up on her. Too boring.

Feeling a little sorry for being so dull, Jane offered, "I was in the attic yesterday and found something interesting."

Ethel's upright posture became even more erect. " 'Found something'? What did you find?"

"A box of old toys. I haven't had the time to look through them."

"I remember your mother showing me some of her childhood toys. There was a mechanical bank—cast iron as I remember—and some china-headed dolls, tops, things like that." Ethel's expression grew distant. "The toys you found were probably your mother's. Daniel was never given anything 'frivolous' as a child. I fared better because our father had mellowed by the time I came along." Ethel shook her head slowly. "You might think that Daniel would have resented me and the better treatment that I got, but he was such a wonderful brother. So kind." Ethel used her napkin to dab at her eyes, leaving a smudge of powdered sugar on the bridge of her nose.

Jane reached over and gently flicked the sugar away.

Daniel and Ethel were actually half-siblings, but Ethel had always looked up to him and loved him so dearly that rarely did anyone remember that they had had different mothers.

"I'll bet he took good care of you, didn't he, Ethel?" Lloyd asked.

"Oh my, yes." Then she launched into a long memory of how Daniel would send her little gifts when he was away at college or studying for the ministry. Then she segued into a story about a bag of marbles, a girl with long golden curls, hopscotch and a purloined lunch.

Knowing that this recitation would take some time to wind down, Jane patted her aunt's hand. "I want to hear the story sometime, but I need to talk to Clarissa. Would you excuse me?"

"Run along, dear. We'll come for dinner one night next week, and I'll tell all three of you girls the whole story."

Jane was not sure she had made much of a bargain. Now she would not only have to listen to one of Ethel's rambling stories, but she would also have to cook dinner for Ethel and Lloyd.

"Hello, Jane. I didn't hear you come in," Clarissa said. She looked tired.

"Were you lifting and carrying things you shouldn't have been?"

Clarissa chuckled. "You mean like coarse, heavy buns and cookies hard as rocks? Why, Jane, you know my baking is always light as a feather."

"You should take it easy, that's all."

"Now you sound like my children. They're always saying, 'Take it easy, Mom. Don't work so hard.' *Harrumph*. As if they don't know that my work sent them to college."

"I'm sure they appreciate your work, Clarissa, but maybe they just think you should slow down a little."

Furrows formed across Clarissa's brow. "If I slow down, I may stop. And if I stop, I'm done for."

"Whatever do you mean?"

"Oh, it's Arthur. He's been giving me some trouble lately."

Jane searched her memory banks for someone named Arthur and could not think of anyone in Acorn Hill.

Clarissa laughed at the expression on Jane's face. "You don't know about Arthur? Arthritis. *Arthur-itis*. Get it?"

"You caught me that time," Jane admitted. "That joke is so old that I forgot all about it."

"I'm old, it's old, but you didn't come in to hear my antiquated jokes, now, did you?"

"I actually did have a purpose for stopping by. I wanted to talk business with you."

Clarissa did not respond, but waved at Lloyd and

Ethel, who were making their way to the door. When they had gone, Clarissa looked at the empty display case. "I'll just close up shop first. I'm already eaten out of house and home." As she moved to lock the door and pull down the shade that indicated to the town that she had run out of baked goods for the day, Clarissa spoke over her shoulder to Jane. "I hate to admit it, but I like to close up before the end of the day once in a while. I'm glad when I've misjudged the product I need and run out early on." Then she returned to the counter and filled two cups with the last of the coffee. "Cream or sugar?"

"This is fine."

Clarissa bent under the counter and came up with an old-fashioned cake plate holding two cinnamon scones. She smiled impishly. "And look what I found just for an occasion such as this."

"Who were you saving those for, Clarissa? Surely not me." Still, Jane helped herself to one of the luscious beauties when Clarissa offered it.

"I usually keep something back for myself at the end of the day. I'd be round as a ball if I didn't limit myself to just one sample a day. And I always save two, hoping my last customer will have a few minutes to visit."

"Then I'm very lucky this afternoon," Jane concluded.

"No luckier than me." Clarissa sank into a chair with a sigh. "Ah, that's better."

Jane eyed Clarissa's feet. The woman wore white,

lace-up, support shoes, the kind Alice wore for work. Jane could only imagine how many hours a day Clarissa was on her feet. And she could not be younger than seventy-four or -five. No wonder she was tired.

"Maybe this isn't the best time to ask what I've come to ask," Jane ventured. "Why don't I come back tomorrow, when you've rested up?"

"Don't try wiggling out of it," said Clarissa, wagging a finger at Jane. "Now you've tickled my curiosity. What's that inventive mind of yours hatching now?"

Jane's heart sank. Clarissa's eyes were tired behind her smile, she had flour and cocoa powder up and down the front of her apron, and a wisp of gray hair had escaped her hairnet.

Oh well, Jane thought. *Say it anyway.* "You know all the hubbub about the reunion, and how we talked about the catering being too much for a restaurant not set up for events this large?"

Clarissa nodded suspiciously.

"Well, it's come to this. Orlando's has bowed out of catering the breakfasts in Acorn Hill, and the committee has asked me to cater them and the afternoon socials."

"So late in the game? The reunion is practically upon us." Clarissa whistled under her breath. "Better you than me."

"That's the challenge, Clarissa, it won't happen unless it's me *and* you." Jane hurried on before

67

Clarissa could say no. "I don't have the equipment to cater. The only way we can provide for the reunion guests now is if everyone pitches in. The Coffee Shop is willing to make pies, Wilhelm's Time for Tea will be offering afternoon tea, and church ladies from around town will be serving coffee. I can't even name everyone who's volunteered to help out. But the only one who has the skill and capacity to do the baked goods is you."

Clarissa's eyes lit for a brief moment, then faded. "I'd love to, Jane, but the Good Apple will keep me busy enough. I've already started getting orders from townspeople who are having a gaggle of relatives staying with them. There's no way I can do it. I'm only one woman."

"What if you were two or three people?" Jane asked.

Clarissa chuckled. "Then I could do about anything. But I have enough trouble just keeping someone here to help in front while I'm baking. Catering an event the size of this reunion? I don't think so."

Jane's shoulders sank. She knew Clarissa was right. She also knew that she was fresh out of ideas for making it work any other way. Lloyd had suggested they have everything made in Acorn Hill so, as he put it, "we can strut our stuff." Pride, the downfall of nations. Maybe it just was not meant to be. Jane dreaded breaking the news to Lloyd and Ethel.

She put her hand on Clarissa's. "I understand, but if any miracles occur back there in the bakery and somehow you can manage it, let me know."

"I'd love to, Jane, you know that, but it would have to be a miracle."

"Then I guess I'll start praying that the right thing happens—whatever it might be. I can be content with that." Wanting to change the subject, Jane went on, "Is Olivia coming home for the reunion?"

Olivia, usually called Livvy, was Clarissa's oldest daughter, a dark-haired beauty who had recently become the superintendent of a large school in Oregon. She was smart, organized and used to taking the helm. Louise often talked about what a good example Livvy must make for her students. Livvy was a loving but formidable person, much, Jane had heard, like Clarissa's late husband.

"Oh yes, Livvy will be here. So will my sons, Kent and Raymond. They're coming together for a quick trip and will bring their families along later when I'm not so busy. Kent is a youth pastor now, you know. He's married and has two young children. Raymond still runs the automotive garage in South Dakota. It will be good to get my children all together again." Clarissa said the last part so oddly that Jane looked at her questioningly.

"Oh, I love my children with all my heart, it's just that sometimes . . ."

"Yes? I'm all ears."

"Well, they're the *bossiest* group of human beings on the planet. Each of them calls me up all the time to tell me what to do with my life. Sometimes they turn the tables on me and treat me like a child. 'Mother, do this. Mother, do that. Get a new stove. Save your money. Move to an apartment. Retire.' Mercy, sometimes those children drive me nuts."

"They love you and they think they're helping."

"Well, they aren't. I may be an old gray mare, but I'm not ready for the glue factory yet." She paused to chuckle. "And if they'd heard me say that, they would have told me to 'get with it' and not use those old sayings anymore."

"You're worried that the reunion will be a prime time for them to gang up on you and give you some unhelpful advice."

"That's it in a nutshell. And if they saw me tackling the reunion baking alone, they'd have me committed."

"You know best, Clarissa," Jane said gently. "You're one of the smartest businesswomen I know. But remember, miracles can happen."

"I know. I've seen many in my lifetime, but never in the back end of my bakery."

Laughing, the two parted: Clarissa to go home and soak her feet, and Jane to tell the committee that she was not going to be able to pull the catering together.

Lloyd and Ethel, knowing exactly when the sisters sat down to eat, sometimes managed to arrive for a visit just in time for the evening meal. Jane would put a couple of extra pork chops in the pan or stretch dessert by adding a few Madeleine and Daughters candies to the plate and invite them to stay.

Tonight, however, Jane was way ahead of them.

She had been feeling a strange urgency about Mr. Enrich ever since he had checked into the inn. He spent most of his time either in his room or in Daniel Howard's library reading her father's old books on philosophy. For whatever reason, Jane felt compelled to reach out to him in a way she usually did not for their other guests. The inn's policy was to provide only breakfasts for guests, but sometimes, on certain occasions, the sisters would invite them for a light dinner in order to get to know them better.

That was Jane's intention for the evening. She made a gigantic pot of white chicken chili, crusty baguettes, and a caramel apple cheesecake for dessert. She invited Mr. Enrich, Ned and the Colwins to join them for dinner. Ned, as Jane thought he would, declined so that he could catch up on paperwork at the pharmacy, but the Colwins agreed eagerly. Mr. Enrich also agreed, but in a somewhat confused manner.

Alice put an extra leaf in the dining room table, and Louise set out red-and-white-checked placemats and napkins while Jane made a centerpiece of fresh fruits and vegetables. The table was festive and welcoming by the time the guests arrived.

Chapter ❦ Four

They that will not be counseled,
cannot be helped.
If you do not hear reason,
she will rap you on the knuckles.
—Benjamin Franklin

That was one mighty fine meal," Lloyd said as he pushed away from the table. "Mighty fine indeed." He dusted the crumbs off his vest and sighed contentedly.

"It was delicious, my dear," Ethel agreed, "even if chili is supposed to be red and not white."

"Just great," Nancy Colwin said. "We want your recipe."

"Jane's going to do an entire cookbook," Ethel informed the Colwins proudly. "Then you'll be able to get all of her recipes."

"Terrific. Where do I sign up?" Zack asked.

Jane enjoyed the young couple. They were so enthusiastic and full of energy—as she had been early in her career. Jane was, of course, still enthusiastic and energetic, but her energy would not last forever. Jane thought of Clarissa and how her business had worn her down.

"I hear all three of Clarissa Cottrell's children are coming for the reunion," Ethel announced.

Louise's eyes brightened. "Good. I would love to

see Livvy again. She was an excellent pianist, very talented. She played for me one summer when I was here visiting. I do hope she has kept it up."

"Probably," Ethel said. "If she made up her mind to do something, she never gave up. Remember all the trouble she gave her mother over redecorating the Good Apple?"

"Redecorating?" Jane frowned. "The Good Apple hasn't changed much over the years."

"Oh, Clarissa held fast. Said people didn't come in to see psychedelic colors and lava lamps. Fortunately, the older Livvy got, the smarter Clarissa seemed to become too.

"A couple years back," Ethel added, "Clarissa told me Livvy had admitted that she was *glad* Clarissa hadn't changed the store. Too bad she didn't figure that out before she caused her mother all that gray hair."

"Now, with the responsibility of being superintendent of a big school district," Alice said, "she probably needs all that fire and more."

"What became of the boys?" Louise inquired.

Jane noticed that the Colwins and even Mr. Enrich seemed pleased by the homey conversation. She said nothing as Ethel happily repeated to the guests what Clarissa had told Jane earlier.

"Kent is a youth pastor in Oregon," Ethel informed them. "He was so quiet I never thought he'd be able to speak in public, but Clarissa says he's wonderful with children."

"Such a kind young man," Alice recalled. "He was in our church youth group at one time."

"How long have you worked with Grace Chapel's youth?" Nancy inquired.

"For the past twenty-five years." Alice put her hand to her cheek. "My, that certainly dates me."

"And Ray still has a garage in South Dakota," Lloyd added. "Always loved working with his hands. Never had much time for talking, that one."

"He is the one with Clarissa's sense of humor, though," Louise said. "His eyes were always twinkling over something."

"Do you know *everyone* in Acorn Hill?" Nancy asked. Jane could hear wistfulness in her voice.

Ethel stared at her as if she had sprouted a second head. "Of course. Why wouldn't we?"

"Nancy came from a smaller community in Michigan. I lived in a city where we never knew many people outside our immediate friends and family." He turned to his wife. "Maybe you're a little homesick."

"I think it is so . . . cozy . . . here," Nancy said. "I love it. I hope you all realize how nice you have it— friends, extended family, community, fellowship."

Zack's head bobbed. "Growing up, I would have given anything for that." A longing expression flitted across his face. "But the city is what I'm accustomed to."

Lloyd emitted a horrified sound. "Terrible! That's no way to grow up."

Jane smiled to herself. Lloyd's ideas about cities

were similar to his ideas about freeways and traffic snarls—no place for human beings to be.

"Well, getting back to Clarissa, she has a talented family, no doubt about that," Lloyd concluded. Something in his tone seemed to add, "But . . ."

"But bossy?" Jane put in.

Although Louise tried to look aghast at Jane's and Lloyd's candor, the description was no surprise.

What was a surprise however, was Mr. Enrich's foray into the discussion. "Sometimes being a smart-aleck catches up with you," he said, looking startled even as he said it.

To make him feel comfortable, Jane said, "I agree. It's not until we figure out that we don't know much of anything and submit to God's wisdom that we get wise."

That brought nods from around the table, and Mr. Enrich retreated into silence.

"Since we're speaking of Clarissa," Jane began, dreading to tell Lloyd and Ethel her news, "I'm sorry to tell you that she's not able to do the baking for me. I'm afraid that means that I won't be able to cater the reunion breakfasts."

"Doesn't she know how important this is?" Lloyd sounded shocked.

"I'm sure she does. She also knows that she's the only one baking. There's no way she can do it alone."

Ethel cleared her throat. "I'm afraid she's right, Lloyd."

The three sisters just about sprained their necks

swiveling them to stare at their aunt. Ethel, not agreeing with Lloyd? Would wonders ever cease?

"I've done a fair amount of baking in my day, and that much work would be difficult for anyone—especially one getting on in years."

Lloyd sputtered, "But, but . . ."

"When's this reunion of yours?" Zack asked.

Jane gave Zack the date.

"That's barely a week away."

"Yes, that's why everyone is in such a tizzy."

Zack sat in thoughtful silence for a moment and then said, "We'll still be on vacation. If you'd like, maybe Nancy and I could help out your friend. It would be okay with you, wouldn't it, honey?"

Nancy looked surprised, but not annoyed. "I suppose so."

"You can't break into your holiday to work for complete strangers," Alice protested. "This is your vacation."

"Why not? It's a worthy cause, right? We can sightsee with Grace Chapel Inn as our home base as well as using any other spot in Pennsylvania," Zack said cheerfully. "If a couple days of help would make it easier, let us know. Besides, it might be fun. Sounds like the reunion parties are going to be an event."

"You aren't serious, are you?" Jane asked.

"Nancy and I will talk it over tonight."

The entire group turned to stare at Nancy.

"Someday I'll grow accustomed to Zack surprising me like this," Nancy said, looking unfazed. "His parents are always volunteering in a soup kitchen or nursing home. Last year when we arrived for Thanksgiving, we found a note on the door saying 'Meet us at the Mission on Fourth Street. You two are serving turkey and dressing.' He comes by it naturally." She appeared resigned, if not delighted.

"We'll let you know for sure in the morning." Zack paused. "But even if we can help, maybe your friend doesn't want to do it at all. You should probably consider other options anyway."

"I'll deal with Clarissa." Lloyd announced this with an authority that everyone knew was all bluster, but the entire table could see how grateful he was for the offer.

"One thing at a time," Jane suggested. "On the off chance you *do* help out, we insist that you and Nancy stay on at the inn. The reunion days will be free of charge, of course."

Louise looked surprised. "But the rooms . . ."

"Oh, we'll manage just fine," Jane said confidently. "Alice and I have bunked together before. We can always set up a cot in the library for an emergency. Someone might need a place to stay and would be willing to rough it for the weekend."

"Maybe I could stay in the library."

Mr. Enrich had stunned them twice this evening. No one had anticipated his having any input into the conversation, considering how uncommunicative he had been. And after his critical comments about the inn during his first days there, no one had dreamed that he would want to bunk in the inn's library.

"You?" Louise blurted. "Why?"

"What my sister meant," Alice hurried to explain, "was that since you aren't an alumnus . . ."

"I know I'd planned to leave before your reunion guests start arriving, but it looks like it might be . . ." his face twisted, as if he had difficulty spitting out the next word, "fun."

Everyone stared at the man. *Mr. Enrich is looking for fun?* Jane thought. *Who would have guessed?*

"If it's a problem . . ." he added.

"Not a problem at all," Jane said firmly before Louise could speak. "None at all. We'll be delighted to have you. We'll consider you 'family' during the reunion, if you don't mind."

Louise and Alice looked at Jane as if she had lost her wits. This was not how they treated guests, banishing them to sleep in the common rooms of the inn.

Mr. Enrich, however, seemed faintly pleased. "I don't have any other plans. And it's been . . ." he paused to search for something to say, "nice, here. I didn't really expect to be around this long." A strange, pained look crossed his face. "But here I am." Even he looked mystified.

"It's settled then," Jane said. She had no idea what drew her to this odd man or made her feel responsible for him, but she had learned in her life that it was always wisest to follow God's nudging, even when it sent her in a strange direction. Why she thought this was from God, she was not sure, but she also knew that if the reclusive Mr. Enrich expressed any interest whatsoever in what was going on around him, it was worth encouraging.

"If you're willing, I'd appreciate your giving me a hand during the reunion. We'll be very short on help, and it might make the weekend more interesting for you." Where had that come from? Since when did she order her guests to work?

Since just now, she decided, as Mr. Enrich nodded.

God, this is too weird for words, but I believe You're behind it, so take it and run with it and let me know what I'm suppose to do, she prayed silently.

"Well, well, well," Lloyd spluttered, his face red and beaming, "if everything falls into place, this is going to be a dandy reunion."

"Dandy." Jane certainly hoped so.

"You look like the dog ate your socks," Jane commented as she entered Sylvia's Buttons. Sylvia Songer was sitting on a high stool by her cutting counter staring at papers that were spread out across it like leaves after a windstorm.

"If only that were it," Sylvia moaned. She and Jane had become close friends since Jane's return to Acorn Hill, but lately they had not been seeing as much of each other socially as they would like. The all-school reunion was taking every waking moment—and some of Sylvia's sleeping ones too, by the look of it.

She pushed away the piles of papers and supported her head with her hands. "This reunion is never going to work. Never."

"I don't believe that for a moment," Jane said calmly. "I'm going to make tea." She went into the back of the store where she could always find hot water in an insulated carafe and a basket of assorted teas from Tea for Two.

She put two bags of peppermint tea into a small pot, filled it with water and carried it on a tray with two cups to Sylvia, who was still at the table. Jane poured the tea and set a cup in front of her friend.

Finally Sylvia roused herself. Taking the steaming cup in her hands, she moaned, "The logistics of this are going to kill me. Whatever made me think this would be fun? I'll be a pariah after the debacle I've created."

"What's today's crisis?" Jane asked evenly. Sylvia had been on a roller coaster of emotions for weeks, and her state was getting worse as the reunion date neared.

"Too few booths for vendors, too many people wanting places to stay, too few parade entries, too many complainers and," she eyed Jane glumly, "too few caterers to get the job done."

"Maybe, and maybe not." Jane told her about the Colwins.

"What did Clarissa say?"

"I haven't asked her yet. I'm almost scared to do it."

"Think she'll say no again?"

"Possibly. But she's feeling so tired that I'm almost afraid she'll say yes." Jane tugged on her own hair. "I'm getting the idea that Clarissa's children won't enjoy seeing Clarissa working that hard either."

"Clarissa knows her own mind," Sylvia assured Jane. "Just because she's got gray hair, it doesn't mean her mind is aging too. My mother always said her biggest frustration was that when she got older, people wanted to treat her differently."

Jane nodded in agreement. "I know I feel younger than I am, younger than when I was young, actually. I have a much stronger sense of myself and my relationship with God and others. I finally understand what Shaw meant when he said that youth is wasted on the young."

Sylvia nodded, sighed and went back to shuffling her papers.

Clarissa, somewhat to Jane's surprise, was delighted that the Colwins were considering working with her.

"You mean it? You found help for me? Somebody who's actually had experience?"

Jane retold the story of Zack and Nancy's offer. "They haven't said for sure. They were going to talk it over last night, and I left the inn before they came down for breakfast, but I think they will help. So, what do you think?"

"I think I've been feeling sorry that I couldn't contribute any more to the reunion and was saying 'poor old me,' last night." She gave a happy grin. "The only thing worn out about me is my body, Jane. I want to be involved. Maybe this will allow it."

"They're pretty young," Jane warned. "They might think they have better ideas than yours."

"Don't worry about that. Remember, I raised Livvy, the most opinionated young woman in three counties. I can handle them. In fact, after Livvy, the Colwins will be a pleasure."

"Has anyone seen Mr. Enrich lately?" Jane asked as she entered the kitchen and found her sisters poring over the inn's finances, their heads nearly touching as they studied the books in front of them.

"No. Not since breakfast." Alice looked up from the ledger and pushed her hair away from her face.

A few minutes later, Jane ran into Mr. Enrich coming out of the library. He had not shaved. A stubbly shadow covered his jaw. Neither had he combed his hair, which stood in dark spiky points on his head. As always, Jane was startled by the haunted look that never seemed to leave his eyes.

"Been reading?" Jane eyed the C. S. Lewis books under his arm. She doubted that some of her father's books had been read since Daniel passed away, so she was glad someone was finally using them.

"You've got quite a library," Mr. Enrich commented.

"My father did. He'd rather buy himself a book than a pair of shoes or trousers." She chuckled. "That may or may not tell you something about the look of his wardrobe."

A stiff smile contorted the corners of Mr. Enrich's lips.

How long has it been, Jane wondered, *since the man's laughed?*

"Mr. Enrich, I've been noticing the titles you've chosen. Most of our guests read the lighter fare. You've even had out a few books my father used when he was in seminary years ago."

"Never read anything like that. Thought I'd try."

Wendell at that moment came strolling out of the room yawning and stretching. He was even staggering a little, as if he was having difficulty waking from the deep sleep he had been enjoying. He glided over to Jane and wound himself around her ankles, purring.

"I see you had company for the day," Jane said. "I wondered where he'd gone."

"He kept meowing at the door until I let him in. I hope that was okay."

"Sure. Wendell actually owns the house. We simply live here as his slaves. He was my father's cat and grew accustomed to long days in the study, dozing, while Dad read."

Mr. Enrich looked at her oddly. "I've never been in a place quite like this," he said after a long pause.

"The inn, you mean?"

"Where people are so willing to share what they have with others. Even the cat is sociable. My wife had a cat and it didn't like anyone but her. It never did quit hissing and spitting at me when I came within three feet of it."

His life was none of her affair, Jane reminded herself. None at all. But Mr. Enrich must have felt her curiosity.

"I had a turn of bad luck with business and was spending an inordinate amount of time working. One night I came home late and went to bed. It wasn't until I woke up in the morning that I realized that not only was my wife's side of the bed not slept in, her clothes, her cat, our son and the living room furniture were gone." He seemed to marvel as he said it. "Can you imagine?"

Then, like a clam snapping shut, Mr. Enrich closed his mouth. It was clear that he regretted his revelations.

Although he had just said more about himself than he had since he first arrived, Jane knew that this information was just the tip of the iceberg.

As Jane slowly maneuvered the staircase carrying a load of freshly washed linens, she heard low, urgent voices coming from the Colwins' room at the top of the stairs.

"If you'd just make up your mind it would be much easier."

"Make up *my* mind? You're the one who's changing her ideas every five minutes."

"That's not fair, Zack. I think the restaurant we work at is just fine. Pretty soon, we'll have saved enough for a down payment on a house and we can start a family. . . ."

"And support it with what?"

"It's you, Zack, who keeps thinking there's something big over the horizon, some pie in the sky, a jackpot. We don't have to have a fancy restaurant right away. Maybe we'll never need one. I'd rather have a little house and a family, remember?"

"Come on, Nancy. Be realistic. Kids cost money. Houses cost money. We've got to get our finances in order before we start any of that."

"But what if there's always something else out there that you want to do first." Her voice had a painful catch in it. "I grew up in a sweet little neighborhood like this one. I want my children to experience the things I had."

"And just who is going to pay for all that? My folks didn't have any money. I know how that feels, and I also know it's something I never want to experience again. First things first."

"That's what I am doing, putting first things first— a baby, a happy life, settling down and not thinking up one fantastical thing after another to pursue. One day you're going to run out of rainbows, Zack."

Jane had just reached the top step when the Colwins' door burst open and Nancy, tears glistening on her cheeks, shot past Jane down the stairs and out the front door. Zack closed the door to their room without looking after his wife.

First Mr. Enrich and now this. What was wrong with her guests? She had never seen such turmoil and distress.

Mr. Enrich wandered into the dining room and was obviously surprised to find a tea party in session. Josie and Jane were having one of their frequent tête-à-têtes over miniature sandwiches and cookies. "Oh, excuse me," he stammered and started backing toward the door.

"Would you like to join us?" Josie asked, sounding forty years old as she said it. She pointed a finger at one of the empty chairs. "Just don't sit on my doll," Josie instructed firmly. "You may have your own chair."

Josie, wearing a pair of Louise's old dress shoes, a shawl Alice had dug out of her closet and a floppy hat of Jane's, presided over the tea party. The chairs around the dining table were filled with teddy bears and ragtag dolls that Josie had dragged from home.

It always delighted Josie when Jane dressed up for these impromptu play dates. So, Jane wore a flowing golden pants and blouse outfit with sandals made of faux-leopard leather. She completed the ensemble with a wide-brimmed, tan felt hat decorated with colorful feathers and a beaded band. She looked as exotic as a day in the Serengeti.

"Tea?" Jane asked primly. Jane loved these play teas she and Josie concocted. Normally they were held in the kitchen, but today they had decided to be special and use the dining room.

"*Puleeeze,* Mr. Enrich," the little girl cajoled as the man shook his head and began backing from the room again. "It would make me *sooo* happy."

He stopped, then walked stiffly toward a chair. The child was impossible to resist.

They ate with their pinkies in the air at Josie's insistence. When Josie decided that her baby doll needed to be changed and trotted off to do some intense mothering, Jane and Mr. Enrich switched from cookies to the plate of Madeleine and Daughters chocolates Jane had set on the table.

"Do you do this a lot?" Mr. Enrich asked.

"Quite often," Jane said. "It's kind of fun, don't you think?"

"Yeah . . . *er* . . . fun," he muttered as Josie returned.

Moments later Lloyd, Ethel and Sylvia found them there, looking like escapees from the Mad Hatter's Tea Party, finishing up the tea and the tidbits left on the plates, pinkie fingers all high in the air.

Chapter ❦ Five

Were it offered to my choice, I should have
no objection to a repetition of the same
life from its beginning, only asking the
advantages authors have in a second edition
to correct some faults in the first.
—Benjamin Franklin

I'm sure you're a wonderful chef," Alice said to Zack as they visited after breakfast the next morning. Everyone had finished eating, Ned had left for the pharmacy and Nancy had gone upstairs. Mr. Enrich sat unsmiling as usual but had not made a move to leave the table.

"Yeah, and I love it. I had a great job as a salad chef and then pastry chef at a well-known restaurant. I saw how a famous restaurant works—from the ground up. Ever since then, I've known I want to create my own special signature place." His eyes were shining. "What a great challenge!"

"How fortunate you have such a wonderful vision for your future. I wish I could say the same for some of the young people I've been working with lately. A few of them can't see the future beyond their own noses. They can't imagine how good their lives and relationships could be and how much they have to offer the world."

Mr. Enrich unexpectedly cleared his throat and spoke. "What if they don't have anything to offer and no fulfilling relationships? What if there is no good future for them?"

Alice gave as emphatic a response as Jane had ever heard from her sister. "Of course they have a future."

"How do you know?"

"Because God made them, of course. He knit each one of us in our mother's wombs. He gave us gifts to use and a reason for being. It's up to us to bring out the best of His gifts."

"You say that like you believe it," Mr. Enrich said mildly.

"With all my heart." Alice straightened. "In fact, I'm staking my life on it."

"What are you two up to?" Louise asked. "What are those bumping and scraping sounds coming from the library?"

"Mr. Enrich and I have been putting up his cot," answered Jane. "We're also going through that carton of toys that I brought down from the attic. I just came in for a drink of water."

When she returned to the library, Mr. Enrich had unwrapped all the toys and was just removing a smaller box from the storage carton. He handed it to Jane.

"Hmmm," she said as she knelt on the floor and opened it. Whatever it was had been packed with newspaper dated from the nineteen-fifties. She lifted a paper-wrapped object out of the box and peeled away the layers. "Well, look at this."

Mr. Enrich stared curiously.

It was a vase about eight inches tall—flat on one side and curved like a regular vase on the other. The colors, mostly orange and black, covered an embossed surface. When she turned it over, Jane saw a flat picture hook on the back. "Looks like this was meant to hang on the wall. I wonder what they put in it."

"Air ferns," Mr. Enrich said.

"What are those?"

"My grandmother used to have little vases like that all over her house. She'd put in some rootless little ferns that she called air ferns. As a child I thought the ferns must be magical because they never needed water or soil. I never did find out what they actually were—maybe something like dried flowers."

Jane stood up with the odd little container in her hand. "Let's see what Louise knows about this vase."

As they entered the kitchen, Louise announced, "I am making lunch."

"Great. What are we having?" Jane asked.

Louise paused. "*Er,* what were you planning?"

"I've spoiled you, haven't I?"

"You *have* spoiled us," Louise admitted. "I have begun to assume that when I open the refrigerator door, my meal will be there." Louise pulled at the refrigerator door, and it opened to reveal a plate of ham sandwiches cut in triangles and covered with plastic wrap. There was a bowl of potato salad decorated with parsley and next to it a pitcher of lemonade. "And you never fail us."

She wagged a finger in Jane's grinning face. "You could have told me you had already planned lunch."

"And Louie, you could have thought of cooking something earlier."

"You like to tease," Louise accused her.

"It's good for you," Jane retorted happily.

Shaking her head, Louise set the table with woven straw placemats and yellow napkins. "What have you got there?" she asked, nodding at the box in Jane's hands.

Jane held up the vase.

"My, my. I haven't seen that in years."

"You remember this vase?"

"Why, yes. It hung on the dining room wall for years. I think Uncle Bob bought it on a trip he and Aunt Ethel had taken somewhere. I was visiting Father when Alice took it down and packed it away. Odd little thing, isn't it?"

"You were right, Mr. Enrich," Jane said to the man

who had followed her into the kitchen. She looked again at Louise. "He remembers these from his grandmother's house."

Impulsively, Jane held out the little ceramic vase to Mr. Enrich. "Here."

"What am I suppose to do with it?"

"I don't know. Hang it in your room. Take it home with you and put it in your living room. Keep it as a reminder of your grandmother and of the days you spent at Grace Chapel Inn."

"I couldn't do that." He sounded shocked.

"Why not? No one here has a great attachment to it, and you, at least, seem to have fond memories connected with it. We'd like you to have it, wouldn't we, Louise?"

"Certainly. Our walls are full to overflowing as it is."

Jane thrust it toward him.

Mr. Enrich reached out and respectfully took the small decoration. "I loved my grandmother's house," he said, almost in a whisper.

"Good. Enjoy. Think of us when you look at it."

He stared at her so strangely that Jane felt a shiver down her spine, but he took the vase and carried it carefully to his room.

After the lunch dishes had been cleared, Jane began cooking.

"May I come in?" Nancy Colwin stood in the kitchen door and observed Jane. The sleeves of Jane's pale denim shirt were rolled to her elbows. She was browning sausage for the *strata* she was making for the next morning.

"Sure. I'm just putting this together for breakfast tomorrow," Jane responded. A glass baking dish filled with crustless bread sat nearby. Eggs, milk and an assortment of spices were on the counter close to Jane's elbow. "It needs to be in the refrigerator overnight."

"Yum." Nancy pulled a stool nearer the counter and sat down to watch Jane cook.

"These days I have to be on my toes because Mr. Enrich is always so prompt for breakfast," Jane said as she moved the pan of sausage from the burner. "For that matter, so is Ned. He likes to get to the pharmacy early to prepare for the day. But he moved to the Parkers' house this morning to make way for our reunion guests, so I don't have to worry about him right now." She whisked together the milk, eggs and seasonings. "I like this recipe because it's delicious and it's easy. I'll just pop it in the oven in the morning, cut fresh fruit, make coffee and we'll be set."

"You're a wonderful cook," Nancy commented.

"That's a real compliment coming from another professional," Jane said. She was happy to see Nancy so cheerful. The Colwins, though obviously in love, certainly had a tendency to bicker and easily to take offense at each other's words. Maybe this was part of the reason they were on vacation—to recover from the stresses of their lives that made them so short with each other. Jane silently prayed that they could find common ground on which they could grow together.

One of Jane's own failings was impatience when she was tired or under stress. Fortunately, the pace of Acorn Hill did not tire her much, and the stress of living with her sisters again was practically nonexistent now. In fact, Louise's and Alice's quirks and foibles had become endearing. Ethel was the one who could still most easily upset Jane, but when Ethel was meddling, she was usually trying to do some good or was suffering from boredom or loneliness. The more troublesome she became, the more Jane felt like giving her a hug.

"I ran into Mr. Enrich in the hall," Nancy said idly. "He's not much of a talker, is he?"

"That's an understatement. You're probably lucky if you got him to say 'hello.' "

"Oh, he did that. I even got him to talk about the breakfasts we've had. He says he likes your Belgian waffles best."

"My my, a regular chatterbox," Jane said with a chuckle. "I'll put Belgian waffles on my menu this week."

"What's his first name?" Nancy wondered. "All I've ever heard anyone call him is 'Mr. Enrich.' "

Jane paused and set down the mixing bowl she was holding. "I have no idea." She wiped her hands on the big colorful apron she wore. "I'm going to get the reservation book and find out."

She returned a moment later, shaking her head. "It's the strangest thing, but we don't know his first name.

The reservation, the slip he signed when he checked in, and his signature in the guest book are all just 'Enrich.'"

"Weird," Nancy commented.

It is *weird,* Jane thought. That, she was sure, had never happened before. Alice, who enjoyed taking reservations and checking in visitors, was always very conscientious about getting as many details as she could about their guests. If there was something special a guest liked—a certain soap, flavored coffee, or a late sleep—the three sisters wanted to know so that they could make his stay more enjoyable. For Alice not to get someone's first name was almost beyond belief. Unless, of course, Mr. Enrich did not care to divulge it. He was one of the most reclusive guests that they had ever had. He seldom talked, never used the telephone and rarely went outside the inn. There was so little that they actually knew about him. They had no idea what he did for a living, although Jane and Louise had speculated that he might be a writer since his light seemed to be on all night.

"I'll have to ask Alice," Jane said. "There is a slim chance that she just forgot to write it down."

"Where's Zack?" Jane asked.

Nancy shrugged her shoulders nonchalantly. "I'm not sure."

Jane looked up sharply. "Is something wrong?" she asked, and then added, "Please feel free to tell me if it's none of my affair."

"Zack and I really want our own business sooner or

94

later, but the way we're going, it's going to be later, much later." Nancy's eyes grew teary. "It's the first major issue that Zack and I haven't agreed about, and it's a huge one."

"Tell me more." Jane sealed the baking dish with aluminum foil and slid it into the refrigerator. Then she took out a tea chest filled with gourmet teas from Time for Tea and set it and two cups on the counter.

"We, being chefs and all, both want to have a restaurant, but our visions of what it is that we want are so different that we aren't getting along well."

Jane put a plate of oatmeal raisin cookies and sour cream bars in front of Nancy. Then she pulled up a stool and sat down.

"Zack has an image of himself in a high white hat, concocting new recipes and creating perfectly artistic presentations of food. He wants to open something trendy, the kind of place people go for special occasions, for meeting friends and for out-of-this-world food. Something unique."

"That sounds lovely," Jane said, thinking of the Blue Fish Grille and all that she had left behind when she moved from San Francisco back to Pennsylvania. "And you?"

"Me? I'm a down-home girl. Meat and potatoes, fresh vegetables, fabulous hearty breads and soups— comfort food. Customers like something delicious that they don't have to identify with a foreign-language dictionary. No morels or sushi. I can make cheesy-potato bread that, served with chowder or soup, will make a banquet. Belly-warming stews and, of course, desserts—that's really what I'm about—decadent chocolate cake, homemade ices and ice creams, Frisbee-sized chocolate chip cookies served with a bottomless cup of great coffee."

"I'm getting hungry just thinking about it," Jane acknowledged, "but I also see your problem."

"Zack wants to make a name for himself somewhere. He'd love a place that's a diner's destination. You know, so good that people would be willing to drive from other places just to experience his food. He's already got a name picked out. Zachary's." Nancy said it a little scornfully. "Great name, huh?"

"And what would you name *your* place?"

"I'm not sure . . ." Nancy gestured at herself. "I'm not fancy. I love comfortable clothing and shoes, the natural look. I'd like a place that would be open only during the day." She blushed a little. "I'm ready to start a family. I'm just plain, I guess."

Plain nothing, Jane thought. Nancy had a healthy fresh-scrubbed look that most other women would give their eye-teeth to achieve.

"Maybe I'd name it something like the places in Acorn Hill," Nancy speculated. " 'The Coffee Shop.' There's no doubt what they offer there—great breakfasts, good pie and long conversations with friends."

She called that right, Jane thought. One could get a stack of flapjacks, biscuits and gravy, or any number of other things to fuel up on for the day.

"And I love the bakery's name," Nancy continued.

" 'The Good Apple.' Quaint. Cheerful. Maybe I would name my place 'Nancy's.' " She sighed. "It's no wonder Zack and I haven't been getting along. I'm afraid the situation will turn into one of those if-you-really-loved-me-you'd-do-this-my-way things. Yet if either of us gives in, I know it will be a source of resentment. We've both worked hard learning our craft and making our dreams come true. Neither of us expected that the one standing in the way would be the other, the one we love most."

"You do have a problem," Jane agreed. "Is there a compromise in this somewhere?"

"Not that we've come up with," Nancy said sadly. "I've been praying for a solution, but so far, no answer."

"Don't give up," Jane urged. "If God's got a hand in it, it will turn out right."

Nancy nodded, but by the way her shoulders drooped, it was obvious that giving up was a very real option for her.

Later that day Jane found Zack sitting in a chair on the front porch holding Wendell. Wendell, she had noticed, was very popular with guests who were feeling disheartened or sad. The big cat seemed to know when a person was troubled and would linger on the lap of someone who needed cheering or con-soling. Sometimes Jane wondered if the cat had learned the value of a comforting presence from her father.

"Hi." Zack kept scratching Wendell behind his particularly itchy ear.

"Hi, yourself," Jane responded. "Where's Nancy?"

"She went for a walk."

"I see."

"I wish I did," Zack said, shaking his head. "She's upset with me, and all I want to do is make the best possible life for us.

"*Hmmm.* The best possible life for whom?"

"Us." His voice faltered. "At least *I* think it's the best life for us."

"I see," Jane said again. Zack was doing just fine without her input.

"She doesn't listen to me. I keep telling her that my way is the fastest way to get what we want—a home, children, a successful business."

"And she doesn't listen?"

"No. I kept telling her but . . ."

"What does she do?"

"She just keeps saying that I'm not paying attention to her feelings, that I'm not hearing her . . ." Zack stopped short and considered what he had just said. "Oh."

Jane remained silent.

"Maybe I haven't been listening as well as *I* should, but we're husband and wife. If she really cared about me, she'd try to help me make this happen, don't you think?"

Jane said nothing.

"I do," Zack continued, completely unaware of the

one-sidedness of his conversation. "But I don't want to fight with her. I love her. Even when she's driving me crazy, I love her."

He picked up Wendell and put him gently on the porch floor. "Hey, thanks. I appreciate your input. Maybe I'd better find Nancy and see if we can talk."

Jane watched him go down the walk before she picked up Wendell and buried her nose in his fur. "Wendell," she said. "I see now why you're such a good counselor. I'm going to do it your way from now on. You know how to keep your mouth shut and listen."

Chapter ❦ Six

To be thrown upon one's own resources,
is to be cast into the very lap of fortune:
For our faculties then undergo a development
and display an energy of which they were
previously unsusceptible.
—Benjamin Franklin

Louise came into the kitchen looking distressed. Jane, who had heard her enter the house, had a glass of lemonade ready for her. As Louise sat down, Alice raised one eyebrow as if to say, "Now what?"

"This reunion is going to make everyone in town crazy," Louise announced as she took out her handkerchief and dabbed at her brow dramatically. "Even Pastor Kenneth has been swept up in the nonsense.

Alice, do you know that he is letting the ANGELs use the entire church parking lot for their car wash?"

Alice blushed. "I suggested it, Louise. Where else could we put it?"

"What has happened to the citizens of this community? Everyone is sweeping sidewalks, pruning hedges and washing windows as if the president were coming to town."

"Oh, this is much more important than the president," Jane said. "You know people really like an excuse to fuss, and this reunion is as big an occasion for most people in town as a family birthday, a wedding or a graduation."

"This all-school reunion is going to be the death of us yet," Louise predicted. Then a genuinely concerned expression spread over her features. "I am worried about Clarissa Cottrell for one."

Jane straightened. "Is something wrong with Clarissa?"

"Only that she is about to drop in her tracks. I stopped at the Good Apple on the way home and it was full of people, all buzzing about the upcoming festivities. Clarissa was behind the counter doling out baked goods, looking as though she was about to fall over at any minute. She would not admit it to me, but I know she was not feeling well. Why she agreed to let the Colwins help her just so that she could take on more work for the reunion is beyond me."

Alice frowned. "Maybe I should go over there and check on her. I've got my blood pressure cuff. . . ."

"It would not do any good," Louise said. "She will not stop for you. Everyone keeps telling her what a good job she is doing and what a wonderful baker she is, and you know Clarissa. The more they praise her the harder she tries."

"Well, wouldn't you? Work hard, I mean," Jane said, "if people were praising you all over the place? You love it when people enjoy your playing the piano. Clarissa has her own art form—baking. She bakes and decorates beautiful pastries, and her displays are breathtaking."

"I believe Jane has something there," Alice added. "What people want most is to be useful and to have a purpose. The Good Apple is Clarissa's purpose. It's my thought that she's afraid that if and when she does give up the bakery, she'll lose her personality with it." Alice grew reflective. "One of the reasons our father was so happy in his later years was that he never stopped being useful. Younger pastors would stop by to visit and go away wiser for the experience. And as he slowed down and wasn't so busy with the church, he had time to sit with friends who were ill or to comfort those who were suffering. In fact, in some ways, I believe his ministry deepened as he grew older."

"You've got to give yourself some credit too, Alice," Jane said softly. "It was because you were here, cooking for Dad, making a home for him and being vigilant about his health, that he was able to continue to thrive and to contribute. Not everyone is so fortunate as to have someone like you in his life."

Alice dismissed the acknowledgment of her dedication with a wave of her hand. "It was my gift too."

"Clarissa should be nearer to her children," Louise concluded. "That is what she needs."

Jane recalled Clarissa's words about her bossy family but did not speak. No use judging. She would wait and see for herself just what Clarissa considered "bossy."

"You are surprisingly quiet on the subject." Louise said to Jane. Though she did not say it, her words implied, *for once.*

"I don't blame Clarissa for wanting to stay independent," Jane said. "Her mind is great, sharp as a tack. She'll go absolutely mad if she can't keep active. How can a woman who's run her own business for years suddenly sit down and twiddle her thumbs and be happy?"

"That is what *you* might experience," Louise said, "but is it what Clarissa would feel?"

Jane had a hunch that it was. She and Clarissa both had a bit of the maverick in them. Unlike Clarissa, however, Jane had been born in a time that allowed for individuality.

"I do wish Clarissa could be nearer her children," Alice murmured.

Silently Jane wondered if Clarissa were up to it. Pleasing her family sounded like almost as much work as pleasing her customers.

There was a knock on the door, and then the sisters heard the screen door open and close.

"It's just me." Sylvia Songer appeared in the

doorway. Her red hair looked as if it had been hastily brushed and her light, freckled skin was paler than usual.

Before anyone could speak, Sylvia said, "Give me two minutes to catch my breath before asking me anything about the reunion."

"Seems to me you're going to need two months to catch your breath," Jane observed. "You look awful."

"Thanks so much. I'm so glad I came here for support."

"You're welcome." Jane smiled. "How about a little pick-me-up? I made chocolate-chocolate brownies with fudge frosting today."

"Be still my heart." Sylvia looked around the room. "Where are they?"

Once Sylvia was settled with a cup of calming herbal tea and a plate of brownies, the others watched her with amusement as she took a bite, closed her eyes, leaned back in her chair and purred, *"Ahhhh."*

It took two brownies and a refill of her tea before Sylvia signaled that she was ready to talk.

"You don't know how good it is to have someplace to go where, when I say I don't want to talk about the reunion, they believe me."

"You're safe with us," Alice assured her with a smile. "But. . ."

"I know, I know, you want to be in the loop too." Sylvia arranged her hair with her fingers only making it worse. With her wild red hair and with brownie crumbs on her lips, she hardly looked like one of the masterminds of this upcoming event, or as Sylvia often referred to it, "the logistical nightmare."

"This reunion is like a snowball rolling down the side of a mountain. It's been picking up size, energy and momentum ever since we got the idea for the celebration, and now it's about to crash down upon our village burying us. And," Sylvia predicted gloomily, "I'll be at the bottom of the pile."

"Going that well, huh?" Jane said. "Welcome to my world. Catering is the same way. It sounds easy enough when you agree to do it. A few canapés here, a dessert buffet there, something with swordfish for the entrée. And the date is months away. There's not another thing on the calendar to prevent you from spending all your time making it perfect."

Louise raised an eyebrow but Jane kept talking.

"Then, just when you think you've got it under control, someone comes along and says all the guests are allergic to swordfish and asks if we can serve meatballs and mashed potatoes instead. And there are forty or fifty more guests coming than first planned so the event is being moved across town. And they all love Black Forest cake and want to end with a taffy pull or some such craziness."

"A taffy pull is the *only* thing someone hasn't suggested," Sylvia said. "Don't say a word about it or someone will think that's a good idea too. Where was everyone when we were planning this reunion? Thirty people showed up for the meetings. Now we're getting input from three hundred."

"Other than that, how's it going?" Alice said, chuckling.

"I hate to say this, but Lloyd Tynan and your aunt are going to be the death of me, if Viola and Orlando's don't get to me first."

" 'Now, Sylvia,' " Sylvia mimicked Lloyd's fussy way of worrying a subject to death. Jane could just imagine him looking both vexed and determined not to be left out of the action. " 'You're representing our little town properly, aren't you? There's nothing planned that would make people think badly of us? I heard a rumor that you're considering blowing off those fireworks on the football field. You know how messy fireworks can be. Maybe you could move the fireworks outside the city limits. . . . What? You checked that out and there's not enough parking spaces? And you've already arranged a cleanup crew? Oh my, I hope you didn't make any hasty decisions about that. You can't have just anyone on a cleanup crew, you know. You need someone with some maturity and common sense. Why don't you drop off the list of candidates and I'll tell you who to pick. Then you can call them and give them the word. That's what this committee is for, after all, right?' " Sylvia waved her hand just as Lloyd might and concluded in his tone, " 'Don't worry, it's no problem for me. Glad to be of service. This is my reunion city too . . .' "

Alice and Jane were hooting with laughter at Sylvia's imitation of the mayor. Even Louise, who treasures propriety, was smiling.

"Can you believe it?" Sylvia shook her head. "Everyone is trying to micromanage this event, and they're all getting into the action months too late. My cleanup crews were formed in January, and now we're in the countdown to reunion day. I'm not going to change a thing now, even if Lloyd does think they might be a bit 'immature' or 'flighty.' He nearly had a heart attack when I told him who was in charge of cleanup. What's wrong with Boy Scouts anyway?"

"Lloyd wants you to fire Boy Scouts?" Jane said, still laughing helplessly.

"Oh dear," Louise murmured. "That sounds un-American."

"I wonder if the Brownies are available." Alice hiccupped with mirth. "Maybe he would think that girls are more mature."

"You'd think we needed a medical team to come in and surgically scrub the football field after the fireworks. And you don't know the half of it."

Sylvia pulled out a big calendar with the month of August on it. Across the top of the calendar, she had scrawled "Countdown to Reunion." Then, in red marker, she had crossed out the word *Reunion* and replaced it with the word *Chaos*.

"This whole thing is just bedlam. How will we ever pull it off?"

"You're too close to the action to see how well everything is going," Alice assured her. "How can it not be a success? Most people are having their families and friends come home. There will be food, music, games, even hot-air-balloon rides. There are class dinners, socials and a parade planned. Everyone I've talked to is just happy that you're providing a setting for them to reacquaint themselves with old friends. When you hand out that program of events and locations, the reunion will practically run itself."

Sylvia looked at Jane. "Is that how you see it?"

"It's not quite that simple," Jane said. "I know, having been in on the planning and execution side of things, but Alice has the general idea. If people simply do what they're assigned to do—Boy Scouts clean up, church ladies serve, car washers wash cars—then it will happen."

Sylvia took a deep breath. "The plans look good on paper. We think we've thought of every contingency. I even ordered extra porta-potties and Fred has stocked umbrellas if it rains. . . ."

"And the marketplace is ready?" Jane referred to the sea of white tents Sylvia had planned as marketing booths for anyone who had something made locally that he wanted to sell.

"Yes. It's full. Every booth is taken. Several people are doing pottery, others are making pins and head-bands or dying shirts and kerchiefs emblazoned with the date and logo of the reunion. The committee is selling mugs, posters and T-shirts to pay for our expenses. Several artists, potters and woodworkers have rented tents, and so has a group of ladies who are making personalized reunion sweatshirts and quilts.

There's no need for anyone to forget they've been here for a celebration."

"And the parade?" Louise asked. She was not sure what a parade had to do with a high-school reunion, but at least it sounded like fun.

"Several registrations have come in just in the past two days. First I worried that we wouldn't have enough entries to make a good parade, and now I'm worrying if we have enough streets for the procession to move on."

"And the food?" Alice asked.

Sylvia turned quickly toward Jane. "Jane is the only one who can pull that off."

Jane made a mental note to stop by the Good Apple again and see for herself how Clarissa was faring.

Just then, Nancy and Zack came into the kitchen laughing hysterically. Jane asked them what had amused them so.

"There was this woman . . ." Zack doubled over and held his midsection.

"And she had a . . ." Nancy, so overcome with laughter that she could not speak, put her hands on the sides of her head and waggled them.

"And it was dressed in . . ." Zack pulled at his T-shirt.

"She was . . ." Nancy made a backward and forward motion with her hands.

"It was . . . the funniest thing . . . we've ever seen."

Jane gestured them into the untaken chairs. "Either the two of you saw an elephant in dress clothes vacuuming, or you ran into Clara Horn pushing her pig Daisy in a baby buggy."

"And Daisy was dressed for the outing," Alice added.

"You *know* about this?" Zack wiped tears from his eyes.

"It's a long story," Alice said calmly. "Just enjoy Clara and the pig and don't ask about the rest. We've all actually become quite fond of little Daisy."

"In fact," Jane said, "Alice helped to save her life when she was very ill from eating a plum pit."

Nancy and Zack broke again into hoots of laughter.

By that time, the noise had roused Mr. Enrich, who had been reading in Daniel's library. When his face with its questioning expression appeared in the kitchen door, *everyone* started laughing.

Although he blushed, Mr. Enrich did not skitter away. Instead, he held his ground while Jane explained to him about Clara Horn and how she enjoyed taking her pig Daisy for walks.

"By the way, we stopped at the Good Apple and introduced ourselves to Clarissa," Zack reported.

"We just loved her," Nancy added. "She will be so easy to work with—and fun too."

"She's got a great kitchen with plenty of room. I'm sure we can handle whatever you want done. We're actually looking forward to it."

Nancy looked at Zack with such intensity that Jane deduced they had been talking about their futures again. She felt a small, uncomfortable flip in her stomach. *Why,* she wondered, *did so many troubled people and people in transition land on their doorstep?*

Because God wanted it that way, that's why. There was no doubt in Jane's mind that God was using her and her sisters and the inn for some bigger plan. There were times, however, when she wondered what, exactly, it might be. She had a true sense of rightness and belonging here that could not be wrong. She had followed her instincts to create some of her best entrées, her best artwork and her most amazing jewelry. Surely, she could use it here at the inn with the people who passed through.

Looking from Nancy and Zack to Mr. Enrich, Jane had an overwhelming feeling that she needed to follow her instinct with these guests. God had something in mind. She just knew it. What she did not know was what part she was to play in it.

Chapter 🍇 Seven

Any fool can criticize, condemn
and complain and most fools do.
—Benjamin Franklin

Jane had taken to stopping daily at the Good Apple to see how Clarissa was faring. Today the bakery was busy when Jane arrived, filled with customers stocking up for the frenetic days ahead. Clarissa, tall and straight as if she were seventeen instead of seventy-plus, was filling orders, chatting with customers and generally running an efficient ship. And, Jane observed, she was beaming.

". . . best in town."

"My Becky says she wants these for breakfast every morning."

"And Jim immediately asked if they were from the Good Apple . . ."

"You're the best, Clarissa. I hope you'll make extras tomorrow because I'll be back for more . . ."

The praise and pleasure were fast flowing around Acorn Hill's resident baker, and she was soaking it in like a sun-bather enjoying the warmth on a summer's day. It took, Jane noticed, at least fifteen years off Clarissa's age to see her so happy. How could Clarissa even consider quitting something she loved so much? Jane knew the answer resided with Clarissa's children. They wanted their mother happy, of course, but by their own definition of happy: safe, secure, no long hours on her feet, near them so they could stop in when they were free. Clarissa's definition of happy, Jane mused, was probably quite different: busy, purposeful, needed, independent.

Clarissa caught Jane's eye and waved her into the back of the bakery. "Help me put out some more buns and doughnuts, will you? I'm almost out of cookies and rolls and it's barely noon. I'll have to double my batches tomorrow."

With practiced hands, Jane did as she was told. When the crowd had subsided and the stragglers went off lamenting the empty shelves, Clarissa poured two cups of coffee and invited Jane to sit down with her.

"Feels good to take a load off," Clarissa sighed.

"You're having fun, aren't you?"

Clarissa grinned and her face pleated with happy wrinkles. "I've loved this my entire life. Sometimes I've worried about making a living in this little town, but this reunion is becoming its own little gold mine. I'm going to have some money to bolster that retirement fund of mine." The grin faded. "Not that I want to use it anytime soon."

"That's just being prudent, not a sign you're going to quit."

The frown cleared. "You're absolutely right, no matter what she says. . . ." Clarissa's words drifted off.

"Who says?"

"Oh, Olivia called last night. She's asked for a couple extra days off from work and will be here tomorrow. 'To help you, Mother,' she said. *Harrumph.* Help me into an early grave, most likely." She put her thumb and index finger to the bridge of her nose and rubbed the soft indentations on either side.

"You're one of the most self-sufficient, independent women I know," Jane reminded her. "Don't let Livvy make decisions for you if you don't agree with them. You're perfectly capable of deciding things for yourself."

Clarissa looked doubtful, as if Livvy were more than a daughter—more a force of nature to be reckoned with, perhaps.

"What *do* you want?" Jane asked.

"What am I going to be when I grow up, you mean?"

"Something like that."

"I feel like a teenager having an identity crisis, Jane," Clarissa admitted. "I know it's happening all because the kids are coming home for the reunion. They haven't been in Acorn Hill together since high school and I have this bad feeling that they're going to 'gang up' on me."

"For what?"

"Look at me. I'm past 'retirement age.' They all have the idea that they're being 'bad' children if they don't make me stop working. I can handle their phone conversations one at a time, but all three of them here at once. . ."

"That has to do with their own self-imposed guilt. They just want people to think they're doing the right thing for their mother."

"And the 'right' thing in this case is to leave Mother alone," Clarissa said. "If that was only possible."

Jane could see Clarissa's worry and her frustration and was glad that she and her sisters had never tried to talk down to their father or assumed that just because he was old he was unable to think for himself.

"What do your kids want you to do, Clarissa? What are your options?"

"The only option is for me to stay in the bakery business until they carry me out like a sack of flour." Clarissa's eyes crinkled and twinkled again. "It's my kids who think there are other options."

"Such as?"

"Assisted living, an apartment near one of them, a 'companion' to help me, maybe a nursing home. Nothing I'm interested in, that's for sure." Clarissa took a sip of her coffee. "I've been considering getting a new car. I've got nearly a hundred thousand miles on my old one. And the kids are trying to talk me out of renewing my license."

"Not very tuned in to you, huh?"

"They only get back here once a year or so. How could they know how I live? When they're here, of course I get exhausted. I'm cooking all their favorite meals, watching the little ones so they can go out, doing laundry, picking up toys . . ."

"The bakery's a breeze compared to that, right?"

"Piece of cake, if you don't mind my saying so." Clarissa smiled. "I love them all dearly. Ray is most like me but they all resemble their father, bullheaded, opinionated and loyal as the day is long. It's just that their best qualities are sometimes also their worst ones." She wiped a tear from her eye. "I wish he were here. He'd know what to do."

"Perhaps it won't be as bad as you're anticipating. Maybe they only want to have a good time at the reunion."

Clarissa looked at Jane as if she had lost her mind. "Maybe. But don't count on it."

After leaving Clarissa's, Jane ran a few errands and when she returned to the inn she indulged in some work on her jewelry projects. Then she showered, changed and headed over to Sylvia's house for dinner.

"This is great beef stew," Jane said, dabbing her lips with her napkin. "Is there any more in that pot?"

Sylvia nodded and carried the pot over to Jane. "I'm flattered. I'm always a little scared to invite the great chef Jane Howard to dinner for fear my cooking won't stand the test."

"Don't be silly. Sometimes I'm so tired of cooking that I'd give anything for someone to wait on me. This is absolutely perfect, Sylvia. You're a wonderful cook." Jane looked at her friend speculatively. "Did you ever think of settling down with someone special? Or do you like your independence too much?"

"Oh, I thought about it all right. In fact, I assumed that I'd have been married for twenty years by now. Funny how things turn out sometimes." She went to a shelf that held several pictures and chose one in a small silver frame. "And this is who I'd planned to marry."

Jane studied the black and white photo of a military man. He was stern and handsome, staring directly into the camera lens.

"That's James Marcot Wilson," Sylvia said softly. "The love of my life."

Jane held the framed photo gently. "Tell me more."

"Oh, there's not so much to tell. The older I get, the smaller the portion of my life was spent with James. We were college sweethearts." A smile played on Sylvia's soft features. "I was so in love with him that

I barely remember a class I took. He wasn't much better but managed to graduate with honors anyway. He became a military pilot. Doesn't he look handsome in that uniform?"

Jane studied the photo again, and then nodded. "What happened?"

"Life intruded on our love story." Sylvia picked up a dishcloth and scrubbed an already clean area on the table. "He decided that the best route for us was for him to stay in the military. I didn't mind. All I could think about was having a military wedding." She smiled ruefully. "I'm a sucker for a man in uniform."

"I didn't know you were married."

"Oh, I wasn't. I only dreamed of it. James spent a lot of his time flying. He loved that more than anything. He talked about his plane with as much affection as he did me."

Sylvia's expression became distant, remembering something long since past. "He promised to take me up in a plane some day."

"And did he?"

"No. There was an accident and James quit flying. A fire broke out in the plane on a routine mission. His crew was badly burned trying to put it out. He was able to land the plane and come out unscathed but for a broken leg, but his navigator didn't make it. He died a month later from the effects of the burns. He was in excruciating pain and James wouldn't leave his side."

"I'm so sorry."

"It was awful," Sylvia said. "I thought James would

lose his mind. He felt responsible for what happened."

"And then?"

"And then he changed. He couldn't get over it and he couldn't forgive himself for the accident. James did this." She opened her hands wide and then slowly curled her fingers in upon themselves until she made tight little fists. "He refused to talk to a counselor or anyone who might have helped him. It was as though he wanted, or needed, to do penance for what had gone wrong."

Sylvia recounted her story in even, unemotional tones, but Jane knew that her outside calm was only a cover for the emotions eating away at her. "He changed after that, became distant and absentminded. Sometimes it was as if he didn't even hear me when I spoke."

"But the wedding . . ."

"We kept putting it off, hoping that he'd be better soon. But he never got better."

Sylvia shifted in her chair. "I never lost hope, even after his first breakdown. I thought that once he was out of the hospital, things would get back to normal, but for James, there was no 'normal' anymore. He was in and out of institutions for six years before I accepted that the man I'd loved didn't even exist anymore. All that was left was a pale shadow that I didn't even recognize. James disappeared in front of my eyes."

"Where is he now?" Jane's heart ached for Sylvia.

"I don't know. As long as his parents were alive, I

kept in touch with them. He'd live at home and work for a while at some job or other and then disappear. Eventually he'd come back to try to pull himself together and the cycle would start again. They never gave up hoping something would turn around for him, but they went to their graves waiting."

"So he's just . . . gone?"

"His sister writes to me every couple of years to tell me if she's heard from him. The last I heard she didn't know where he was."

"Oh, Sylvia, I am so sorry."

"I wouldn't have believed it if I hadn't seen it for myself. He could never forgive himself for his friend's death and could never quit reliving it or punishing himself for letting it happen."

"But it wasn't his fault. It was an accident."

"I know that and you know that. Even James knew it on some level, but he just couldn't get beyond it." She looked at Jane sharply. "Things happen to a person that can have a profound and lasting effect. It doesn't always make sense. It may be perfectly clear to everyone else how to deal with whatever it is, but to the one who's hurting . . ."

Sylvia looked at Jane with a speculative expression of her own in her eyes. "But you know how that is, to have something that happened in your youth affect you for years to come."

"Shirley Taylor, you mean?" Shirley had been on Jane's mind a lot lately. She had been replaying the video of that fateful moment in high school in her mind. She felt a pang of empathy and sadness for James Marcot Wilson. The burden he had carried was far, far worse.

"She probably had no idea how deeply the wound went," Sylvia commented. Her eyes were warm and compassionate as she looked at Jane. "Just as none of the rest of us ever really knew what James had felt." Sylvia was steering the conversation away from herself and back to Jane. "What was Shirley like? Otherwise, I mean."

Jane sat back and pondered the question. "Quiet, mostly. She never seemed to hang around with anyone special. She just attached herself to whatever crowd was available. She was like a . . . a chameleon, changing colors to blend in. The only time I ever really saw her animated was when she was around a couple of the guys on the football team."

"Really? I wonder why?"

Jane's expression grew distant. "Jeremy Patterson, my high-school sweetheart, was on the team. Jeremy Patterson. Quarterback, weight lifter, all around cutie. He was so sweet to me—and to everyone."

"How so?" Sylvia tucked her feet beneath her and settled in for a long story.

"He just was. It was his nature to be considerate and thoughtful. He always saw things that no one else seemed to see. He knew when people were hurt, upset or disappointed and he always acknowledged it, even when he couldn't do a thing about it." Jane sighed. "For a time, I really thought I loved Jeremy."

"And?"

"And I suppose I did—not mature love so much as appreciative love. I was so grateful that I was fortunate enough to know a person as kind—and handsome—as he."

"A lovable teddy bear," Sylvia murmured.

"That pretty much sums up Jeremy."

"Where did you meet him?"

"He belonged to our church, Grace Chapel. He was the only boyfriend I ever had that my entire family approved of. Even Father trusted Jeremy." Jane felt sad. "But after the trouble with Shirley, even the thought of Jeremy couldn't keep me in Acorn Hill."

"What if that was her motive? Maybe she loved Jeremy too."

"Of course. Everyone did."

"I mean *loved*. You were in her way. Maybe she thought that if you weren't in the picture, Jeremy would be free to love her."

"No . . . that couldn't be . . . even if . . . he wouldn't have . . ." Jane paused to stare at Sylvia. "You could be right. It wouldn't be surprising if she cared about Jeremy. Every girl did. Not romantically, of course, but as a friend. There's no way she could have known. . . ." Jane's voice trailed off.

"Known what?" Sylvia persisted.

"That she was one of the few people that Jeremy actually didn't like. He was uncomfortable around her."

"No wonder," Sylvia commented. "Good intuition, that Jeremy."

Jane sat back and pondered the discussion. "And I was oblivious to it all."

"That's how it is with the popular kids, Jane. They have no idea how jealous others can be." Sylvia's eyes clouded. "Believe me, I know. I was on the outside."

Jane was overwhelmed with compassion. "Were you hurt a lot?"

"Not so that it broke me. I was lucky. I was always wearing these amazing clothes my mother made for me. I might have been poor, but I was also interesting. It gave me an edge."

"Would you like to see James again?" Jane asked.

"I'm not sure. In some ways, I want to remember him as he was when we met. And in others . . ." she sighed.

"Yes?"

"I suppose I still love him. I love who he was, if not what he is now." Her eyes misted. "But I would also be afraid."

Then she seemed to shake off the melancholy that thoughts of James inspired. "One more question," Sylvia said. "Whatever happened to Jeremy Patterson?"

"Is that a dragonfly? Why do they call them dragons? Are they really dragons or is it just because they look like them? What do real dragons look like? Do they breathe fire like they do in storybooks? My mom says . . ."

Jane closed her eyes and shut out Josie's endless

string of questions. It had seemed like a good idea at the time to invite the little girl to join her at Fairy Pond. The child, after all, had been playing in the inn's driveway, patiently waiting for her mother to get home from work, which was nearly two hours away. Better her here than dodging traffic, right?

"Fern is a funny word, isn't it, Jane? Furrn—like on a kitty, right? Fur-urn. Why are some ferns like lace and others kind of clumpy and not very pretty? Why do they call them all ferns? My mom says that her grandmother always had a fern on a stand in her living room. Fern. Fuuuurrrrrrnnnn. Furn. Furniture. Furnace. Fern . . ."

Josie, even sitting still, seemed to be in action. Her little bottom bounced on the tree stump that she had claimed as a chair and her curls seemed to be animated by a life of their own. Her mouth never stopped. It was always smiling or asking questions. And given permission, her pert nose would poke into everything and everybody's business.

There was to be no soothing, mind-releasing sketching today, Jane thought. With Josie around, the only thing she could think to draw were whirligigs, Ferris wheels and children doing cartwheels.

Suddenly Josie stopped squirming and turned to Jane. "Is the ree-union going to be fun?"

"I hope so."

"I've never been to one before. Mom says I'm not old enough to have a ree-union. But I'm old enough to go to this one, aren't I?"

"Oh yes. And I think you'll like it. There'll be lots of food, a little carnival, music . . ."

"And a car wash!" Josie chortled. "Mom says it's *Alice's* car wash. Isn't that funny, Jane? I didn't know Alice liked to wash cars." Josie giggled and kicked her feet.

"Alice's car wash." That, actually, was what it had come to be called, much to Alice's dismay. Every streak and spot left unpolished on those cars would be Alice's responsibility. Poor Alice was having a minor nervous breakdown over the entire affair. She had never washed a car in her life, other than using the automated one at the gas station. As the reunion neared—and it was almost the Day—Alice became more and more edgy.

When Jane had finally gotten Josie to settle down with a pad of sketch paper and a handful of colored pencils, she started drawing the large old stump that had been challenging her on her last few visits. The thing had personality with its gnarled shape and rough bark. It was a very old stump and sometimes Jane tried to imagine what the tree had seen in its lifetime—and what the stump had seen since. Generations of birds, rabbits and deer, squirrels and fox, insects and humans, no doubt. As she tried to imagine the old stump alive and speaking, she could see a crack in the base that could very well be a mouth. And the knot-hole to the left, an eye, definitely an eye . . .

She was so engrossed that it took her some time to realize they were no longer alone at Fairy Pond.

The crash and clatter of footsteps breaking their way through the delicate environment sounded like a harsh intrusion after the whirr of wings and warbles of birds. Even Josie's little voice had seemed at home in this place, but not the loud clomping that was coming their way.

Jane was about to gather Josie close to her when Mr. Enrich broke through the wall of forest and stumbled into the magical land of Fairy Pond.

His clothes were rumpled, as if branches and twigs had been pulling at him, and his hair was decorated with leaves and spiderwebs. He looked utterly out of place in the severe dark clothing he always wore, and it was obvious that the trek through the woods had damaged his shoes.

It was he, not Jane and Josie, who was startled. "You!"

"Hi, Mr. Enrich, how are you today?"

"What are you doing here?" Josie asked.

Jane had thought to ask the same thing but the question sounded much sweeter coming from the child.

"We came to draw pictures and paint," Josie went on without waiting for an answer. "Sometimes Jane brings me here. Do you want to see what I drew?" Josie dived for the picture, which might have been the ferns around the pond—or just about anything else in the woodsy tangle of greenery.

"Very nice," Mr. Enrich stammered, taken aback at finding someone here, in the middle of nowhere.

"Did you come to draw too?" Josie inquired. "Do

you want to use some of my paper?"

He looked so out of place and befuddled in his black loafers, dress pants, and dark shirt and tie that Jane had to stifle her laughter. No doubt he had left his suit coat in the car before venturing into the woods.

"No, I, *ah* . . . I just wanted to take a walk."

"And you found us!" Josie concluded delightedly. She turned to Jane. "Isn't it time for lunch yet? Can we share it with Mr. Enrich?"

Jane glanced at her watch. "I think it's exactly time for lunch and I made plenty." She looked at Mr. Enrich. "Will you join us?"

It was Josie who had him trapped. She had already dragged out the picnic basket, found the red-and-white checked flannel-backed plastic tablecloth and was spreading it across the tree stump Jane had been sketching.

Mr. Enrich shot Jane a pleading glance, as if to say, "Help me get out of this," but Jane had no intention of doing anything to help him escape. Instead she pulled a bowl out of the basket. "Three-bean salad with my secret dressing. Ham sandwiches, fruit and Josie's favorite caramel cake for dessert."

"And don't forget these." Josie held up a bag of salt-and-vinegar potato chips and a thermos of lemonade. "And," her voice lowered, "Jane says there's a surprise in the bottom of the basket if we're good."

Jane was not sure Mr. Enrich would be tempted to behave by a coloring book and a packet of crayons, but who knew with him, anyway?

He sat down on the ground in front of the stump and gave a little groan, like an old man whose joints had frozen. Misery seemed to be his middle name. Of course, Jane reminded herself, they did not even know his first name yet.

Josie presided over lunch like a queen over her subjects, handing out sandwiches, serving lemonade in plastic cups and generally taking charge.

"Do you want to say grace, Mr. Enrich?" Josie asked. "Jane and I always say grace."

Mr. Enrich's terrified deer-in-the-headlights expression compelled Jane to say, "I'd like to pray today, Josie."

"Oh, okay." The little girl folded her hands and bowed her head. Mr. Enrich, following her lead, mimicked her pose.

"Dear Heavenly Father," Jane began, "thank You for this lovely place You created and the miracle of every tree and bug and flower. Thank You for the food we are about to eat. Without Your gifts, we have nothing and are nothing. And thank You for our little trio of friends today. I believe there are no coincidences, Lord, only God-incidences, and for whatever reason we're here together. Help us to make the most of this opportunity to share food, friendship and support. We ask it in His name. Amen."

Josie heartily echoed, "Amen."

Mr. Enrich made a strangled little sound half way between a sob and a sigh.

Three-bean salad and ham sandwiches seemed to be

on Mr. Enrich's list of top ten foods, Jane observed, and she was glad she had, as usual, packed far more than she and Josie could eat. Generally she sent the leftovers home with Josie so her mother would not have to cook dinner that night, but today there would not be a crumb left behind.

After she ate, Josie spread out on a bed of soft grass, her arm beneath her head, and began to grow sleepy. As her eyelids drooped she struggled to keep them open, but eventually she dozed off.

"I suppose I should move along . . ." Mr. Enrich began.

"Not for me, you don't. Now that Josie's asleep, there's nothing that will keep me from sketching. If you'd like, take a nap yourself."

"It's tempting but . . ."

"But what? You're on vacation."

For a moment, Mr. Enrich looked startled, as if he had not remembered that was his purpose, but he did lie down on his back and gazed at the canopy of green decorated with bright birds and filtered rays of sunlight. When Jane turned from her sketching to speak to him, he, too, was fast asleep. Resting, some of the worry lines in his face faded, and for the first time Jane realized what it might look like to see Mr. Enrich at peace.

She was packing the last of her equipment when Josie and Mr. Enrich awoke.

"Done already?" Josie asked disappointedly.

"It's been over two hours, sleepyhead."

"Two hours!" Mr. Enrich sat up straight. "I haven't had a two-hour nap in . . . well, I can't remember when."

"Good. It was time then. Come on, Van Gogh, come on Raphael, it's time for me to see what's happening at the inn."

They trudged back to the road and to what Jane called "civilization," though she had always thought Fairy Pond was one of the most civilized places she knew.

Alice met Jane at the door. "Jane, would you do me a favor?"

"Sure. What's up?"

"I have a meeting at the church. Could you go to the Good Apple? I left an order with Clarissa for the meeting's refreshments, and she said she would have it ready about now."

"Okay, I'll be back in a few minutes. I'll take them to the assembly room for you."

"Thank you, Jane." Alice put her hand to her head. "I've had so much to do. . . ."

Poor Alice, Jane thought as she jogged toward the Good Apple. If her heart were any bigger for the youth of the church, it would burst. It was not an easy job keeping up with that kind of youthful energy.

When she got to the Good Apple, the door was already closed and the blinds pulled. Clarissa must have run out of baked goods very early today. Jane walked around to the back of the building and called through the screen door. "Clarissa? It's Jane. Sorry I'm late to pick up Alice's order. I didn't think you'd be closed this early. . . ."

A small gasp escaped Jane's lips. The large wooden kneading table in the center of Clarissa's kitchen was piled high with baked goods—bags of buns and cookies, loaves of bread and two intricately decorated cakes. Clarissa was obviously not out of product.

"Clarissa!" Jane called more loudly. The lights were turned off in the back of the bakery, but she stepped into the dimness anyway.

"Don't trip."

The voice came out of the far corner where Clarissa's tiny office was located. It, too, was dark, but as Jane's eyes adjusted to the dimness, she could see Clarissa inside, sitting in the dark, leaning back in the old office chair she had had since before her husband had died.

"Are you okay?" Jane made her way toward the office. "Why are you sitting here in the dark?"

"I'm hiding, mostly." Clarissa sighed. "You're welcome to hide out with me if you like."

Eyes adjusting, Jane found a second chair and sat down just outside the doorway of the office. "What are we hiding from?"

"Reality, mostly."

"Would you like to explain?"

"Olivia arrived this morning."

"How nice."

"Yes." Clarissa sounded as happy about it as she had

when the plumbing broke at the bakery a few months back.

"Not so nice, then? Let me try to interpret this," Jane suggested. "Livvy arrived even earlier than expected and caught you working here in the wee hours of the morning. She thought you were working too hard and scolded you about it."

"Close." A chuckle grew out of the dimness. "When I wasn't at the house, Livvy, unable to believe that I still went to work that early, decided I'd had a heart attack or been kidnapped or wandered off in a vacant elderly haze. Without even checking out the bakery, she went to Fred Humbert, because she knew he is always willing to help, woke him out of a sound sleep to come with her to find me." Clarissa shook her head. "That girl has been watching too much television."

"And what did Fred say?"

"Not a thing. He knew Livvy as a little girl and recalled all her theatrics. He just went along with her. Said he'd be happy to go along and 'save your mother's life.' Besides, he stops at the Good Apple for coffee almost every morning before I open the store, so he knew good and well where I was."

"And when she saw you, was your daughter embarrassed over her histrionics?"

"Not in the least. She said it just proved that I worked much too hard and that I needed 'more care' than I was getting."

" 'More care?' As in . . ."

"A retirement home, probably, so I can start acting like the grandmother I am."

"I hate to say it, Clarissa, but your daughter is a little deluded about you. . . ."

"Livvy is dead set on 'helping' me quit working."

"Do you want to?"

"Not on your life." Clarissa paused. "It wouldn't hurt to ease up a little, to take a trip once in a while or sleep in until six, but that's as much 'quitting' as I want to do."

"So tell her that."

Clarissa gave Jane a withering look. "Livvy's a woman in search of a cause, Jane. I'm afraid this is her cause at the moment. And things are going to be even worse when her brothers come along."

"Wow." Jane sat back and folded her arms over her chest. "Do any of them know how unempowering that attitude is?"

"Opinionated, like their father," Clarissa said, as if that explained everything. "And I know they love me so much they think they have to 'protect' me. Trouble is, I don't want to be protected. If I can just get through these next days without the people I love most in the world driving me crazy, I'll consider the reunion a success."

She paused. "Oh, by the way. That nice young couple stopped in, the ones who are going to help me during the reunion. I think we'll get along just dandy. Thanks, Jane, for finding them for me."

"For Acorn Hill, more accurately, and especially for

Lloyd. He's convinced that an event without your baked goods will fail on that point alone."

They were chuckling when they heard the screen door open and crash shut.

"Mother? Mother? Are you in here? Are you okay?"

An overhead light flicked on, leaving Jane and Clarissa blinking stupidly for a moment until their eyes adjusted.

"What on earth are you doing sitting in the dark . . . oh, hello. I didn't realize Mother had someone with her."

"Hi, Olivia," Jane greeted her.

Olivia Cottrell was even more beautiful than she had been as a child. She was as slim and tall as Clarissa, but while her mother appeared long and wiry, Livvy looked like a model—willowy and regal. She wore her nearly black hair pulled back into a severe knot that accentuated her already exotically slanted eyes. Clad in pristine white trousers, a lemon-yellow cotton-knit sweater and a navy double-breasted jacket emblazoned with the crest of a well-known designer, she looked as though she had stepped off a page of a slick fashion catalogue. Her lips and her nails were an identical shade of blood red and the gold jewelry at her ears and on her wrists was undoubtedly real. She was a beautiful and intimidating woman.

Jane's heart sank a little. She saw immediately what Louise, Alice and Clarissa had meant. Livvy was obviously accustomed to getting her own way. In fact, the way she carried herself and her air of confidence hinted that anyone would be foolish to disagree with her.

"I'm Jane Howard, Livvy," Jane stood and thrust out her hand. "You probably know my sisters better—Alice and Louise?"

"Reverend Howard's family." Livvy gave Jane a beautiful smile. "As a little girl, I thought your father was the most wonderful man in the world. We'd leave church on Sunday mornings and he would reach out to shake my hand, just as he did all the adults, and greet me as if my presence had made his day. Such a good, sweet man."

"I fully agree," Jane said, touched. "He had a love for children."

"I know. I think more than anyone, he influenced me to become a teacher and even a school administrator. I never forgot how valued and respected he made me feel, even as a little girl. I hope I'm doing some of that for the children I have in my charge now."

Jane glanced at Clarissa, who was beaming with maternal pride. No wonder Clarissa loved her so—and no wonder she wanted to avoid any sort of confrontation. A woman with such passion and fervor for her beliefs would be hard to convince that any opinion other than her own could be right.

"Now back to my original question: What are you two doing sitting in the dark?"

"Enjoying the calm before the storm," Jane said deftly. "We're gearing up, that's all."

"What do you think of my mother still working like a slave in this bakery?" Livvy asked.

"I think your mother is remarkable. She and the Good Apple are a tradition in this little town. I'm delighted that we're going to have plenty of opportunity to taste the best baked goods in the entire state."

Livvy opened and closed her eyes owlishly. That was not the sentiment she had expected—or wanted—to hear. "But don't you think it's hard on her? Isn't it time for her to relax and enjoy herself?"

"Quit talking about me like I'm not here, child," Clarissa chided.

Livvy rolled her eyes a bit as she turned toward Jane, as if they were discussing an errant child just out of earshot.

"Maybe the bakery is a way for her to relax and enjoy herself," Jane suggested. "Granted, it's been hectic lately, but generally it is a wonderful way for her to see all her friends every day when they come to shop."

Clarissa nodded emphatically at that.

"But think of all the *fun* things there are to do. Mom, you could be in a craft club, doing senior water aerobics, going on the senior bus to plays and concerts . . ."

"Crafts! More stuff to fill my house with? And water aerobics? Livvy, have you ever, in your entire life, seen me enjoy the water?"

"You went fishing with Papa and me once."

"And sat on the shore and waved at you two in the boat."

"And you came to every single play, concert or

event any of us kids were in during our school years."

"Got my fill then," Clarissa retorted. "Honey, my fun, my relaxation and my hobby is this business. Don't try to take that away from me."

"I've seen how stiff you are in the morning."

"And coming here limbers me up."

"You were tired when I arrived, I know you were."

"And a cup of coffee with my regular customers wakes me right up and cheers me for the entire day."

"And you're not as young as you used to be."

For that, Clarissa had no answer.

Chapter ❧ Eight

She laughs at everything you say. Why?
Because she has fine teeth.
—Benjamin Franklin

Is there something wrong with you?" Louise asked Jane. "You have been moping all morning."

"I'm not moping, really," Jane said, "but I am concerned." She told her sisters about the conversation she had had with Livvy and her mother.

"Frankly, they both have a point," Louise said reasonably. "The Good Apple *is* a lot for Clarissa. She will admit that to anyone but Livvy, because Livvy is set on making her mother take it easy. Clarissa wants to decide for herself what her next step might be."

"Livvy doesn't realize that the most fun her mother ever has is in that bakery," Alice said. "Why, Clarissa told me once that decorating cakes day and night would be her idea of a good time. As long as I've known Clarissa, she's never had another hobby other than her work."

"And, you might have just hit the nail on the head," said Jane. "If she weren't at the bakery, I think Clarissa might just die of boredom."

"Well, she will not be bored this week," Louise said. "Nancy and Zack went to visit with her. They are eager to get started." Louise shook her head. "That is another topic of conversation. I wish those two could agree on what they want to do with their lives."

Clarissa and Livvy. Nancy and Zack. Mr. Enrich. All troubled souls. As Louise poured more coffee for herself and Alice sipped her tea, Jane reached for the small Bible that always lay somewhere in the kitchen and flipped to the thirty-seventh chapter of the Psalms:

"Though he stumble, he will not fall,
for the Lord upholds him with his hand."

Lord, Jane prayed silently, *there are people here who are stumbling. Reach out Your hand to each of them and send them on the right path, the path You want for them. Amen.*

At that moment, Nancy arrived in the kitchen. "Jane, Zack sent me to tell you that you should come and convince Mrs. Cottrell to take a break this afternoon. We can handle the bakery now that we've got our strategy planned for the reunion. He thinks she should rest up. What do you think?"

Poor Clarissa. Everyone was either trying to send her to bed or out to pasture—and they all thought they were being kind doing it.

"She's sturdier than Zack thinks, but it's lovely of him to be so considerate." Jane paused before adding gently, "Next time, you might just ask *Clarissa* what she feels like doing."

Nancy bobbed her head agreeably, as if that were an option that neither of them had considered.

When Nancy left, Louise spoke up. "Why does everyone think age is a disease? Clarissa could teach those youngsters a thing or two."

"Everyone has to reinvent the wheel," Alice said quietly. "I see young people do it every day. It's as if they know a better way than anyone who's gone before them."

"You did not do that to Father," Louise pointed out. "You always deferred to his wisdom."

"That's because he had so much of it," Alice said. "I still miss the talks we use to have."

"I wish Livvy would listen to her mother. She could learn a lot too."

There was a knock at the door, interrupting their conversation. "Anybody home?"

"Hi, Vera, we're back here," Jane called, recognizing their friend's voice.

Vera came into the kitchen looking frazzled. "Do you have any vacancies for the reunion? A single would do."

"Sorry, Vera. We're full. Did you get an unexpected guest?"

"No. Everybody is expected and everyone is coming."

"Then who's the room for?"

"Me." Vera dropped into a chair and groaned. "I told Fred we might as well install a revolving door on the front of the house. Both girls are here and some of their old classmates have descended already. It's like high school all over again but worse because they have no curfew and I can't say, 'No, you can't do that, not as long as you live under my roof.' And they're the best behaved of our relatives. The rest of them will flock in, leaving Fred and me to cook and clean while they can go out and enjoy the reunion."

"Don't cook or clean," Jane suggested. "There will be plenty of things to eat—especially for breakfast. I've never been known to skimp on portions. And you can clean the house after they leave. That's when it will need it."

"See? That's why I need to run away from home and come to a place where there's some common sense. I can't even think in my own house."

"We are full—top to bottom—or we would help you out. Every nook and cranny is filled, even some that should not be," said Louise.

"What do you mean?"

"Mr. Enrich is staying for the reunion and has agreed to sleep in the library on a cot, of all things," Louise told her. "Jane thinks it is a fine idea but I think it is awful—what kind of innkeeper would do that?"

"The kind that won't kick someone out onto the street because they want to hang around and enjoy the fun," Jane said calmly. "Besides, it makes him happy. I think he's enjoying this."

"How can you tell?" Louise said dryly.

Jane shot her sister a look. "I think I saw him smile yesterday."

"Who made that miracle happen?" Louise asked.

"Josie."

"Oh. That explains it. She can make anyone smile."

Vera glanced at her watch. "If you can't take me in, can you at least promise that if things get too out of hand, I can come and sit in your garden instead of my own?"

"We'll even give you some iced tea—and an aspirin," Jane assured her.

How, Jane wondered, was she supposed to get Clarissa out of the bakery mid-afternoon to take a rest? Zack and Nancy were trying to be considerate of Clarissa, but getting her to leave the bakery was nearly impossible. On impulse, she picked up the bag of sketchbooks and pencils that she and Josie had used the other day as she was walking out the door.

Sylvia waved her down as she was walking toward the Good Apple. She looked surprisingly calm, considering that the countdown clock to the reunion was ticking noisily.

Jane commented to that effect.

"Oh, I've given up," Sylvia said cheerfully. "What happens, happens. We've tried our best. Now all we can do is point people in the right direction, put out fires and hope and pray for success. It's in the hands of our volunteers now. I'm going to start enjoying things."

At that moment, Wilhelm Wood joined them on the sidewalk. He addressed Jane. "I've got everything settled about the beverages and more than enough helpers. When the time comes, speak up and tell them what you need them to do."

"Then I think we're set." Jane turned to Sylvia. "Everything's covered."

"Music to my ears."

"Not quite everything," Wilhelm interjected. A smile played around his lips.

Sylvia leaned forward. "What do you mean?"

"Obviously Viola hasn't found you yet this morning."

"I've been hiding from her, actually. She's in a twist over the books we've asked her to order. 'Too silly,' according to her."

"Oh, it's more than that now. . . ."

Wilhelm's comment was interrupted by a vociferous *"Yoo-hoo! Yoo-hoo!"* from across the street. Viola charged toward them without looking to the right or to the left. Poor Carlene Moss, editor of the *Acorn Nutshell,* had to slam on the brakes of her car as Viola trotted in front of her.

Viola was a palette of color in her teal blue pantsuit

and rainbow-colored scarf. Her face was bright pink under her rouged cheeks. "I must make a statement."

"Yes?" Sylvia asked tentatively.

"I want to file an official protest with the reunion committee. I have been forced to order boxes and boxes of books, tapes and CDs that will never be purchased. I will have to return them all. That 'good idea' to have a reunion bookstore in the marketplace was misguided. Who will purchase ridiculous tapes of music from the sixties and seventies? What kind of character would want to read a book, *Autobiography of a Flower Child* or *What They Wore in 74* or some such nonsense? Reminiscing is one thing, but . . ."

"Actually," Sylvia said, "I'll buy a copy of *What They Wore in 74*. I don't have that one in my collection of books on fashion. Do you have any others like it? Since I started collecting vintage clothing, the word's gone out about it and I get calls from people searching for certain garments. The seventies are far enough in the past to be collectible. Please put one aside for me. I'd hate to have them sell out without getting one."

The look on Viola's face was worth a thousand words. No, maybe a million, Jane thought.

Deflated, Viola walked off, now apparently worrying that she might be in danger of actually selling some books and thereby ruining her reputation for carrying fine literature.

It was not until she disappeared around the corner that the trio erupted in laughter.

"Shame on you, Sylvia," Wilhelm chided. "Being interested in a 'silly' book."

"Hardly silly. I didn't even know it existed until now. I can't wait to see it."

"I'm not sure what Viola fears most, not selling her books or selling them." Jane glanced at her watch. "I should go. I'm a woman on a mission."

When she arrived at the bakery, Clarissa was sitting out front having a conversation with Craig Tracy from Wild Things. Nancy was behind the counter pulling empty trays from the displays and replacing them with full ones. Jane could see Zack moving around in back with swift, efficient steps.

"Hi, Craig. Are you ready for the onslaught?"

"As ready as I'll ever be. How about you?"

"If I've learned anything over the years, it's plan well, hire the best and enjoy the ride. The planning is done. We obviously," and Jane tipped her head toward Clarissa and then the Colwins, "have hired the best. Now all that's left is enjoying the ride."

"Well said, Jane." Craig clapped his open palms on his thighs before he stood up. "I'm going to take your advice. I'd better go back to the store and make sure my floral orders are caught up. Cheers, Clarissa."

Clarissa waved.

"Look at you," Jane said to Clarissa after Craig had departed.

"Sitting around like a queen," Clarissa acknowledged with a smile. "I had no idea it could feel so good."

"Just 'sitting around,' you mean?"

"No, sitting in my own business and overseeing a staff as smart and quick as the Colwins. I should have hired help years ago."

"What's stopping you now?" Jane inquired.

Clarissa's eyes twinkled. "At the moment? Livvy is stopping me. She got some of those stubborn genes from me. I want it to be *my* idea, not hers. Livvy understands children and school systems but I think that girl needs to learn a little more about old people. They don't like being bossed about and having decisions made for them any more than young people do. I may be wrinkled but I'm not weird. And I'm younger up here," Clarissa tapped her head with her index finger, "than many people. Probably even Livvy."

"I love it." Jane sat back and grinned. "You teach 'em, Clarissa. But how about an even bigger break from the grind before this reunion gets into full swing and engulfs us all?"

"What do you have in mind?"

"Josie and I were at Fairy Pond yesterday and it was just lovely."

"Fairy Pond. I haven't been there in years. Why, my hubby and I used to go out there to," Clarissa blushed, "spoon."

Jane smiled, trying to imagine Clarissa and her husband kissing under the canopy of foliage encompassing Fairy Pond. "Then it's past time that you make a return visit. I've got apples and water in my bag. It's not much, but we can pretend it's lunch."

143

"I've got tuna fish sandwiches," Clarissa offered. "And all the cookies we can eat."

"Done."

"Done." Clarissa rose to get ready for her first picnic in twenty years.

"It's even more beautiful than I remember." Clarissa sat on the stump Josie had used the day before for a table. "How everything has grown. Some of these trees were just saplings and now they're giants."

"It's one of my favorite places," Jane admitted. "I come here to sketch or design jewelry. There's inspiration here."

"I see that."

"Do you draw, Clarissa?"

"Just my breath, nothing else."

"I can't believe that. Look at all the beautiful cakes you've made over the years."

"That's with a pastry tube and a little butter and sugar, hardly the real thing."

"Don't sell yourself short." Jane reached into her bag and pulled out the sketchbook Josie had used. "Want to try it?"

"Sure. Then you'll see that I'm telling you the truth, and I can shut my eyes and take a nap out here." Clarissa reached for the paper and colored pencils Jane handed her.

They were quiet then, Jane intent on her design for a brooch that reflected the mist of ferns hovering near the lake. Neither spoke for a long time.

Finally, the design satisfactory, Jane looked up. Clarissa was absorbed in sketching, her tongue caught between her teeth and her brow furrowed. Whatever she was drawing, she was working hard at it.

Clarissa raised her head and looked embarrassed. "This is kind of fun."

"I think so. May I see your drawing?"

"It's not much yet, but . . . ." She held up a full-page drawing of Fairy Pond dotted with lily pads. From one of the lily pads, a frog was jumping, his green body stretched its full length and, Jane wasn't quite sure how Clarissa had managed it, an intent, do-or-die sort of expression on his tiny face. His mottled green skin seemed to glisten in sunlight.

"That is absolutely marvelous!" Jane exclaimed. "And you told me you couldn't draw."

"Didn't know I could." Clarissa studied the picture. "Huh. How about that? I started working at the bakery when I was a little girl and just never quit. My parents never thought to encourage me to do anything but the family business. I learned to decorate cakes by watching my parents do them. I never saw either one pick up a pencil to draw." She held it out and squinted at it. "It kind of looks like the pond, doesn't it?"

"Clarissa, it is an amazing likeness. And you've even improved upon the pond. I love that frog."

"His name is Ed."

Jane did a double take. "What?"

"The frog's name is Ed. I drew a few other sketches of him and decided he needed a name." She flipped back the pages to other sketches. Ed poised on the lily pad. Ed diving into the water with only the back half of his body showing. Ed sitting on a tiny stool, and Ed on his back legs peeking through a faint sketch of a window.

Jane laughed out loud. "This is marvelous! How inventive. Clarissa, I've seen children's books illustrated with much less creativity than this."

"Go on. You're just trying to make an old lady feel good about herself."

"Not where art is concerned. This is great. Maybe *I'll* start decorating cakes for practice."

"Don't be silly. This is nothing like what you do."

"No? Probably not. It has the potential to be even better."

Clarissa rolled her eyes at that.

"I wonder how your kids will react when they learn that you can do this."

"It will be a surprise. All they ever saw me do was work—at the bakery, at home, in the garden, at church. Of course, I didn't have much choice once their dad was gone. I had to earn a living and keep them clean and fed." Clarissa's expression saddened. "Sometimes I wonder if Livvy's work habits are my fault. I didn't teach her much about resting."

"And the boys?" Jane sensed this was a direction Clarissa wanted to go.

"They're a little better. I'm thankful that they married wives who made them slow down for the sake of their families." She leaned back and gave a gusty sigh.

"I wish I'd thought to bring them out here."

"It's not too late. You have grandchildren, you know."

"They're far away and I'm an old woman now. . . ."

"Now that's the lamest excuse I've heard in a long time."

Clarissa chuckled. "It sounded pretty bad to me too. But until I get Livvy—or the bakery—off my back, I'm not going to have much time for anything else. That girl has practically said that she thinks it's time I consider a nursing home. Well, maybe not that, but somewhere I can have 'meals, a social director and company my own age.' "

Jane wrinkled her nose. " 'Company your own age'? What fun is that? Variety is the spice of life."

"Tell that to Livvy."

"Just promise me this. Now that you've started drawing, will you keep it up?" Jane took extra sketchbooks, pencils and a little watercolor kit with brushes from her bag. "I want you to have these."

"I couldn't take those. They must have cost you a fortune."

"I'll trade you then. For one of your pictures."

"You're getting the raw end of that deal," Clarissa said, shaking her head.

"That's for me to decide. Will you take them?"

Clarissa looked longingly at the equipment at her feet. "It was fun to draw that frog. . . ."

"Then do it for Ed."

That settled it. Clarissa gathered the art materials and stuck them in her own bag.

"Jane, someone from your graduating class called to remind you about 'the big party.' " Alice was carrying clean towels through the kitchen toward the upstairs bedrooms.

" 'Big party?' Isn't that what this entire reunion is? One big party."

"No, something else. Something formal. She said you should bring a guest."

Jane groaned. "Oh, that's the reception for all the graduates on Friday night. Every school in the county is having one in their hometown. You're going to it, aren't you? After some mingling time, the classes are supposed to congregate. I suppose that's when we get to look one another over and see who's got the most gray hair, jowls, wrinkles and chins."

"Well, it certainly won't be you. Sometimes I think you're even prettier now than you were in high school, so . . . what is it the kids say? . . . so 'together.' "

"That is very sweet of you, Alice, but I can already feel my insecurities flaring. Besides, someone had the brilliant idea that this event should be a formal affair. Can you believe it? What are we supposed to do? Squeeze into our old prom dresses and tuxedoes? Ridiculous."

Louise, who had entered the room mid-speech asked, "Insecurities? You? Jane, whatever do you have to feel insecure about?"

Alice shot her older sister a look.

"Oh, you mean that thing Shirley Taylor said? Do

not pay one bit of attention to that. You were both young."

"Of course," Alice said slyly, "you don't want to go to the formal party without an attractive man on your arm—just like in high school."

"I don't need anyone else with me to feel complete." Then her eyes began to sparkle. "I have to admit, though, that it would be fun to bring a handsome man to the festivities just to get people talking. I know the women from my class would find it most interesting." Then she groaned. "Even saying that makes me sound like an adolescent."

"Reunions do that to people. Frankly, I think you should get one. A handsome man, I mean."

Louise and Jane stared at Alice as if the top of her head had come off.

Alice looked girlish as she spoke. "For fun. I know *I'd* like to come to the reunion in a lovely dress with a good-looking man on my arm instead of wearing a rain slicker and working a car wash. At least one of us should go the glamorous route." She looked at Louise. "Unless you want to be the one."

Louise held up a hand. "Do not look at me. I am committed to helping Viola with the bookstore and keeping her sane. I already have my hands full. Besides, at my age, my classmates thought something more sedate might be in order."

"And Pastor Ken and I promised a pizza party with movies to our young people. He is going to hold down the fort until I get there after the reception."

"That doesn't sound like much fun," Jane commented. "Doesn't he want to get out and see the celebration?"

"He says that as a newcomer to Acorn Hill, it's his duty to see that everyone else is free to enjoy the event. He's happy to be chaperoning the kids."

"And what about you? Are you happy?"

Alice considered Jane's question for a moment. "Actually, I am. Next to nursing, the most rewarding thing I do is work with these young people. Besides, my classmates have things planned throughout the reunion. I'll barely miss a thing."

"It is settled then," Louise said unexpectedly. There was an impish glint in her eye that her sisters rarely saw. "Jane will represent the family as the beautiful, successful one." She turned an eye to Jane. "You will, will you not?"

Jane had heard that tone in Louise's voice before. Louise had made up her mind and nothing was going to change it.

"I can't . . ."

"You most certainly can. Let's go upstairs and look through your wardrobe."

"I don't have a handsome man in there."

"Then I will make a call. Is Ned Arnold handsome enough for you?"

Louise, who had not "sprawled" on anything for a number of years, had done so, in a ladylike fashion, of course, across Jane's bed. Alice was perched beside her, eyes bright. How on earth she had gotten into this

Jane would never know. *This was like the years her sisters had called conferences to decide what Jane should wear on dates,* she thought as she modeled yet another evening dress for her sisters. In San Francisco, she had gone regularly to dressy occasions, gallery openings and the like. Here, her formal clothes had been in retirement—until now, the most unlikely of circumstances, a blind date set up by Louise and Alice.

"This reminds me of you two playing 'dress up' with me as a child," Jane complained as Louise spun a finger in the air, telling her to twirl around for them again.

"You always looked like a little doll," Alice said mistily. "Remember how we used to braid her hair, Louise?"

Jane's heart melted. They were having fun. This reminded them of their youth, when the most important thing was making sure their baby sister was as pretty as she could be. It was harmless. Why not let them have that fun again?

Besides, Jane admitted to herself, maybe she would feel a little more comfortable wearing a dynamite dress when facing her nemesis for the first time.

They settled on a graceful, sophisticated, white-beaded dress with a dipping back. It was Jane's favorite dress. It fit her like a glove and the shiny flecks of beads danced in the light when she moved. The dress had been a hit at several parties and, Jane had to admit, it made her feel confident and poised.

"I think you should wear your hair up," Louise was saying.

"But not too severe," Alice said, "you know, something messy but elegant. Like those women in magazine ads."

Jane grabbed her thick hair, twisted it at the back of her head and secured it with the nearest thing she could find, a pencil.

"That's it!" Alice said delightedly. "Except, of course, it can't be a pencil."

"You and Ned will make a lovely couple," Louise said with a note of satisfaction in her voice. It had been she who had reached Ned at the pharmacy and had explained the situation. Ned graciously told her that he would *love* to escort Jane to her party. (Jane did not want to know exactly what Louise had told him. The whole thing was far too humiliating already.)

Louise's eyes twinkled. "I think he likes you, you know."

Jane, as she had as a youngster, clapped her hands over her ears. "Louie, don't even go there."

Louise settled in with an enigmatic smile. Jane thought that was almost worse than her saying something. Louise's prediction for the reunion had come true—everyone *had* gone mad—including Louise.

Jane met Mr. Enrich in the hall. He had struck up a bit of a friendship with Joe and had been advising him on certain issues with rosebushes and mulch. He had a little color in his face although a smile was still missing.

"I believe you're getting a tan," she said by way of greeting.

He put his hand to his cheek. "Well, that's a change." He tipped his head and entered the library.

One of many, Jane thought. Mr. Enrich was eating more and talking more at breakfast. She had heard him out on the porch in an involved conversation with Josie about the state of health of some of her dolls, and he had begun opening doors for people and performing other small civilities around the inn. And he had moved into the library, made his own bed and settled in to read even more of her father's books.

She could not imagine how many of them he had already read. Jane had noticed that most of those he carried with him to the porch or garden were spiritual in nature.

Alice always had extra Bibles on hand, and Jane reminded herself to give one to Mr. Enrich when he decided to leave. He still had not mentioned his departure date. That was very strange since initially he had promised, "I won't be here much longer." Oh well. He had become part of the fabric of the household now and whenever he did leave, he would be missed.

Lloyd and Ethel were both on the verge of heart attacks.

It might appear, Jane thought, that her aunt and the mayor were in total charge of all aspects of the reunion and were run ragged by it when, in reality, they were primarily spectators who were wearing themselves out cheering on the home team.

Lloyd had taken to wearing bow ties in red, white and blue or those of Acorn Hill's school colors, yellow and burgundy. They were not colors meant for a bow tie. They made Lloyd's corpulent chins appear to be tied in gift wrap. Ethel, meanwhile, recently had had her hair dyed and the vivid red "Titian Dreams" color had not had time to soften or fade. She could be seen coming from a block away.

The mayor had also begun carrying a little red notebook in which he scribbled at intervals. Sylvia had told Jane that no one on the reunion committee had appointed Lloyd record keeper, judge or jury. He had taken the task on himself.

"Cars are pouring into this little town like maple syrup onto pancakes," Lloyd announced. His similes were colorful but inspired odd mental images. "We've got people out parking them in fields. I've just been to Fred's Hardware and bought every flashlight so our parking attendants can direct people out of the fields at night."

"And tell him about the bug spray, Lloyd," Ethel instructed.

"He's already sold out and he ordered two extra cases. We're fogging the town, but I gave him strict orders to get more spray in here tomorrow. We can't have people going home bitten up and complaining about Acorn Hill."

I'll bet Fred loved that, Jane thought. Aloud, she

said, "Everyone coming to the reunion once lived here, Lloyd. They're probably well acquainted with the hometown bugs."

Ignoring her, Lloyd continued. "Ethel and I did a check of every store in town to see that they were well-stocked. Joseph had threatened to close the antique store for the reunion, but I told him he'd be crazy to do it. He'd lose a lot of money not being open on the busiest days of the decade."

"He is on the reunion committee," Jane reminded Lloyd. "Maybe he has too much to do."

"That's why *I* found someone to work for him," Ethel said proudly.

Jane did a double take. Ethel? Temporary employment agency?

"Josie and her mother Justine were in the Coffee Shop. She told me she had the reunion days off from work and I hired her on the spot."

"You did? For Joseph?"

"I did." Ethel snapped her slightly pudgy fingers. "Just like that."

"And Joseph was delighted." Lloyd added. "He's going to pay her a commission on everything she sells, besides an hourly rate."

"Good for her," Jane said. Justine struggled financially as a single mom and extra income would make life easier for her.

"If she works out," Ethel confided, "he might hire her to work for him full-time."

Jane smiled. Things were going swimmingly.

The inn was hopping. Alice had checked in all but one guest—Shirley Taylor—and Louise was busy keeping the fruit bowl full and giving directions.

Today Jane would see if this Shirley Taylor was the same woman with whom she had attended school.

A knock on the door made Jane spin around. A handsome man with dark hair stood in the doorway.

"Yes? May I help you?"

"I'm looking for Jane Howard. Is she here?"

"I'm Jane." She had an odd feeling in the pit of her stomach.

"I'm Ray Cottrell, Clarissa's son from South Dakota. My mother's had some bad news, I'm afraid, and she wondered if you'd mind coming over."

Without a second thought, Jane grabbed her wide-brimmed straw hat and headed out the door.

Chapter ❦ Nine

Many people die at twenty five and
aren't buried until they are seventy five.
—Benjamin Franklin

What's happened?" Jane's long legs could barely keep up with Ray's even longer ones.

"Mom just got a call from an old friend. It seems her sister, an even closer friend of my mother's, has had a stroke. They aren't sure how much damage has been done although they do believe it's not life-threatening.

Mom always handles things like this so well, but this time she just fell apart. Livvy—who isn't great at a big show of emotion—is beside herself. My brother Kent is a pastor, but apparently it's more difficult to comfort one's own mother—too close and too concerned, I suppose, to be of much help. Anyway, it was you that Mom asked for."

He grinned and Jane saw Clarissa's playfulness in him. "She said she needed someone with a 'good head on her shoulders' and she didn't mean any of her children."

"I'm sorry . . ."

"Don't be. We all know that Livvy has a heart of gold. It's just hard to find it, sometimes, especially when she's upset. The more worried she is, the more she wants to be in charge of everything, as if when she's directing traffic nothing will crash. And my brother's heart is almost too big for him. It hurts for everyone. I'm the practical one in the family." He held out his work-worn hands, and Jane could see dirt and grease imbedded so firmly beneath his fingernails that nothing would get it out. "I'm an auto mechanic. It breaks and I fix it. That makes sense to me. Livvy and Kent are always trying to change the world. I'm just trying to make it easier and more pleasant for people one person at a time."

He grinned again, and Jane was smitten. "And I've got a good business and loyal customers too."

"I'll bet you do." She looked at him as they walked. "You're the most like your mother, aren't you?"

"So they say." He stopped and stared at her somberly. "I have a gut feeling it's not my mother's sick friend that is causing Mom's distress, but something has triggered this and I'd be very grateful if you could help us figure it out."

Jane took a deep breath. Mind reader. One more skill for her résumé.

When they arrived at the house the air crackled with tension. Livvy was pacing the floor. Kent, who looked much like Livvy but with soft brown hair, jumped to his feet.

Jane introduced herself to Kent and inquired, "What's happening?"

"Mom lost it. Her friend's sister said she believed things would be okay, but that she thought Mom would want to know about the stroke. Mom really took it hard."

"It's because of that bakery." Livvy pointed out. "She's working too hard. No wonder she doesn't have any emotional reserves left."

Clarissa had more "emotional reserves" left than most people had ever had, Jane thought as she climbed the stairs to Clarissa's room.

"It's about time someone sane came to see me," Clarissa said. She put the Bible she had been reading on the table next to her easy chair.

Jane chuckled and walked in. "What's this about you being so terribly upset because of a friend? Is it serious?"

"For Mimi? I doubt it. Not according to her sister, at

least. They wanted my prayers for her, not to tell me she was dying."

"I'm glad to hear that. Then what's the fuss about? Your children said you 'lost it.' Livvy says your 'emotional reserves' are low because of how hard you work at the bakery."

"Educated mumbo-jumbo," Clarissa muttered. "I thought I taught that girl to speak English."

"Don't be too hard on her. She loves you and she's worried about you."

"No need to be. I'm fine when no one is telling me I'm an old, weak, incompetent woman."

"Then why did you react so strongly?"

Jane sat down on the edge of the bed across from Clarissa's chair.

"That could have been me. I could have been the one who had a stroke."

"It could have been any of us, for that matter."

Clarissa's eyes bored into Jane's. "This age thing is getting to me, Jane. I don't feel old up here," she pointed to her head, "but here," Clarissa rubbed her hip, "it's not looking so good. When that young Colwin couple came in and started helping me, I realized just how much I've slowed down. Do you think Livvy and her brothers are right? *Am* I too old for this?"

"What do you think?"

"I'm not willing to give it all up, Jane, but I'm not sure I can keep it all either." She chuckled humorlessly. "I guess what the baker in me is saying is that

I can't have my cake and eat it too. If I give up the Good Apple, what would I do? Livvy thinks I'd be happy crocheting doilies and doing crossword puzzles. Where's the meaning in that?"

"It sounds like it's not the bakery that you don't want to give up as much as it is the meaning and purpose in your life."

Clarissa chewed on that a bit and then nodded. "You're right. I'm needed at the Good Apple. People come and visit and take baked goods home to their families. Through the bakery I can make people's lives a little more pleasant and easy. When I feel like it, I can bake extra and give it away."

Jane did not say anything, but she did know that Clarissa had been more than generous to Justine and her daughter as they struggled to make ends meet. Justine had told Jane that some nights Clarissa made the difference in whether they had something to eat for supper.

"I need to have some meaning in my life, Jane. I want to have the ability to contribute. And Livvy doesn't see that."

"She's not here every day, how could she? I feel a little guilty for the predicament you're in right now," Jane confessed. "If I hadn't snared you into doing all the work for the reunion, Livvy wouldn't be so concerned and you wouldn't be so frustrated." She reached out and took her friend's hand.

"Livvy is just like her father. He'd keep coming at a problem from the same angle until he wore himself out." Clarissa looked misty. "And I loved him for it. I knew he'd never give up on us or stop working for his family."

"So when it's good, it's very good and when it's bad . . ."

"It's one big nuisance." Clarissa was smiling again.

"Why don't we turn it over to God and let Him figure it out."

Together, they bowed their heads.

"Dear Heavenly Father, one of your children has a problem. Help Clarissa to know what You want her to do. She's beenYour steward in the Good Apple all these years and now things are changing. What's the meaning of this, Lord, and what do You want her to do about it? Her children want to help her, her friends want to support her and her customers love her. Unfold the answers for Clarissa that only You can provide. And, Lord, let her children see what their mother really needs—freedom to make her own decisions, support, not force, and love, not lectures."

"And take care of my friend who's ill and get us through this reunion, please," Clarissa added.

"Amen," they chorused together.

Clarissa squeezed Jane's hand. "*Whew.* I feel better. But how do I go downstairs and explain to my family that I took a temporary leave of my sanity?" Clarissa wondered aloud.

"No explanations necessary. You get to feel what you feel. You were upset and now you've turned it all over to God. You're trusting Him to deal with it now."

"That's exactly what I'm going to say." Clarissa looked at Jane. "I'm glad God brought you back to Acorn Hill. I think He did it just for me."

"And just for me. Otherwise, I'd still be in San Francisco, estranged from my home and family."

"Mysterious ways. Definitely mysterious ways." Then Clarissa's eyebrows shot upward. "Before we go downstairs, I have something I'd like to show you." She went to her closet and pulled out a large, flat box. "You got me thinking, out there at Fairy Pond." She opened the top flaps of the box and Jane gasped. There inside, was a startlingly realistic portrait of Livvy, showing the fire, the compassion and the stern set of her lips—beautiful, complex and sweet.

"I've done the boys too." She lifted the portrait of Livvy to reveal portraits of her two sons.

Jane almost laughed out loud at the twinkle in Ray's eyes and the commonsense set of his jaw. In Kent's sketch, Clarissa had captured the empathetic good-heartedness he wore like a garment. He looked a little puzzled too, as if he were baffled and perplexed at all the negativity in the world. "These are amazing!"

"You think so?" Clarissa studied the visual renderings critically.

"Absolutely. Your talent is remarkable—and so is finding it so late in life."

"A regular Grandma Moses, huh?"

"Do your children know about this?"

"No, and I'm not going to tell them right now. When they boss me around, I escape to my room to 'nap,'

162

because that's what they expect of me. That's when I draw. I think Ray is on to me because he's the one who sees me most clearly, but even he has no idea what I'm up to. I'm planning to give them their portraits on their way out the door after the reunion." Clarissa's eye twinkled. "That'll teach 'em to think I need all those naps."

As Jane accompanied Clarissa downstairs, she could feel Livvy's eyes on her.

When Clarissa had made her declaration that she was "just fine," Jane tried to take her leave. Livvy caught her as she said her good-byes.

"What do you think?" Livvy asked breathlessly.

"About what?"

"Mother, of course. Is she . . . you know . . . losing it?"

"Livvy, your mother hasn't lost a thing. She's smart, clear-headed, talented and wise. She's remarkable. I count her as a dear friend. She might be twenty-five-years older than I, but her mind is as good as mine. Better, maybe."

Livvy looked as though she and Jane were discussing two different people. "That can't be . . . not at her age."

"Why? I know people twenty-five years old who act as old as the hills. Your mother's mind is barely twenty-five now." Jane took Livvy's hand. "I know how much you love your mom and want to take care of her. She loves you that much in return. But if you love her, then empower her. Let her make her own choices as long as she's able."

"But is she able now?" Livvy wondered, her trepidation clear.

"More than most, Livvy. More than most."

"You can't see past your own nose, Zack Colwin."

"Aw, Nancy, I'm just being practical. You've got this goofy idea about picket fences, a dog in the front yard and some quaint little diner, but diners are history. Blue-plate specials are passé. Inventiveness and creativity are in."

The voices came from the dining room. Jane winced as she passed through the hall. This was the same old argument. Nancy had fallen head over heels in love with Acorn Hill—its size, its ambiance, its people.

"I want to live in a place like this," she had told Jane. "Of course, you've got all the food establishments you really need, with Potterston so close and all, but there's got to be somewhere similar, a place that needs a good restaurant."

"What does Zack say about this?" Jane had asked. She had not liked the troubled expression the question had brought to Nancy's face.

"Zack has got his head in the clouds. He wants to be a famous chef someday. He thinks you were crazy to leave San Francisco. He's heard of the Blue Fish Grille. He'd give almost anything to have the job that you walked away from."

Jane could have told Zack that she rarely thought of the Blue Fish anymore. When she did, it was with fond memories—and no desire to go back. He would not believe her, of course. There were certain things about life that one had to learn for oneself.

Now Jane heard Louise come in the back door. She had been practicing at the church, judging from the music she was carrying. The two sisters could hear the pair in the dining room in intent discussion. Casting her eyes heavenward, she asked, "Not again?"

"Why don't you start playing some of that music you're carrying," Jane suggested softly. "We need a change of pace around here."

"If you think it will work." Louise went into the parlor and over to the piano. She put her books on the piano bench and slid in beside them. With more gusto than she usually displayed, she began an enthusiastic rendition of "Jesus Loves Me." Then she began to sing. "Jesus loves me, this I know, for the Bible tells me so. Little ones to Him belong, they are weak but He is strong. Yessssss, Jesus loves me! Yessssss, Jesus loves me. Yessssss . . ."

Louise's voice was nearly as good as her piano playing. Jane, however, had been absent when that particular talent had been handed out. Still, knowing that if pretty music might not cause some interest, her off-key vocalizations always would, she sang along.

The bickering stopped almost immediately, partially drowned out by the performance. Jane smiled and kept singing. Louise shook her head at her and played on.

Soon, two curious faces peered around the door-jamb.

Jane waved them in and invited them to sing. Nancy looked at Zack and smiled. They stepped into the room and, standing next to Jane, began to sing.

After several choruses of "Jesus Loves Me," Louise switched to another old favorite with a catchy chorus. "I've got a home in glory land that outshines the sun, oh, I've got a home in glory land that outshines the sun . . ." and they all chimed in again.

Then, surprisingly, another voice joined the group. This voice was low and on key. Mr. Enrich had entered the room and was standing behind them, singing, his face stiff and somber, his eyes intent. Zack impulsively threw his arm around the older man and invited him into the fold.

"Do, Lord, oh do, Lord, oh do remember me . . . Michael row the boat ashore . . ." Alice had now joined them and they were all smiling—even Mr. Enrich—when they finished.

Nancy clapped her hands and Zack gave her a hug. "That was fun."

Jane watched them exchange a fond glance. These two were so in love with each other and so at odds about their futures. At least for the moment, the quibbling was forgotten.

"You have a wonderful voice, Mr. Enrich," Alice said. "As good as Jane's is bad."

"Hey, are you complaining about my singing?" Jane teased.

"Just the tune, dear, not the volume."

Mr. Enrich blushed and escaped from the room.

Later, when the sisters were alone, they discussed what had happened.

"It was a miracle, really," Louise commented, "Mr. Enrich *singing.*"

"And smiling," Alice added. "Or at least trying to. The gentleman has come a long way since he arrived." She looked at Jane. "In no little part, thanks to you."

"We've all been praying," Jane pointed out. "And it looks as if God is answering."

"I wonder," Louise mused, "what it is that Mr. Enrich needs to hear."

The countdown was over. This was the day of blast-off. The reunion was about to begin.

Walking through the streets of Acorn Hill, Jane marveled at the number of cars in the streets and people milling on the sidewalks. Many were hugging and laughing, and a few were already on overload, sporting glazed expressions even though the party had not yet begun.

She ran into Sylvia coming out of the Coffee Shop. "Well, the big day is here."

Sylvia bobbed her head and dabbed at the corner of her mouth. "I just had a piece of pie to fortify myself. Are you ready for the formal gathering tonight?"

"My sisters will have me ready. They've been fussing over me like mother hens. They picked out my clothing and even found me a date."

"No kidding?" Sylvia's eyes grew wide. "Louise

and Alice? Or do you have other sisters hidden away somewhere?"

"They have it in their heads that since Shirley Taylor is coming to the reunion—and staying at the inn—that I should look pretty and successful." Jane grinned widely. "It's fun. I'm seeing them as they used to be—always hovering over me, trying to make sure that everything was right. I didn't appreciate it then, but now I realize just how sweet they were trying to be."

"And you don't mind?"

"Actually, I'm pleased to have a place to wear some of my old clothes. There are not many occasions for sparkles in Acorn Hill."

"And the date?"

"Ned Arnold. He's being such a good sport about it. Besides, he says it gives him the opportunity to enjoy the reunion as a participant rather than as an observer. He's looking forward to it."

"And that's it?" Sylvia looked intently quizzical. Then she waggled her eyebrows.

"That's it. No romance. Just friendship. But, if you can believe this, Louise told him to be very attentive to me this evening. She told him that an old boyfriend of mine would be there and the woman who tried to 'steal' him away. Isn't that hilarious?"

"I've known Alice a long time, and Louise as long as I've known you, Jane, and I must say, when you arrived, you brought some new excitement into their lives."

Jane thought back to their first difficult days. Back

then, she had wondered if she represented too much excitement. Now, it seemed, Louise and Alice had turned the tables and were giving her a run for her money. "Like Louise says, it's all in good fun. I appreciate the fact that they don't want an old rival to get me down, but they do seem to forget that I can handle myself."

"Enjoy," Sylvia advised. "Are they coming to the reunion too?"

"Louise is coming later with Viola. Alice will come as soon as all the guests are checked in and her responsibilities with the car wash are finished. Even Nancy and Zack said they might stop by and peek in. I heard them ask Mr. Enrich if he'd like to come along."

"You're getting to be quite a cozy little family over there, aren't you?"

Jane had not thought about it in quite that way, but she supposed Sylvia was right. Since they had opened the inn, their family had grown to encompass everyone who passed through their doors. Right now, it seemed that some of their more needy family members were in residence.

"Where have you been?" Louise demanded when Jane walked through the front door. "You have to start getting ready."

"I've got over an hour before I meet Ned."

"*Humph.* Ned will pick you up. We discussed it this morning."

Jane opened her mouth to protest and then shut it

again. "Enjoy," Sylvia had said. And she would.

"You had better go upstairs and shower," Louise instructed.

"Are you bossing her around?" Alice asked as she came from the kitchen. "You know how she disliked that as a child."

Jane laughed inwardly. Then she noticed the serious expression in Alice's eyes.

"What's wrong?"

"Shirley Taylor checked in," Alice said in a whisper. "I had Justine watch the inn for an hour while I went to check on the kids' schedule for the car wash and she came while I was gone."

A little flutter of butterflies waved their wings in Jane's stomach.

"I'm sure we'll all have a wonderful time," Jane said cheerfully. "Louise is right. I'd better get ready."

For once, her hair did exactly what she wanted it to do. She had lost a few pounds since the last time she had worn the dress, a result of all the hard work she had been doing at the inn, no doubt. So it glided over her slender hips like a dream. Louise insisted that she wear the diamond drop earrings that Eliot had given her for their twenty-fifth wedding anniversary. Alice surprised her with a small, silver-mesh evening bag that had been Madeleine's.

Jane returned the favors by giving both Louise and Alice brooches she had made especially for them, commemorating the years of their own high-school graduations and color-coordinated to the dresses they planned to wear. Both were delighted.

Mr. Enrich came out of the library and into the kitchen as Jane stood there doing one last check of her catering list before Ned arrived. Mr. Enrich had obviously had his suit dry-cleaned and his shoes polished. She was not sure, but she thought he had also had his hair trimmed.

"Don't you look nice."

"I feel like a fool," he growled. "Look at me, dressed up for a party I'm not invited to."

"Nonsense. This is a party for anyone who's ever lived in or loved Acorn Hill. That means you. Besides, Nancy and Zack are thrilled that you've agreed to go with them. They won't know anyone else either so you'll be able to converse with each other—and me and my sisters, of course. I even think Joe Morales might make a showing. He's never been to a formal party, he says, and he's curious. Perhaps you can befriend him if he comes."

Mr. Enrich looked at her oddly. "You watch out for everyone, don't you? You care. Why?"

Jane was taken aback. "Why not? We're all God's children. It's only right that we care about one another."

"This is the strangest place I've ever been," Mr. Enrich mumbled in bewilderment. "Extraordinary."

Jane took that as a compliment.

Ned was prompt, ringing the doorbell at the appointed time. Jane heard her sisters go to answer the door.

How many potential suitors had those two scared off when she was in high school? Who knew? And if they were not intimidating enough, Daniel Howard would emerge from his study to question those young boys about their plans and the hour they would have her home. Jane marveled that she had ever had a male friend at all.

Jeremy Patterson had been the one boy who had not seemed intimidated by her family. Football player, all-around athlete, honor student and genuinely nice guy, Jeremy had been a high-school heartthrob as well as Jane's boyfriend. It was the word *friend* that defined their relationship. Both Jane and Jeremy had their eyes on dreams in the future and, because of their similar aspirations, had become united in their desire to hurry through high school and to get on with their lives.

It was a concept not shared with most of their classmates, who had been more interested in the here and now—dates, social status and popularity. So, while everyone saw Jane and Jeremy as a "couple," they viewed themselves as collaborators on their futures.

But that was the past and this was the present. Ned, looking incredibly handsome in a dark suit, a crisp white shirt and a red tie, was standing in the front hall waiting for her.

Jane said good-bye to her sisters and got Ned out the door, before Louise or Alice could suggest taking a photo. She had enough of those stored in a shoebox somewhere. In each one, she and her date at the time stood stiff and uncomfortable posing for the Kodak moment.

"Sorry about the abrupt departure. My sisters are acting as if I'm going to the prom. I was afraid they'd bring out the camera."

Ned threw back his head and laughed. "No teenager ever looked as good as you do tonight. You're absolutely lovely, Jane."

"And I might say the same about you."

He chuckled. "I guess I do clean up rather well. It's a pleasant change to wear something other than a white lab coat for a few hours."

"Is it busy at the pharmacy?"

"Surprisingly, yes. Treatments for poison ivy, sunburn and stomachache, mostly." He gestured toward his silver sports car. "Here we are."

As they pulled up in front of the high school gymnasium, which had been transformed by the reunion committee into something that resembled a silk purse more than the sow's ear it actually was, she felt a thrill of excitement. She also noticed that what seemed to be the entire male population was hanging around the school's entrance and was now focused on Ned's car. The whistles of admiration, she knew, were not for her.

Okay, Lord, here we go. Whatever goes on tonight, let me be a representative of You.

In the gymnasium, there was much squealing going on as old classmates recognized one another—or not.

For a moment, Jane could not pick out a single person she knew.

"All friends of yours, I presume?" Ned breathed into her ear.

"I have no idea. I don't recognize a soul. It appears that everyone has gotten old but me."

Ned laughed out loud. "You have that problem too? I went to my own reunion and wondered where all these old folks had come from. For a moment I forgot that I was the one with totally gray hair." His eyes twinkled. "Prematurely gray, of course."

"I wonder if I look as old as everyone else," Jane mused, more to herself than to Ned.

"Not a chance," he whispered.

Slightly comforted, Jane ventured forth, grabbing Ned by the hand and pulling him with her.

Suddenly faces were becoming recognizable. "Martie?" Jane ventured as she walked toward a cheerfully round-faced woman with pink cheeks and bottle-blonde hair.

"Jane?" There was dumbfounded amazement in the voice. "Jane Howard? What time warp did you get caught in? You don't look a day older."

Jane only smiled and reached out to give her old classmate a hug. Martie did look days, months and years older, but her ebullient personality was still intact. "Have you seen Sarah and Jean? They're over by the refreshment table. And wait until you see Mr. Longer. Remember him? Our math teacher. When we were in school I thought he was ancient, but now I realize that he was only about six years older than his students. He looks great. Not, of course, as great as you . . ."

They wound their way through the crowd, Ned's hand firmly planted in the small of Jane's back, greeting friends and neighbors. Music was playing on the stage, a string quartet. There would be an oldies group coming later.

"Jane? Martie told me you were over here and she said you were beautiful. I had to come and check it out for myself." Linda Watson and her husband Glen, both classmates, were looking at Jane with studied awe. Glen, who had had a full head of black hair as a youth, was bald as an egg. Linda's own beautiful red hair was giving way to gray.

"What have you been up to?" Linda asked.

"I'm a chef and have been for several years. I also paint and design jewelry. And you?"

"We own a photography studio in Kentucky. I love it there, but there's something about Acorn Hill that always makes me nostalgic." Linda leaned toward Jane confidentially. "What's your secret?"

"Do I have one?" Jane puzzled.

"You're thin, you're lovely, your dress is amazing and you are being escorted by a man that could be a model. I want to know how you managed all that."

"I've trained myself not to eat much of my own cooking, and my sisters pulled the dress out of my closet and fixed me up with the handsome man, that's all."

"You're holding back on me," Linda accused cheer-fully, "but the reunion isn't over yet. I'll learn how you found the fountain of youth."

Jane and Ned laughed and then moved on with the flow of people.

"You're a hit," Ned whispered in Jane's ear.

"Thanks, I think."

"You aren't sure?"

"All everyone is looking at is the outside, the appearance, the shell. What really counts is what is inside people—how they think, where they hurt, what they believe. I may look fine, but I've had my trials just like everyone else in the room. This doesn't feel quite real."

"That's only because you are so real, Jane, so down-to-earth and unpretentious. And for tonight, at least, before everyone lets down their guards and become the people who aren't trying to impress anyone any-more, you may have to grin and bear it."

She squeezed his hand in appreciation and he smiled down at her as if she were the only woman in the room.

They were not alone, however. Jane could feel a gaze drawing her like a magnet. She glanced around, but could not locate the source of the feeling. Who was here that she was missing?

Then a pleasant-faced man approached. He was portly, a little jowly, but his eyes gave him away. They were startlingly blue and intent and, as always, seemed to be looking almost past her into the future.

"Jeremy!" Unthinking, Jane threw her arms around her old boyfriend and gave him a hug. Then she stepped back, embarrassed. That quickly faded, however, when she saw the delight in his eyes.

"I can't tell you how many times over the years I've thought of you, Janie. I've wondered where you were, what you were doing and if you'd accomplished any of those big dreams we used to spend so much time discussing."

"I've managed a few. I'm a chef and an artist. How about you?"

"I made some money in technology before it hit the skids. Now I have a company that manufactures medical equipment. It keeps food on the table."

"I'll bet." Jane smiled at him, delighted that all their hopes for him had come to fruition. "Jeremy, I'd like you to meet my friend Ned. Ned, this is Jeremy."

Graciously, the two men greeted each other and a bond was set. Before Jane knew what was happening, they were discussing the medical field, pharmacy, pacemakers, implants and the like. She chuckled to herself. Ned and Jeremy had more to discuss with each other than she did with either.

She turned to glance around the room and saw Ethel and Lloyd bearing down upon them. Ethel had outdone herself. She wore a bright pink dress that clashed with not only her own hair but with nearly every other garment in the room. On the dress she wore a corsage. It was long, curving at least ten inches down from her shoulder, and incorporated flowers in every shade of pink and burgundy. Greenery sprouted every which way and a reddish-purple ribbon decorated the stems.

"Great flowers, Aunt Ethel." Jane gave her aunt a hug, being careful not to crush the spray on her chest.

Ethel beamed. "Lloyd gave them to me. Aren't they wonderful? Oh my, I can't even think how many years it's been since . . ." Her eyes grew misty.

Touched, Jane reached out and hugged Lloyd too. "How sweet of you," she whispered in his ear. He blushed the same color as Ethel's dress.

"And the dress matches perfectly," Ned offered politely.

"Thank you so much for noticing. Why, I feel like a schoolgirl tonight," Ethel practically giggled. "Come, Lloyd, I think they're serving cranberry punch at that table over there. It's your favorite, you know."

And off they went in a happy haze.

"Well, well," Ned said politely. "Isn't that nice?"

"They are just too cute. And they do a beautiful job of keeping each other entertained."

Chapter ❦ Ten

Whoever feels pain in hearing a good
character of his neighbor, will feel a pleasure
in the reverse. And those who despair to rise
in distinction by their virtues, are happy if
others can be depressed to a level of themselves.
—Benjamin Franklin

Before long, Jane and Ned were caught up again in a throng of people and memories. From the corner of her eyes, she saw Nancy, Zack, Joe and Mr. Enrich enter through the front door. Zack, taking charge, steered the little group toward the music and refreshments. Jane was pleased to see a flicker of interest in the usually blank expression of Mr. Enrich. Joe was utterly wide-eyed and amazed.

Jane noticed a couple near the band, swaying to the music. Both had long gray ponytails snaking down their backs. She quickly looked around for Vera, but could not see her. The couple was Betty and Bill Paige, the "flower children" that Vera had wondered about. Jane laughed to herself. Some things just never changed.

Louise and Viola came in later. Louise looked elegant in a steel-blue silk dress from Nellie's, one Jane had insisted she buy, because "it gets you into the new millennium, Louie. You don't have to look like a piano teacher every moment of the day."

Viola, of course, was swathed in a long scarf and made her entrance like an opera diva coming onstage.

Alice, in a smart black evening suit, arrived with Rev. Thompson shortly after. Both were smiling, which meant all had gone well that evening with the car wash. Jane hoped that her sister was enjoying her moment of respite, because she knew that once the business started again tomorrow, Alice would have her hands full.

"Do you know everyone here?" Ned finally asked, after being introduced to dozens more people than he could possibly remember.

He was the ultimate escort, Jane decided, courteous, thoughtful, never forward or pushy and handsome besides. Her sisters had outdone themselves this time.

She saw Louise edging toward her through the crowd and affection welled up within her. Who would have thought it? Louise was set on having her baby sister the prettiest girl at the ball—and with the most handsome man, too. Jane knew why she and Alice had done it and loved them for it.

"You look fabulous, Louie," Jane said when her sister drew nearer.

"Vera said that until tonight she thought I owned nothing but skirts and sweaters."

"Well, the way you look in this dress proves that you should vary your 'uniform' more often."

Louise smiled and gave Jane a hug. "Are you having fun?"

"More than I expected. As I talk to people the years

simply fall away and it's like we'd been apart months instead of decades."

"Good. Have you seen . . ."

There was a commotion near the punch table. One of the waiters had spilled the sticky red drink down his white shirt and onto the floor. The ensuing fuss created by several people trying to clean up the mess with paper napkins drew Jane's attention to the far side of the room. As she turned in that direction, the tiny hairs at the back of her neck began to tingle eerily. Jane scanned the room for what—or who—was causing this strange sensation.

On the far side of the room, Fred and Vera Humbert were laughing together with a pair of classmates. Over to the left side, Viola had found a listening ear in a gentleman who was struggling not to yawn, and on the right side, Lloyd and Ethel were moving clockwise, slowly making the rounds as unofficial greeters. It occurred to Jane that those two had made this entire event their own personal party.

As she continued to look over the crowd, she finally found the person whose eyes were boring into her. It was a woman who looked to be in her late fifties. She was quite beautiful, but hers was a hard-edged beauty, a kind with which Jane was familiar. Many of her patrons at the Blue Fish were women her own age who had started in business thirty years ago when the work climate was much less welcoming to females. Many had had to work doubly hard for their success, often developing a tough veneer. They had paved the way for younger women of today—often at a personal cost. Jane had a hunch that the person staring at her was probably younger than she looked. Her hair was artificially dark with streaks of paler highlights. The effect was formidable rather than soft. It was cut and styled close to her head with dramatic wisps of hair framing her face. Even these had been tamed into perfection with plenty of gel and hairspray. *Literally,* Jane thought, *not a hair out of place.* The woman wore a tight-fitting sequined top over black tuxedo pants with the jacket studiously arranged over one arm. And her eyes never left Jane.

"What's wrong?" Ned leaned close to Jane's ear and whispered the question. "I just felt you stiffen."

She put her hand on his arm gratefully. "There's someone staring at me."

"Everyone is staring at you, Jane. Everyone we've talked to says you look just like you did in high school, but prettier, and no one can get over it. Frankly, if you could bottle whatever your secret is, I could quit being a pharmacist and retire on commission selling it for you."

She beamed up at him. Another point for Ned and his charm. "Let me rephrase: She's not staring, she's *glaring.*"

Ned gave a low whistle as he turned to look at the woman. "Wow. Ice wouldn't melt in her hands, would it? Who is it?" Their heads were close together and Ned had put his arm around her waist to lean in and hear her over the din.

"I have no idea. She doesn't look like anyone I remember."

"Shall we go over and talk with her?"

Jane had turned her back to the woman but felt the antagonistic gaze burn through her shoulder blades. "I'm not sure." Then curiosity got the best of her. "Let's casually move in that direction. Maybe we'll run into someone who can tell me who it is."

Nonchalantly but methodically, Jane and Ned wound their way through the crowd. When the woman began to talk to one of Jane's classmates, Jane nudged Ned. "Let's go. She's talking to Wenda Carson. Maybe we can get close enough to hear something that will tell us who she is. If she's someone who I should know, I don't want to make a fool of myself by failing to know her name."

Deftly Ned steered her through the crowd. Jane was thankful for him because, for some reason, the single unfriendly stare in the room had unnerved her. *Silly,* she thought. *It's probably that her shoes are uncomfortable. If my feet hurt, I'd probably be frowning too.*

As they neared, Wenda caught sight of Jane, put her hand in the air, and waved. "Jane! Jane Howard. Over here."

"Here goes," Jane muttered to Ned, who was still faithfully sticking to her side.

"You look twenty years younger than the rest of us," Wenda said in greeting. "Everyone from our class is raving about you. It is so good to see you." Wenda wrapped Jane in a warm embrace. Then she set Jane

183

back a bit and turned to Ned. "And who is this good-looking man you have with you?"

Ned, as if on cue, said smoothly. "I am Ned Arnold. I'm a pharmacist here in Acorn Hill."

"Lucky you," Wenda said slyly. Then she turned to Jane. "And lucky *you.*"

Before Jane could open her mouth, Ned smoothly turned to the smaller woman watching the exchange. "Hello, I'm Ned." He reached out to shake her hand, and she laid a well-manicured hand in his. "It is so nice to meet Jane's old friends."

"I'm sorry, where are my manners?" Wenda apologized. "This is another classmate of mine and Jane's, Shirley Taylor. Jane, of course you know Shirley."

"Of course." The words nearly stuck in Jane's throat. "Hello, Shirley." This was Shirley? Up close, Jane realized that Shirley was wearing a skillfully applied but substantial layer of makeup, kohl eyeliner and heavy blush, as if she were going onstage.

Shirley was beautiful and glamorous, but unapproachable.

Shocked, Jane took a step backward and ran into Ned's solid warm chest. He caught her by the upper arms to steady her. Shirley's gaze did not miss a thing.

"I had just asked Shirley what she was doing now. Go ahead, Shirley, tell us about your life," Wenda encouraged, oblivious to Jane's discomfort. "What have you been up to these past few years?"

"I run my own company." Now Jane recognized

her—by the sound of her voice, which was familiar though lower and more studied.

"Really?" Wenda sounded impressed. "What kind of company?"

"Real estate."

"Oh, that sounds wonderful. I'd love to go through homes all day. I must say you didn't seem the business type in school." Wenda was having the time of her life reuniting with two old classmates. The two old classmates, however, were not enjoying it all that much.

"I've changed since school, and there were a few things that you most likely didn't know about me," Shirley said abruptly. "Probably no one did."

"Is your business successful?" Wenda probed.

"Very. Actually, I deal in commercial real estate. There's more profit in that."

Ned suddenly became Jane's cheerleader. "Jane and her sisters own some valuable real estate right here in Acorn Hill, the Grace Chapel Inn. In addition to being the chef for the inn, Jane does amazing oils and watercolors and designs jewelry as well."

Jane noticed Shirley's jaw tighten. Otherwise her face was completely passive and expressionless.

"I've heard about the inn and how wonderful it is, but an artist . . ." Wenda was impressed. "Tell me more."

Although Jane's mouth was stuck in neutral, Ned's was not. As he spoke, he made her sound like some sort of female Van Gogh, but she was too preoccupied to correct him.

This was Shirley Taylor? She made Jane, who wore light make-up and the classic beaded gown, feel almost under-dressed. Shirley's commanding, almost aggressive, presence made Jane feel somehow out of the race. Then Jane smiled inwardly. That was exactly how she wanted it. She was done with making an impression for business, always being "on." For a moment, she had nearly been drawn into what Shirley seemed to represent. Jane had been there, done that and was no longer interested.

". . . And that is, of course, why she's had so much success as a chef. I eat at the inn a lot and the presentation is always beautiful."

"A chef too? Jane, you're a Renaissance woman. I had no idea of all your interests." Wenda was still carrying the conversation and was oblivious to the undercurrents.

"I noticed a little placard on the table over there filled with those beautiful candies. 'Chocolates donated by Madeleine and Daughters Candy Company.' I never knew her, of course, but your mother's name was Madeleine, wasn't it? When I'd stop at your house, your father would often mention her."

Again, Ned picked up the slack in the conversation. "That's Jane's company, named after her mother."

Wenda appeared delighted. "Both you and Shirley run businesses! My goodness, and I was excited to tell everyone about my little gardening service. Compared to the two of you, I haven't done a thing."

When Shirley didn't speak, Jane jumped in.

"There's nothing more delightful than a garden, Wenda. The one at the inn has been a big challenge for us. We aren't sure what truly old-fashioned plants would be appropriate for a place like that. Maybe I could hire you to consult."

"Why don't we get some punch, Jane?" Ned suggested. He asked the others, "Would either of you ladies care for some? No? Then if you'll excuse us . . ." and he spirited Jane away.

"Thank you," Jane breathed as they approached the punch table. "I was about to babble, wasn't I? Seeing Shirley Taylor blew me away."

"Me too," Ned said with a chuckle. "I stood there comparing the two of you and wondered if two successful women could possibly be more different."

"Back in high school there was some bad blood between us, more than her jealousy over my boyfriend," Jane began. "I should tell you . . ."

"No need to explain, your sisters told me all about it."

"They did?"

"Aren't you glad they did?"

"Well . . . yes." Jane blushed. "Always taking care of me, those two. Whether I need it or not." She looked up gratefully at Ned. "And tonight I needed it. I don't know what I expected, but Shirley certainly didn't fit any image I'd had in my mind."

"Want to talk about it?"

Actually, Jane did. They found a table for two at the far corner of the room, and Jane told him the whole story, and that Shirley was one of the motivating factors that led her to leave Acorn Hill. Ned listened attentively.

They both turned to look at Shirley. Her face was animated now, softer and more pleasing. "Look at them," Jane marveled, nodding her head to where Shirley stood talking with Jeremy Patterson, middle-aged, stout, pleasant Jeremy. His equally nice, mild-looking wife was at his side.

"It's funny, isn't it?" she mused. "At certain ages how tender and impressionable one is. When I was seventeen, what Shirley did to me seemed unforgivable. And now . . ."

Ned raised an eyebrow questioningly.

"And now I realize that I foolishly allowed it to affect the choices I made about my life." Jane suddenly felt very, very tired. Was there ever a time in one's life when one stopped learning? Evidently not. God was sculpting and cultivating her life every day, now more than ever.

"She's an intimidating presence," Ned commented. "Are you feeling okay about all this?"

"Do you mean am I jealous or wishing I was more like her after all these years? Not on your life."

"Then you don't want to leave?" Ned asked, concern written on his handsome face.

"Leave?" Jane considered the irony of the question. "No way. I allowed Shirley to chase me away from something wonderful once, Acorn Hill. I'm not letting it happen again."

"Good." Ned looked delighted. Suddenly Jane noticed that she was delighted too.

Jane was late getting breakfast started the next morning, but everyone else was even later coming down for it. The festivities had gone on well into the wee hours and, if last night had been the only event planned, the reunion still would have been considered a complete success.

Jane had just returned to the kitchen from arranging fruit, breads, yogurts and cereal on the sideboard when Sylvia called softly through the back screen door, "Is the coffee pot on?"

"Sure is."

"I'm sorry to barge in when the inn is full of guests, but I wanted to chat and I figured they wouldn't be up yet."

"I'm glad you dropped by. No one is stirring yet. Sit down and I'll get you some coffee. It's strong this morning, but I'm not sure anything is strong enough for you right now. You look exhausted."

"I ran between Potterston and here last night so I took in two reunions rather than one. If I make it to the end of this weekend, I'm checking in here and having you and your sisters pamper me until I'm rested."

"That should only take a month or two," Jane said. She put two steaming mugs and a pitcher of cream on the table between them. "So far so good?"

"It seems like it. What did you think of last night? You looked like you were having a wonderful time."

"Ned is an absolute gem." Jane told Sylvia about more of her sisters' machinations.

"What a hoot! I'm seeing an entirely new side of Louise and Alice."

"And which side might that be?" Louise's slightly haughty voice came from the kitchen door.

Jane crossed the kitchen and threw her arms around her sister. "The side we knew was there but that you wouldn't let out."

Sylvia moved over so Louise could join them. Alice soon followed.

The guests were obviously sleeping late as no one else had yet ventured down the stairs. The conversation had covered almost everyone at the party when Shirley's name came up.

"I would not have recognized her," Louise said.

"Nor I," Alice admitted.

Then they both remained silent. Gossiping had not been approved in Daniel Howard's household when he was alive—and it was not condoned now that he was gone.

Sylvia, however, had not grown up with the Howard's rules of good behavior. "All I have to say is that I felt as though I were in the presence of an ice queen. Whatever her appeal is, I do not see it. And Jane, well, you were stunning. I loved it."

Jane glanced at her sisters and was amused to notice that they were both bobbing their heads in agreement. "I'm just sorry," Alice blurted, "that Shirley isn't fat and dumpy."

Sylvia's jaw dropped. This was so unlike Alice.

"It does not matter," Louise said. "Jane is more beautiful—and more real." Then Louise touched her lips with her perennial hankie. "Oh, dear, we should not be talking like this."

Gloating had not been allowed in their household either, but Jane knew that Louise and Alice were not so much putting Shirley down as being protective of their sister. The conversation ended when some of the guests entered the dining room. Sylvia left for reunion duties and Louise and Alice served the guests while Jane stayed in the kitchen making phone calls and assuring herself that her catering plans were all on track.

It was almost too easy, she decided, after everyone had assured her there were "no problems" and that she did not even have to come around to check on them. Zack and Nancy had taken over most of the responsibilities, and right now they were spearheading the community breakfast. They had even told her to stay home as long as she wanted, that they would handle everything. They were a pair of hard workers. Jane heartily wished they could somehow reconcile their differences.

When breakfast was over, Louise and Alice left— rather hastily, Jane thought—Louise to help Viola at the book tent and Alice to organize the first crew of car washers. Jane went into the dining room to collect the breakfast remnants.

She was startled to see Shirley Taylor at the table, sipping a cup of coffee.

"Oh, I thought everyone had left. I'm sorry." Jane moved toward the kitchen.

"Go ahead and clean up, don't bother about me." Shirley's eyes narrowed. "I never thought I'd get to see you in the role of waitress." She said it so derogatorily that Jane frowned.

She seemed to want to pick a fight, but Jane was not going to oblige her. "You looked as if you were pondering something. I don't want to interrupt."

This morning Shirley was again painted with makeup. She was dressed smartly in slim white slacks and a black-and-white patterned silk-knit sweater. Jane recognized that her black, quilted handbag was a Prada, which must have cost a fortune.

Jane, in slim-fitting jeans, a trim T-shirt and no makeup, felt like her polar opposite. *Oh well,* Jane told herself, *I look like me—and I'm comfortable.*

"You look very nice," Jane offered.

"And you look so casual."

"I know, but I'll get myself pulled together for . . ."

"I meant it as a compliment." She didn't sound very happy about it.

It was a strange compliment, Jane thought. Where was Shirley going with this? And why had Louise and Alice left so early? They would have been useful in this odd conversation.

"I watched you last night."

So I noticed, Jane wanted to say. Instead she tipped her head inquiringly.

"You're very popular here."

"It's my home," Jane said and realized how very true that was for her now. "What's going on, Shirley?"

"You're an easy person to hate."

Jane felt the breath leak out of her and an emptiness in her chest.

"Frankly, I was disappointed when I saw you. I wanted to find you fat and dumpy, miserable maybe." Shirley talked calmly, as if they were discussing the weather. "You've always had it all and you never even seemed to realize it. Everything was so easy for you back when we were young."

"Easy?" *Things had looked easy?* That was not how Jane had felt as a teenager. And this woman sitting across from her had not helped one bit. Nor was she helping now. Then it occurred to Jane that there was a second message that Shirley was sending. It was unsaid but was as loud as the first.

"Are you trying to say that you've been spending your life trying to catch up?"

The shock on Shirley's face told Jane she was exactly right. That did not make Jane feel any better, however, for no matter what Shirley had in mind, it had never been Jane's intention to hurt anyone. All these years, Shirley had been smarting with jealousy.

"Did you see Jeremy Patterson last night?" Jane grasped for something to say and immediately realized that was perhaps the worst topic she could have chosen.

No amount of makeup in the world could have hidden the scowl on Shirley's face. "Yes. He's aged."

"Haven't we all?"

"Everyone but you, it seems."

Jane felt as though she had fallen into an alien universe in which whatever she said was wrong, twisted into meanings she did not intend.

"I should have known," Shirley added with a bitter laugh.

"Jeremy was a nice boy in high school," Jane stammered lamely.

"You knew him better than I did."

And apparently that was at least part of the problem.

Jane sat down at the table. She was tempted to take Shirley's hand, but resisted. She wasn't sure this woman would allow her to be so personal. "Shirley, I know you hated me back then, although I'm not sure of the reasons why. I know my friendship with Jeremy played a big part in it. But we're grown women, and we're dredging up old feelings that have no place in our lives now. Whatever was between us should be buried. I don't want to be someone whose life's most pivotal events occurred before they were eighteen years old."

She *had* been one of those people for a long time, and it had prevented her from coming home to Acorn Hill for years. She was not like that anymore.

"We all know about the former football stars or cheerleaders for whom the most important events of their lives, the ones they revisit and relive, are from a time that is really part of their childhoods. The big touchdown that saved the game. Being chosen homecoming queen. Silly, but important nevertheless because those are the only things from which those people have taken their identity. We are so much more than our pasts."

Jane kept talking, feeling a little desperate, since Shirley did not respond. "I'm a Christian, Shirley, and I am so grateful I have a God who erases our pasts when we ask for forgiveness. If He can forget our mistakes, surely we can. If I've learned anything since I returned to Acorn Hill, it's that all I can do with the past is learn from it—and move forward with my life. That's what I've done. That's what I want for everyone to do—to start looking forward instead of back."

The chill in Shirley's eyes did not soften. She reached down, picked up her designer handbag and stood up. "That was most interesting, Jane. Something to think about, I'm sure." And she walked out.

Jane sagged in her chair and felt a flood of weariness wash over her. *How dense could that woman be? Could she not see?*

Then it was almost as if God tapped her on the shoulder. *You could not see either, not for a long, long time. What if I had given up on you?*

Okay. I get it. This isn't about me anymore. It's about Shirley, who's struggled a lot more than I. Jane leaned back in her chair and looked up to the ceiling. She thought of Shirley, of Zack and Nancy, of Mr. Enrich and of the numerous other guests who had come through the doors of the inn needing help and comfort. Then she prayed, *After the reunion, Lord, could You send us a few easy visitors? Just so we can rest up.*

• • •

"Look at all the candy I've got." Josie held open a bag filled with wrapped candies, small toys and an occasional coin. "They're just throwing them off the floats. Isn't that *silly?*"

"Is this your first parade, Josie?" Jane asked.

"Uh huh. Momma said I've been to others but not for a long, long time."

"Well, the people on the floats are throwing the candy to you, Josie, because they want you to have it. It's part of the fun."

Just then a big flatbed truck hauling a community band drove by. Josie dropped her bag and covered her ears. "They sound funny."

"That does not tell the half of it," Louise muttered in Jane's ear. "I thought they would practice before they got on that float."

"I think they did. Sylvia told me I should have heard them before."

"Here come some clowns!" Josie clapped her hands with pleasure. "The clowns always have lots of candy." And she darted off, her eye on an orange-haired fellow in a purple-and-red striped suit.

"She's having fun."

"I am happy for her, but I will be glad when all these antique cars go by. Is every single year and make of car since the Model T represented here?"

"Sylvia requested a few extras when she thought the parade wouldn't be long enough. Looks like she overdid it." The procession did look more like a traffic

196

jam than a parade at the moment. "You will have to wait to see the horses, Louise. You can't give up now."

Louise sighed. "I wish I had worn tennis shoes and borrowed a baseball cap to shield my eyes from the sun. And a stool, I should have brought a stool."

Jane grinned through the rest of the parade, all the way to the last clown who had cleanup duty behind the horses, just imagining Louise perched on a stool wearing jogging shoes and a hat advertising John Deere tractors.

"Like clockwork."

"Easy as pie."

"Not a hitch."

"More fun than anyone had had in years."

"We must do this again in five years. With the same committee, of course."

Jane had been collecting comments and compliments about the reunion to share with Sylvia and Joseph, who were not only busy making sure the reunion was on course, but also staving off their personal nervous breakdowns.

Things *were* moving as smoothly as oiled gears. The makeshift catering was a hit. The programs were entertaining. The marketplace was booming and food was being consumed by the truckload. Even Viola was happy.

"I cannot believe how many books I have sold," she gushed to Louise and Jane as they stood in the now sparsely inventoried Nine Lives book tent. "Not only have they practically emptied me out here, but the store has been busy too. And I've been selling *history* books, isn't that wonderful?"

Jane did not point out that some of the "history" books were *The History of Disco, When Swing Was the Thing* and *Collecting Muscle Cars of the 1950s*.

"I'm so glad I did this."

Jane blinked. Had not the committee dragged Viola kicking and screaming into this venture? Had not she been the one to predict certain doom for the effort? Apparently, Viola was one among a number of people with conveniently selective memories.

Lloyd and Ethel approached the tent beaming. They had spent the morning at the breakfast tent telling everyone that all the food was lovingly prepared and served by Acorn Hill residents just for them. They added that, if they had not stepped in and saved the day, Acorn Hill alumni might have been eating rolls and Danish shipped in from who-knows-where. Jane had listened to them for a while, amused. She was happy that at least the Good Apple and the church ladies were getting credit for their efforts.

"They are outrageous," Louise said to Jane. "You were the one who pulled the food together."

"Oh, let them have their fun. I'm used to it. Caterers sneak in the back door of the house, provide a banquet and sneak out as if they've never been there and the hostess gets the credit for being wise enough to employ them. It works for me."

"You are certainly laid back about things," Louise commented.

" 'Laid back?' I don't believe I've heard you use that term before, Louie."

Louise reddened. "I have been listening to Alice too much. She has picked up the vernacular of those young people she works with and it is catching."

"Speaking of Alice, do you want to wander over to the car wash and see how business is?"

For two days, no matter that there was a program, a concert or even the parade, the parking lot of Grace Chapel had been full to overflowing with cars to be washed. To expedite the process, Rev. Thompson and Joe had developed a sort of car valet service. Rev. Thompson would park cleaned cars on the back side of the church, and Joe would hand out keys to the owners as they came to collect their vehicles.

Alice, who had been up early every morning and to bed late every night, was exhausted and beaming. "We've made over fifteen hundred dollars," she said to her sisters. "People have been amazingly generous. The kids say people have handed them twenty-dollar bills and said, 'Keep the change.' Now we're trying to decide what to do with all the money. The Youth Group's mission trip is paid for. With their share, the ANGELs want to buy toys for underprivileged children at Christmas and to set up a visitation program for the children's ward at the hospital in Potterston." Alice's face was glowing. "God is so good. The kids are learning to enjoy working for the good of others, and their faith is growing."

"Amazing, absolutely amazing," Louise said. "The car wash, the bookstore . . . this entire event is a huge success."

Well, almost, Jane thought. She had not been able to get Shirley out of her mind. The woman came and went from the inn as if it were an onerous duty to attend the reunion functions. Even poor Alice had given up trying to draw her out. She wore an entirely different face when with the public. She was . . . networking. Jane could describe it no other way. Even at the reunion, she was offering business cards. There was something mechanical, robotic about the way she approached people. There were exceptions, of course, mostly men who had aged well and were obviously successful.

Jane, however, could not forget their conversation at breakfast. What if God had given up on her before she returned home? She had no idea how she could get through to Shirley, but she knew she could not give up either.

Josie, her mother Justine and Joe converged on the sisters at once.

Justine was all smiles. "Josie's never had so much fun," she said. "It's the biggest parade she's ever seen in her life, and Clarissa gave her cookies for free. Miss Viola even gave her a book on turtles. You know how much Josie loves turtles."

Good will was everywhere, Jane mused. She turned to Joe. "How about you, Joe, are you having fun?"

"It's like a festival. It is wonderful."

"I'm sad it's going to end soon," Josie said. "I'll practically be a grown-up by the time there's another one."

"It hardly seems possible that this is the last day," Louise agreed with the child. "That means we have to make the most of it. If you, your mother and Joe would care for some, I would like to buy ice cream for all of you."

The trio assented happily and disappeared into the crowd with Louise.

"She's loosened up," Jane commented to Alice.

"It's good for her. She gets lonely sometimes with Cynthia so far away. I'm glad Josie has captured her heart."

"Josie is a real blessing," Jane agreed. "Well, I'll leave you to your work. I think I will walk down to the Good Apple and see how my favorite bakers are doing."

Jane felt her step lighten as she approached the shop. Clarissa, Zack and Nancy had saved the day. Clarissa had even been able to spend time with her family thanks to the Colwins' efficiency.

The bakery was fairly quiet. Jane walked around the counter and toward the swinging doors that separated the front from the kitchen. Nancy and Zack were talking in low tones on the other side of the door.

"But I love it here."

"I like it too, Nancy, but it's not for us. If we opened a place like this, we'd be struggling . . ."

"Clarissa raised a family."

"We'll have to do it my way. We'll never make it otherwise."

"Maybe we won't 'make' it at all if we do it your way, Zack. Your attitude is pretty selfish. Can't you at least consider my idea?"

" 'Selfish?' "

"Time out, guys," Jane said as she walked through the doorway. "There's an answer to your problem. We just haven't found it yet."

Chapter ❦ Eleven

Experience keeps a dear school,
but fools will learn in no other.
—Benjamin Franklin

Monday morning. It was over. The reunion was history. Sunday had flown by with the all-faiths church service and the final good-byes. Cars had started pulling out of town in the afternoon and by the next morning Acorn Hill was back to its former size. Although there would be visitors and family who lingered for a few more days, by next week the only tangible reminder of all that had happened would be the brass plaque that had been hung at the school to commemorate the first all-school reunion.

Those who had not served on any committees were already proposing that the reunion-planning group be retained to do another in five years. Those who *had* served on the aforementioned committees were hiding out and making plans to leave town if anyone so much as dared to mention a reprise of the event any time in the next hundred years.

The Antique Store and Sylvia's Buttons were closed and their owners were sleeping late. Fred Humbert was reordering bug spray, umbrellas, fold-up stools and numerous other items that had sold out. Viola was walking dreamily from shelf to shelf in the bookstore admiring all the gaping holes where books had been only last week. All seemed well in Acorn Hill.

But the tug of war between Zack and Nancy had been hanging heavy on Jane's spirit. So had the chill emanating from Shirley Taylor. Odd, Jane mused, since she was the one who had been hurt. Or did Shirley have pain of her own?

Jane, reminding herself that she was a glutton for punishment, poured coffee into a carafe and freshly squeezed orange juice into a chilled glass, put them on a tray, squared her shoulders and marched up the stairs to Shirley's room.

She would make one more try with Shirley. She would not give up. Shirley would have to be the one who ended the conversation. If God wanted Jane to talk to Shirley, then she would, and trust that He would give her something to say.

Jane tapped on the door with her toe and to her surprise, it swung open. "Excuse me, the door just opened. I thought I'd bring you some . . ."

Shirley was seated at the small dressing table applying mascara. The open closet across the room revealed a spectacular selection of clothing and the floor was cluttered with shoes.

"Oh!" Shirley said. "I'm not quite ready."

"I thought you might like some coffee while you were dressing."

"You might as well leave it on the table." Shirley sounded put upon.

"Are you sure? I could come back with it later."

"I'm sure." Shirley said flatly and rotated on the bench to face Jane.

Ooookay. So that was the way it would be. Jane came into the room, set down the tray and started toward the door.

"Wait."

Jane turned.

"Why don't you join me? I have a cup here from my tea last night. I'll use that."

"I . . . ah . . . *er* . . . okay." Jane walked toward the table and sat down on one of the two chairs. *Now what?*

In agonizingly slow motion, Shirley finished straightening her makeup and then poured the coffee.

"So this is how it is to be waited on by Jane Howard. It's rather fun, but why are you trying so hard? I'm sure you think that *I* should be trying to make amends. I'm the one who hurt you."

So she did remember.

"I don't want you to leave here without knowing that everything is forgiven—on my side, at least."

The other woman studied Jane. "You have no idea of what I'm thinking."

"It doesn't matter. I just want you to know that although I'm not sure exactly why you did what you did, it doesn't matter anymore."

"Making that comment about you and your mother, you mean?" Shirley reddened. "I suppose that was a cruel thing to do."

Jane gaped at her. *Suppose?*

"I wanted to hurt you, but you looked *so* injured. I didn't know how to take it back, so I just let it go. I suppose I should have apologized but I was young and angry."

She saw Jane's questioning gaze and continued. "You still don't get it, do you? I hated you." Shirley gave a small sound. "I thought nothing could bother you. You were smart, pretty and popular. You had lots of friends, a boyfriend . . . everything I wanted . . ." her voice trailed off. "And I was so in love with Jeremy Patterson that I thought I'd die of it—and he wouldn't look at anyone but you."

Shirley paused, as if remembering her long-ago feelings. "When I saw Jeremy for the first time this weekend, I nearly fainted. He certainly wasn't the superhero I'd made him out to be."

"Jeremy is a nice, pleasant man with a normal job and a normal family," Jane pointed out, fascinated by what Shirley was revealing and by the cold, calculating tone of her voice.

"Back then, I thought that if Jeremy and I could be together, everything would be perfect." Shirley's eyes narrowed. "Of course that never came about, but I've spent my life trying to make things perfect for myself.

"I suppose I should thank you, really," Shirley commented.

Startled, Jane asked, "What for?"

"For standing in the way, for drawing his attention away from me." Shirley shuddered lightly. "Imagine! If I'd been stuck with him, I might still be living in a one-horse town like this." She eyed Jane's casual attire. "Like you."

Jane read between the lines. *How pathetic to end up here. How pathetic that this is the best place that you can find to live.* Why this woman could still get to her, Jane did not understand. She and Shirley had been tied together for a lifetime in a relationship that was miserable for both of them.

What is your will, Father? What kind of role is Shirley supposed to play in my life now? Or I in hers?

The idea that this encounter was of God's design comforted her. It also reminded Jane that her discomfort was not important, especially if there was something she should say to Shirley or do for her.

"So how has it worked out, the 'perfect' life, I mean?" Jane asked. As *if there could be a perfect life apart from God—and He did not guarantee that until eternity.*

Shirley contemplated the question, and as she did so, Jane thought about how much Shirley's words had changed them both.

"My jealousy gave me drive and ambition," she said frankly. "I wouldn't be where I am businesswise if not for that." She looked around the room and gave a brittle laugh. "I have a lot of money and I'm not still trapped in this town."

"Oh, I'm not trapped," Jane said softly. "When I left, I thought it was because of you. Now I think it was also because of *me*. I felt like a pariah, thinking that my mother might have lived if it hadn't been for me. I suppose it was so shocking because I hadn't known that before. . . ."

"You mean I was the first to tell you?" Shirley put her hands to her lips, rattled for the first time. "I had no idea. . . ."

"It's worked out," Jane said, feeling peace settle at her core. "I didn't realize it for a long time, but returning to Acorn Hill and knowing my life has come full circle here has been a joyous experience. Interesting, isn't it, that we both wasted our energy on that single incident," Jane concluded. "I don't want either one of us to waste any more." She reached out a hand. "All is forgiven?" She sensed Shirley hesitating.

How sad. Even now, Jane realized, Shirley did not see that she had other options, that life could be lived in gratitude and joy, not driven by jealousy or greed.

"You don't have to forgive me for anything, if you don't want to," Jane added. "There doesn't need to be a truce between us now, if it's not genuine. I don't want anything but the truth in my life anymore. It's all right."

"What's the deal with you, Jane?" Shirley asked.

"I've found God, the most significant Forgiver of all."

"Now you sound like your father's daughter." The way Shirley said it made it hard to tell whether the statement was praise or condemnation.

"Good!" Jane beamed. "I'll take that as a compliment, and it's the nicest one I've had all weekend."

"Take it as you like." Frustrated, Shirley simply turned back to the mirror to finish her makeup.

"How did you mean it then?" Jane wanted nothing more than to get away from the unpleasantness Shirley was radiating, but something compelled her to stay. Was it one of God's nudges? Or something curious in her that was fascinated by what Shirley had become?

Shirley spun around so quickly that Jane took a step backward, startled. "Jane, I don't buy your faith or your holier-than-thou attitude or whatever your church is trying to preach today. The bottom line is that if I can't be successful at something, I don't do it. And I was never very successful at being a church-goer, so why bother? I don't think that God is the only one who can do good things for us." She gestured at the closet full of clothing and the jewelry scattered on the dresser top. "I've done pretty well for myself, don't you think?"

Jane felt her heart sinking. It was as though Shirley had doused her with a bucket of cold water.

"No . . ."

"*Yes*. That's how I feel, Jane. You've followed God and look where it's gotten you."

"He's provided me with everything I want."

Shirley's expression was pitying. "And I got everything I wanted all by myself." She looked Jane over again. "And I think I did a better job."

Jane left the room, stunned.

"Well?" Alice asked after Shirley had checked out.

"What happened?" Louise said almost at the same time.

"Not what I'd hoped."

"Oh my," Alice murmured.

"What do you mean?" Louise asked.

Jane repeated the conversation she had had with Shirley.

"She's like . . . like ice . . . where God's concerned. She thinks He's incompetent, ineffective and maybe not even real." Jane sank into a chair and rubbed her forehead with her hand. "Where did I go wrong?"

"Where did *you* go wrong?" Louise echoed. "Whatever makes *you* think that *you* went wrong?"

"I should have been able to say something to get through to her, but it was like a child throwing a dart at a castle wall. Nothing I said had an effect. She was impenetrable."

"Hmmm." Alice sat down at the table across from Jane. "What's wrong with this picture?"

Jane looked up and Louise's expression showed her curiosity.

"What do you mean? Everything's wrong with this picture. Shirley . . ."

"Not about Shirley, about you, Jane."

"Me? I failed to get through to her. I feel partly responsible for the way she is. I . . ."

"You're not giving God any credit whatsoever, are you?" Alice asked gently.

"What do you mean?"

"Here you are, bewailing the fact that you, personally, didn't turn Shirley's life around. Now you're thinking you're ineffective and a poor witness."

"Yes, so?"

"My, what a big ego you have."

"Alice," Louise began, "Jane's feeling bad because . . ."

"Because God didn't choose hers to be the message that got through to Shirley Taylor?"

Louise and Jane stared at their sister.

"Is that what I'm saying?" Jane asked.

"Sounds a bit like it to me," Alice said. "Who knows how God will use this conversation between you and Shirley? Obviously, she's not ready or willing to turn the reigns of her life over to anyone, even God, right now. I have a strong feeling that whatever happened today wasn't even about you, Jane. It was all about Shirley."

"It is true," Louise admitted, "that I often forget that sometimes I am just a tool in God's hands and not the target of God's attention. I suppose we are just being human when we are always so concerned about ourselves and how we feel."

"You're exactly right, Alice," Jane said. "All I was

thinking of was how I had failed Shirley, not how God might be using me in a way I don't understand."

Jane slipped down in her chair and rested her head against the chair back. "What a wake-up call." She sat up again. "You are absolutely right. The Lord does work in mysterious ways. What I should be praying is that I moved His plan forward and didn't interfere with it."

"God still has much work to do with Shirley," Louise commented.

Jane jumped up and knelt between the chairs in which her sisters sat. Then she reached over and took her sisters' hands. "I love you two so much," Jane said. "I wouldn't trade you for all the jewelry in the world."

"*Harrumph.* I should hope not," Louise said.

Jane smiled and then reached over to give Alice a hug. "Thanks for reminding me that I'm not shouldering the problems of the world alone." Then she opened her hands as if to release the burdens she had been carrying. "I've got God helping me."

"And that's the good news," Alice said. "We know He is helping. We'll just trust Him to speak to Shirley in His own time."

" 'God's time—' " Louise murmured, "it is not always our time, but it is always best."

Feeling more at ease but oddly exhausted, Jane went to her room. She needed to sit down with her Bible for a bit. Scripture was her rudder, the thing that kept her in line, and she was very hungry for that right now. She lay down on the bed and reached for her Bible.

She felt humbled by what she had discussed with her sisters.

A slight smile touched her lips. Alice often had commented about the less mature teenagers with whom she sometimes worked at church. "Everything is all about them," Alice would say. "If only I could get them to turn their eyes outward and see the rest of us for a change."

That's me, Jane thought, *suffering from an elevated sense of self-importance.* She picked up the Bible and opened it to the book of Matthew, but before she could read more than a few words, her eyes drifted shut and she was asleep.

She was standing in a vast warehouse. It was something, she imagined, like a furniture distributor might use. As she stood in the middle of one long row, it was virtually impossible to see either end. On the endless shelves were rows of brightly wrapped boxes stenciled with the contents of each. Jewelry. Money. Influence. Accolades. Bonds. Savings Accounts. Beauty. Prestige. Silver. Gold. On the side of each box were photos of the contents of the boxes.

Curious and completely unafraid, Jane moved toward the nearest box. On it was a photo of what looked like a jeweler's display case. There were rings pictured, with multi-carat diamonds; tennis bracelets; and bejeweled brooches. Fascinated as she had always been by jewelry and for new ideas about making her own, Jane did not resist the urge to lift the top of the box and peek inside. A small puff of dust appeared from the interior of the box and Jane sneezed. Carefully, she pulled the box closer and slid the lid away from her until it fell off the back of the box. As she stared inside, a small gasp escaped her lips.

The lovely jewelry pictured on the outside of the box was not there. Instead, in its place, there was a tangle of rusting necklaces and crumbling bits of fake colored glass. Much of the box's contents were covered with greenish-blue mold.

Quickly, she pushed the box away and turned to another marked "Investments." Instead of important looking documents and certificates, this box held nothing more than bits of ashy paper and mouse droppings. Most of whatever had been inside had been consumed by rodents. Shuddering, Jane pushed the box into place and looked around. A pervading mustiness offended her nostrils. As she walked down the aisle, she rapped on the boxes she passed. Most seemed empty and some had foul odors emanating from them. What was this place? Whose things were these? Then, as if in response to her question, wavering bits of light appeared on each box spelling out names of the owners. Only one name leaped out at her, one recognizable name—*Shirley Taylor.* Horrified, Jane took a step backward and screamed.

"Wake up. Wake up. You're having a nightmare, dear." Alice's calm voice broke Jane's dream. "My, my but you can scream. I thought someone had stepped on Wendell's tail."

Blinking hard against the light, Jane pulled herself upright to find that Alice and Louise were peering down at her. "I was dreaming . . ."

"You certainly were. And thrashing around like, oh, I don't know, like there were mice running up and down your legs."

Jane shuddered and closed her eyes, recalling the images that had passed through her dream. "I was in a warehouse," she stammered, "and it was full of boxes. There were supposed to be beautiful things in the boxes, but they were all rotted, rusted or foul in some way. I don't know what I was doing there, but . . . that was the weirdest dream . . ." Jane's brow furrowed. "It was all so familiar. Like I knew who all of the worthless trash belonged to . . ."

"Maybe I do," Louise said. She picked up the Bible that lay open at the place where Jane had fallen asleep and began to read, "Matthew 6:19. 'Do not store up for yourselves treasures here on earth, where moths and rust destroy, and where thieves break in. But store up for yourselves treasures in heaven, where moth and rust do not destroy, and where thieves do not break in and steal. . . .' "

Jane took the glass of water Alice offered. It was still warm for Alice had not taken time to run cold water in Jane's bathroom sink. Still it tasted good sliding down her throat. She thought about what Louise had read. "That was Shirley Taylor's warehouse I dreamed I was in. All the things she's so proud of were worthless. . . ." Jane closed her eyes as if her head had begun to ache. "And all those material things are so important to her. I should have . . ."

"Remember what we were talking about, Jane," Alice said sternly. "You aren't capable of changing the world or every person in it. You did what you could and Shirley ignored you. That's all."

"'All?' But I should . . ."

". . . trust God with this one. He still has His eye on her, Jane, even if you do not." Louise's voice was compassionate but firm.

"You're right, Louie. This is between Shirley and God."

"And you did your best. Now you can pray for Shirley, but you'll have to leave the rest to Him." Alice pointed heavenward. "Now throw some water on your face and finish your grocery list. I'm going shopping."

Nancy and Zack were hardly speaking when they returned to the inn that afternoon from the walk they had taken. Zack loped up the stairs two at a time. Jane touched Nancy on the arm before she too went to their room.

"It's none of my affair and you can tell me to mind my business, but I still have to ask. What's happening between you two? You seem to be more miserable by the minute."

The young woman stared until Jane feared that she had gone too far and intruded too much. Then Nancy burst into tears and threw herself into Jane's arms.

"I love it here," she wailed. "I want to live in a place just like this one. I could work for Clarissa forever but Zack says he needs to 'try out' his dream."

She pulled back from Jane to wipe her eyes on the edge of her sleeve. "This is tearing apart our marriage. He doesn't feel I appreciate him, and I think he's being selfish. What are we going to do?"

Jane patted the young woman on the back. "I don't know, honey. I don't know."

By dinnertime that evening, Jane's faith in miracles was restored: Mr. Enrich had offered to cook dinner.

"No, I insist." He carried two grocery bags into the house from the General Store. "I want to do this as my way of saying 'thank you.' "

"For which part?" Louise inquired. "For sending you to sleep in the library? Or for completely forgetting to give you clean towels? Or would it be . . ."

"Maybe it's that we quit treating him like a guest." Alice gave a quick little shrug of her shoulders. "What's that old saying about treating family like guests and guests like family? That seems to be what happened here."

"And that's what I'm trying to say thank you for." Mr. Enrich said, shaking his head as if he thought the sisters would never figure it out.

Jane happily relinquished control of the kitchen. Even she, who loved to cook, was feeling burnt out.

"Right now I don't care if I see the inside of a kitchen for a month," she announced to her sisters.

The inn had emptied of all its guests but Mr. Enrich and the Colwins, and they were all tired.

"Think about poor Clarissa," Alice said. "I daresay she would have had to sleep at the Good Apple if it hadn't been for Nancy and Zack."

"I noticed Livvy, Kent and Raymond taking turns there too." Louise smiled. "Livvy was a little rusty on the cash register."

"Have they left yet?"

Neither Louise nor Alice knew the answer.

"If she's home alone, I'm going to invite her for dinner too."

"But it's Mr. Enrich's party tonight and he's already invited Nancy and Zack," said Alice.

"If he says there's enough for one more, I'm going to call her."

When Clarissa answered the phone, Jane could hear the strain in her voice. Before Jane could even finish explaining the dinner plans, Clarissa said, "I'll be right over."

"So your children have left then?"

"Left? Of course not. If they'd left already, I could stay home. They're trying to browbeat me into going to live with one of them. They say then they won't have to worry about me. Hah. I don't want to be treated like an old lady until *I* consider myself old and I can assure you that won't be any time in the near future. My hip may hurt and my hair might be gray, but neither of these things has affected my mind. They're talking to me like I'm senile, for goodness sake. I'm old, not deaf and dumb." She sounded thoroughly disgusted. "They've all wandered off for the moment. I'll leave them a note and be right over."

It wasn't more than fifteen minutes before they heard Clarissa's voice at the screen door. Jane walked to answer it. "Hi. I'm so glad you could come . . . what's that?"

Clarissa carried a big flat leather case in her hand. "Something I wanted to show you. I found this case in the attic." She patted the large folder. "Something Ray had when he took a drafting class years ago. I didn't know how else to sneak these things out without having them be seen."

"Did you tell them where you were going?"

"Nope. Just left a note. That was supposed to be good enough for me when they were teenagers. Let's see how they like it." Clarissa was already in a much cheerier mood.

"The cake you made for the reunion was a masterpiece," Jane said. "You could have a full-time job just decorating cakes."

"Now that would be fun." Clarissa looked dreamy. "My idea of the perfect job."

Then she snapped back to her businesslike self. "And, thanks to you, I found something else I like to do. Is there any place to lay this out?"

"Mr. Enrich is cooking supper, and it won't be ready for a while yet. We can spread things out on the dining room table."

"Getting pretty friendly with the guests, I see," Clarissa said, referring to Mr. Enrich.

Jane nodded pensively. "It's odd. I can't explain it, but all three of us have been praying for him ever since he arrived. We're attributing it to a nudge from God and trusting He'll work it out when the time is right."

"He could get involved in a few things right now," Clarissa murmured. "My kids and their insistence that I'm too old to work, that nice young couple trying to figure out what to do with their lives. God could be busy here for a long time."

"Or," Jane said, "He could wrap it up in a single night."

"What have we here?" Louise entered the dining room, and Alice trailed behind her. Mr. Enrich had banished them from the kitchen.

"Jane gave me something to play with the other day," Clarissa explained as she unzipped the large folder. "I wanted to show her what I've done."

As Clarissa pulled the contents from the folder, three jaws went slack with incredulity.

"You did these?" Jane heard the crack in her own voice—joy, admiration, awe.

"Are they bad?" Clarissa frowned. "I thought they looked pretty good at home but now . . ."

" 'Pretty good'? They're fantastic."

Jane picked up the sketch on top.

Fairy Pond shimmered in all its natural glory. Every hue of green was there, the feathering fronds of fern, the canopy of trees above, the lily pads and even the ripples in the water. And there, so delicately and faintly that they were difficult to see at first, were the fairies. They were interwoven throughout the drawing. Green ones were tucked into the ferns. Blue fairies seemed to swim just below the surface of the water, and a pink blossoming flower along the bank was really a cluster of crimson fairies curled into tight balls, each with their wings tucked neatly around them. These were far more sophisticated than the first sketches Clarissa had drawn.

In fact, Jane realized, Clarissa had in effect drawn a picture in a picture. The fairies' limbs and wings made up the leaves and blades of grass. The ripples of the water, if one looked deep enough, were made of faint fairies doing the backstroke.

Jane had seen work like this before, a picture within a picture, one dominant and the other receding into the background of the other, but she had never done it herself. It was painstaking work to accomplish the effect. And Clarissa, in less than a week, had created several of these pieces.

She had sketched Jane leaning against a tree. In the bark of the tree were tiny faces smiling. And Josie! Clarissa had painted her perched on a large flat stone at the edge of the pond, peering into its depths. Josie, in bright yellow like her curls, was a magical creature herself who, owing to Clarissa's talented hand, seemed to hover slightly above the rock to study a tiny reflection of herself sitting on a lily pad.

"You did these all since we were at the pond?" Jane asked.

"I know they were done fast, but I couldn't stop myself. I'd come home from the Good Apple exhausted and see the art supplies you gave me and I couldn't help myself. I'd find myself yawning three hours later with one of these almost done. I'm sure if I'd had time I could have made them better."

"I don't think you can get better than this," Alice said.

Louise nodded her agreement.

"No wonder your family thought you were tired. You were running on only a couple hours of sleep a night," said Jane.

"But it's like a compulsion, Jane. Now that I've tried this, I don't want to stop. I have so many more ideas. . . ."

Suddenly there was a knock at the front door and a voice called through the screen, "Mother? Mother? Are you here?"

Clarissa groaned. "The posse found me," she muttered. "In here, Livvy," she said aloud.

Livvy walked in with Kent and Ray in tow. Her beautiful black eyes were flashing. Kent looked concerned and Ray had an amused grin playing around his lips, as if he were enjoying his sister's theatrics.

"What's the idea of that note, Mother? It isn't funny. We were worried about you running out like that. It will be dark soon and . . ."

"And my old blind eyes won't function properly, I'll

get lost on the way home, fall into a swamp and be eaten by an alligator? Well, Livvy, we don't have alligators here, so I suppose I'd have to be nibbled to death by bunny rabbits or carried into the trees by owls that make me sit on their eggs while they go hunting or . . ."

Jane covered her smile. Clarissa was very imaginative.

"Motherrrrr," Livvy protested.

Ray burst out laughing. "I told you not to run after her like she's a child, Liv. She's been here all her life, why are you getting so worked up about her living here now?"

"She's not as young as she used to be. . . ."

"But I'm not as old as I'm going to be either, honey." Clarissa put her arms around her daughter. "I know you feel guilty that you're way out west and I'm here by myself, but it's okay." She stepped back and eyed her beautiful daughter at arm's length. "I do declare, Livvy, that if I had to be bossed around by you every day, I'd be *much* older than I am right now."

Livvy's displeasure turned to distress. "But you're so alone out here."

"I have more friends than you can shake a stick at." Clarissa gestured at the three Howard women. "Here are some of them."

"But all you do is work. You need hobbies, something more."

"She has this." Jane pointed to the fan of sketches on the table.

"Yes, but . . ." Livvy did a double take as she looked at the pictures. Kent stepped nearer. Ray whistled.

"You didn't do these . . . did you? Are they Jane's?"

"I wish I could take credit for something so beautiful, Livvy, but these are your mom's."

"But when . . ."

"After she got home from the Good Apple," Louise said proudly. "While all of you thought she was resting."

"You are amazing, Clarissa," Alice chimed in. "Working all day and staying up all night to draw. Why, people *half your age* couldn't do that."

"You did these this weekend?" Kent gasped.

"After we went to bed?" Ray whistled again. "You don't need anyone taking care of you." He glanced at Livvy. "I think it's your children who need the help."

Livvy didn't speak. She moved forward as if in a trance to touch the delicate artwork. Her eyes blurred with tears as she reached out to touch one of the creatures Clarissa had so deftly drawn into the foliage. "Fairies."

When she looked up, the tears were running down her cheeks. "When I was little, Mom used to take me to Fairy Pond. We'd make up stories about the animals living there and imagined a community so tiny and fragile that we could only see glimpses of its inhabitants, the fairies."

"Remember the Butcher and the Baker fairies?" Clarissa prodded. "And the Preacher fairy who looked a lot like Pastor Howard?"

"And the Teacher fairy who never made her students stay after school to clean the blackboard." Livvy looked up, her eyes shining. "Mom and I solved a lot of problems at Fairy Pond. She'd tell me to practice talking to the Teacher fairy so I knew what to say when I had to apologize for misbehavior. And the Manners fairy—well, no book of etiquette had anything on her."

Livvy looked at her mother with so much love in her eyes that Jane wanted to put her hands to her heart.

"I'm sorry, Mom. I grew up and thought I had all the answers." She looked ashamed.

Clarissa opened her arms and Livvy flew into them.

"Now that that's settled," Ray said, sounding relieved, "we can . . ."

The screen door slammed.

"You do whatever you want, Zachary," Nancy's voice trembled with frustration. "Start 'Zachary's' restaurant. Cook a scallop, decorate it with pâté and call it gourmet, if you like. I'm more interested in real food. And a real life. I'm going to ask Clarissa if she'll hire me and if she will, I'm staying here."

Nancy flounced past the dining room and was startled to find it full of people. And Clarissa.

"Oh, hi, I didn't mean . . . it's not that you have to hire me . . . I was just going to ask . . ."

Zachary stomped after her to see to whom she was talking. His eyes widened.

"What's the problem here?" Kent asked. "What were you going to ask my mother?"

"I just wanted to know if she'd like an employee."

Nancy turned to glare at Zack. "I'm available."

"But I thought when we were working together at the Good Apple, Zack told me that you were going to start a nightspot," Livvy said. Her arm was still around her mother.

"That's what he's going to do. That's always been his dream, not mine." Nancy smiled through her tears. "I just want to run a little place like the Good Apple."

"Oh, for goodness sake," Clarissa muttered.

Louise was clucking her tongue like a mother hen, and Alice started murmuring, "Oh dear, oh dear, oh dear."

"Well, I could use a little help," Clarissa admitted, "because I found a new hobby I'd like to take up, but I won't hire a wife away from her husband, so I guess you can't count on me for a job."

"But . . ." Nancy looked devastated. She obviously had not planned any course beyond this one.

"Come on, Nance, we'll work this out. When I get my place started and it starts paying for itself, then we can find you something," Zack pleaded.

"Why can't we start *my* place first?"

"Oh, good grief," Livvy suddenly sputtered. "You two sound just like the kids on the playground of my school. Have you listened to yourselves? You're both being terribly childish. If you were my students, I'd make you sit down and write a compromise. What good is having your dreams realized if you don't have anyone to share them with? And since when did marriage become such a throwaway commodity?"

Nancy took a step back, her eyes wide. "But he said . . ."

"But she said . . ."

"That's it," Livvy pointed out calmly. "But what do 'we' say?"

Jane could see why Livvy was such a good teacher. She would not let any student get by with less than his or her best, if this showdown with the Colwins was any indication. It was a very odd scenario being played out at the inn, but Jane had no inclination to put a stop to it. In fact, she was relieved to have someone else asking the hard questions for a change.

" 'We' say we need to get a place where we can do *both* a supper club and a diner," Zack stammered. "But where would we go to find that?"

" 'Find' it?" Louise asked calmly. "Why don't you *create* it?"

Everyone turned to look at her.

"How would we do that?"

"You would have to buy a versatile building that could be used as a diner by day and a supper club at night. Something with either two stories or two large spaces with a kitchen in the middle," Livvy suggested, as if it were the simplest solution in the world.

"Or a bakery and supper club," Nancy said. "I've really enjoyed the work at the Good Apple."

Zack looked at Nancy, the idea taking hold in his mind. "It could have separate entrances but we'd be able to use the same kitchen. That's what's so expensive. Neither business would have to be big if we were running them simultaneously because we'd be open eighteen hours a day. It's a great idea."

"I suppose," Nancy said doubtfully, "but even one building is going to be expensive if it must be large enough for two businesses, isn't it?"

"Not if you can rent it inexpensively enough." Clarissa spoke calmly as well. "Maybe you could go into partnership with someone and add on a second eating area."

"How would that work?"

"Take the Good Apple, for example. If you left the bakery just like it is and built a supper club addition off the back, you could have your main entrance there. Homey in front, classy in back."

The entire room was silent as Clarissa's words sunk in.

"That's a great idea," Zack said. "But where are we going to find someone who wants to do that?"

"Seems like there'd be others besides me who'd consider it. I like the idea myself. If a young couple like you were to do that and let me stay on in the bakery to supervise and decorate cakes, why, I believe I'd be happy as a mouse in a cheese factory."

Livvy's eyes grew large at Clarissa's words.

"Yes, sir, then someone like me could do what she enjoys doing and leave the rest to someone else. And, since they'd be in partnership with this young couple, there would be some revenue coming in every month. Why, it sounds like a perfect deal to me."

"You mean you'd consider . . ." Zack began as

everyone in the room held their breaths.

Just then, Mr. Enrich came through the kitchen door holding a large spoon. His white chef's apron was spattered with spaghetti sauce.

"Dinner's done. Time for you to sit down and eat."

Chapter ❧ Twelve

Fish and visitors smell in three days.
—Benjamin Franklin

Mr. Enrich's eyes grew wide as he took in the crowded dining room.

Jane could practically hear him wondering where all these people had come from, calculating the amount of food on the stove and dividing it by the ten people present. The mathematics of it must have worked, because Mr. Enrich turned to her. "You haven't set the table yet."

Suddenly, everyone started to scurry. Clarissa and Livvy whisked the sketches off the table and propped them lovingly on the sideboard so everyone could look at them during supper.

Louise scooped a bowl of Swedish mints from the middle of the table; Alice whipped a tablecloth from a nearby drawer and snapped it into place.

Ray and Kent hustled for the extra chairs stationed around the room.

And Zack and Nancy stood in the middle of the melee crying and hugging.

Jane walked up to Mr. Enrich. "Do you have enough food?"

"I learned to cook in the Army. I'm not very good at cooking for any less than twenty-five. We should be fine." Then he frowned. "Except I forgot Caesar salad dressing. I remembered the anchovies but forgot the dressing."

"No problem," Jane said. "I have some in the refrigerator that I made this morning. I was planning on not making anything but salads for dinner for the rest of the week."

"Perfect." Mr. Enrich looked as pleased as one could be—one who was unaccustomed to smiling, that is.

The enormous tossed salad was rich with bite-sized romaine and crumbly croutons. Mr. Enrich had purchased loaves of Italian bread. He had heated them, then basted them with butter and garlic, and heated them again so that the tops glistened and the bread was chewy on the outside, soft and white on the inside.

He had also cut carrots, celery, broccoli and cauliflower, arranged them on a bed of lettuce and decorated them with radish roses and cherry tomatoes. He had found vegetable dip at the General Store and a crystal bowl to serve it in. There was a fresh fruit platter, sparkling water and the largest pot of spaghetti Jane had ever seen.

Mushrooms, beef, Italian sausage—the sauce had it all. After everyone had been served, Mr. Enrich went around the table with a chunk of fresh Parmesan and grated it for each guest.

When he grated the cheese over Zack's plate with a flourish, Zack turned to him and said, "If you ever decide you want to work in the restaurant business, I'll hire you. You'd be a great maitre d'."

Mr. Enrich, Jane noticed, scowled but flushed with pleasure.

When Mr. Enrich returned to the table at his place, Alice folded her hands and bowed her head. "Lord, we thank You for this marvelous gift of food and the cook who made it for us. Mr. Enrich has been a blessing and we thank You for bringing him into our lives as well as all the people at this table. Work Your will and let us experience the wisdom of Your ways. Amen."

When Jane raised her head, she realized that Mr. Enrich had tears running down his cheeks.

"You actually would consider something like that?" Zack asked, leaning forward. The Colwins and all the Cottrells were gathered around the table eating dessert and having a high-level planning meeting. Dessert, flaming cherries jubilee, had been a rousing success even though Louise feared the tablecloth would go up in flames and Alice eyed the chandelier for smoke smudges.

Jane, Alice, Louise and Mr. Enrich sat in a huddle in the corner of the room drinking coffee, too polite to pull up to the table and too curious to leave the room.

"If you and Nancy ran the Good Apple as it is," Zack went on enthusiastically, "and we managed to build an addition without shutting the kitchen down for too long?"

"And that way, our business wouldn't compete with that of the Coffee Shop," Nancy said happily. "I'd be happy to do what Clarissa's always done during the day and open the restaurant after the Coffee Shop closes for the night."

Clarissa nodded emphatically, liking the idea.

"Then," Zack said excitedly, "when that's done, we'll build Clarissa her own cake decorating room."

"My 'studio,'" Clarissa corrected impishly.

"And we can put in a glass wall so everyone can watch her work," Nancy finished.

Clarissa frowned. "Does that mean I have to start dressing up? I don't want to feel like I'm on television or anything."

Nancy laid a comforting hand on the older woman's arm. "You get to do exactly what you please from now on."

"*Humph.*" Clarissa eyed her daughter. "I can manage that."

Livvy had been alternately laughing and crying all evening. Laughing every time her mother came up with a new idea or a quick retort. And crying, Jane guessed, every time she thought about how little credit she had given Clarissa for being the clearheaded independent woman that she was.

"And when you're ready, or," Livvy corrected herself, "when you *feel* like it, you can come and stay with any of us."

Clarissa eyed her family. "Now that's what I like to hear. You could have put it that way in the first place."

"You're never going to quit teaching us lessons, are you, Mom?" Kent rubbed his mother's shoulder.

"Now's the time you could ask me what I'd like to do," Clarissa hinted.

"And that is?" Ray said.

"I'm looking forward to the idea of doing only cake decorating and helping these two get their feet on the ground. I'd love to visit each of you for a month or so out of the year. Maybe more, depending on how it goes with my new hobby." She gestured toward the pictures. "Jane thinks that if I had these made into note cards, they'd sell well here at the inn and probably around town. Wilhelm could supply gift cards in Time for Tea and Viola wouldn't say no to selling them at Nine Lives."

"So you'll be starting a new business," Alice exclaimed. "How exciting."

"I guess it isn't true that you can't teach an old dog new tricks," Clarissa commented. "This old dog still has plenty of tricks up her sleeve."

The others were laughing when Jane caught Louise staring at her intently.

"What is it, Louise?"

"When I get old, in twenty or thirty years, that is, I hope you do not try to do anything foolish with me."

" 'Foolish'? Maybe you should define that for me a little more fully."

"Telling me I cannot think for myself anymore, unless, of course, I am truly unable to do so or talking about me as if I were a helpless child."

"I thought they'd talk all night," Alice said after the Cottrells had left and Nancy and Zack had gone upstairs. "I've never seen such an excited group."

"With good reason." Louise cleared plates from the table. "By the way, has anyone seen Mr. Enrich in the last hour?"

"Is he in the kitchen?" Jane jumped to her feet. "I forgot all about him."

Mr. Enrich was buffing the butcher-block counter to a high gleam when Jane entered. Foamy warm water bubbled in the sink and the dishwasher door was open for the last of the dishes. Otherwise, the kitchen was immaculate.

"Wow. You're good. Zack was right. You'd be great in the restaurant business."

"Yeah? It sounds kind of fun. Maybe I could work with Zack. But, of course, we'd have to call the place 'Enrich's.' "

Both burst out laughing as Louise carried a tray of cups and saucers into the room.

"What are they doing here so late in the evening?" Alice wondered. She had stood to look out the window and had seen Ethel and Lloyd trotting down the driveway to the inn. Only the three sisters and Mr. Enrich remained on the first floor. Louise, Alice and Jane liked to have a quiet moment at the end of the day whenever they could to reflect and give thanks. Mr. Enrich, who was usually the first to disappear, seemed reluctant to do so tonight.

"They're probably still on 'reunion hours.' I bet those two were the last to leave every event they attended. I wouldn't be surprised if Lloyd swept the floor and Ethel turned out the lights before they left." Jane had her feet up, still enjoying her night off from the kitchen. "If nothing else, the reunion was memory-making for them."

"*Yoo-hoo!* Is anybody home?" As usual, Ethel did not wait for an answer but came right in, towing Lloyd with her.

They were both bursting with enthusiasm. Lloyd's pink cheeks were even ruddier than usual and Ethel's bottle-red hair was in surprisingly attractive disarray. Ethel was getting all the mileage she could from her corsage even though it looked more out of place than ever on the orange jacket and slacks set she wore.

"Our little town did itself proud!" Lloyd announced pompously. " 'Course I knew it would all along. I just came from the football field. I checked up on those Boy Scouts and they did a fine job picking up after the fireworks. Clean as a whistle, it was. I knew that they would be the best choice for a cleanup crew. You can't beat the Boy Scouts."

Jane marveled at the selective memories Lloyd and her aunt sometimes possessed. Before long, in Lloyd's memory, Sylvia would be demoted from the one who planned the reunion to the one who did her best to foul it up by not hiring the Boy Scouts for cleanup duty.

"We ran into Nellie," Ethel said. "She's pleased as

punch with the way things turned out for her. She sold every one of those 'Countywide Reunion' T-shirts she ordered, as well as so many gift items she could barely count. Even your jewelry went, Jane. Nellie ran out and needs some more."

"*Even* your jewelry?" Alice whispered into Jane's ear. "My my, the tourists must have been desperate for things to take home."

"Very funny, Alice. You know she tried to make that a compliment."

"She's not very good at it, is she?"

"Out of practice, that's all."

Lloyd waved his arm to catch Jane and Alice's attention. "And," he said with some amazement in his voice, "the rumor is that Joseph sold that ugly statue he's had in the antique shop since he opened it. Whoever bought it paid good money for it too. Can you imagine? For something so ugly?"

Jane tried to recall which of the statues in the antique shop might be billed as ugly. Joseph and his wife had excellent taste and chose wisely for their store. She had a hunch that Lloyd and Ethel dismissed the place only because much of what Joseph considered "antique" had been new and modern when they were young. It was, Jane thought, a little like the time she had visited the Smithsonian and found toys from the fifties and sixties on display behind protective glass.

"We stopped at the Coffee Shop for breakfast this morning," Ethel continued. "Hope said her feet are about to fall off from standing on them, but they had a steady stream of customers throughout the weekend. She wondered if we should have these reunions more often for all the business they brought to town."

Louise, Alice and Jane all sighed.

"But I have saved the best news for last," Ethel announced. She turned to Louise. "Have you talked to Viola?"

"Not in the past few hours. Why?"

"Because she earned so much from her sale of books that she's going to be able to fulfill a lifelong dream of hers."

"What's that?" Jane mentally explored the possibilities—an addition to the store for selling rare first editions? A basement where the popular fiction could be stored in an even *lower* spot at Nine Lives? Or perhaps a little boutique that sold only scarves and boas in every color under the sun?

"A rescue shelter for stray cats." Ethel looked enormously pleased with the announcement. "You know how much Viola loves cats, so she's going to convert that little house she owns on the south side of the fire hall for that purpose. It's practically kitty-corner from the store."

"'*Kitty*-corner?' How convenient." Jane could not resist.

Ethel, of course, did not catch the pun and rolled on with her story. "You know that she inherited that house from an old aunt and has been wondering what on earth to do with the place. Although it's very sweet from the outside, it needs a lot of interior work to be rental property and Viola's not made of money. But," Ethel said gleefully, "the cats won't care."

"Let me get this straight," Louise managed in a strangled voice. "Viola is going to fill her house with stray cats?"

Lloyd, who had been unusually silent until now, stepped in. "That was my first question too. Being the mayor, I didn't want anything strange or foolish happening in town, but Viola's got it all figured out. It's going to be a rescue and adoption center. She has promised to limit the number of cats and make sure that they're being adopted out to good homes nearly as fast as they come in. Why, Viola's goal is for every house in Acorn Hill to own a cat."

Jane glanced at Wendell, so relaxed that he appeared boneless on his pillow. "I've heard of worse things, I guess."

"And best of all," Lloyd said, "people who come to pick out a cat will do a little shopping here, maybe have pie and coffee and then leave." Lloyd loved it when people had reason to visit Acorn Hill but had no excuse to stay.

Wacky as it was, the idea was harmless and rather sweet, Jane decided. Besides, it would give Viola something to do other than trying to talk people out of buying the books of which she didn't approve.

"Indeed," Louise said to no one in particular.

Jane had no doubt her sister would be discussing the idea with Viola at the first opportunity.

"I don't know about the rest of you," Alice suddenly

announced, "but I'm exhausted and must go to bed. Sorry I can't stay up to visit, Aunt Ethel, Lloyd, but that car wash wore me out."

"Another big success," Lloyd said delightedly. "Only positive comments, and the kids set a lot of people's minds to thinking." He patted his shirt pocket. "I've been carrying around that little message of faith they handed out."

"Come, Lloyd," Ethel tugged on Lloyd's hand. "I want to stop in and see how Sylvia's doing, too. And these girls need to get their beauty sleep."

After the pair left, the three women collapsed into laughter.

" 'These *girls* need to get their *beauty sleep*'?" Alice wiped a tear of laughter from her eye. "Then I'd better get to bed right now and not get up till a week from Wednesday. I do love Aunt Ethel. She makes me feel so young."

Shortly it was only Jane and Mr. Enrich left downstairs. She eyed him speculatively. "I'm going to make a cup of herbal tea to take upstairs. Would you like one?"

Even though she had asked, she was surprised when he nodded and followed her to the kitchen.

"We all appreciated your supper very much," Jane said as she put water on to boil. "It was very generous of you to do that. And you even had enough for our unexpected guests."

"My pleasure—and it's you and your family that I appreciate."

"A mutual admiration society of sorts, then," Jane said as she put the steaming brew in front of him.

"I don't understand." Mr. Enrich looked genuinely mystified.

Jane gave a little huff of frustration. "Maybe that's the problem. You put people off because you don't believe you're likable."

"*Likable?* That's a word I haven't heard in a long time."

"You were likable tonight, serving dinner."

"It's different here. You people are very . . . accepting."

"And other places you've been are not?"

Mr. Enrich was silent so long that Jane began to grow uncomfortable. Maybe she had overstepped the limits.

When he spoke, there was heaviness in his words that wrenched at her heart. "This is the only place I've been in several years where I began to think it might be all right just to be myself."

Jane waited.

He looked at her and their gazes locked. "May I tell you something? I'll understand if you're tired and . . ."

"Tell away." She settled deeper in her chair.

"I made a complete mess of my marriage," he began softly. "It might not have been perfect to begin with, but I did nothing to help. I thought that a man had to be a good provider for his family. It really never occurred to me that financial support was only a fraction of what was expected of me.

"My wife was always angry when I was never home for meals or gatherings—sometimes I wasn't even home for holidays. I chased that almighty dollar as hard as I could and it still got away from me. That, and everything else."

He raked his fingers through his dark hair and Jane saw pain etched in his features. "When the baby came, my son Mitchell, I guess I thought she'd be entertained by him and would quit nagging me, but it only got worse. I missed the baby's first tooth, his first word, his first step, and I didn't understand why she was so furious about it. I was giving them what I thought I was suppose to give—debt-free living, nice clothes, food and shelter. And it was as if she hated me for it.

"Pretty soon we were so angry with each other that we just quit talking. I suppose Mitch was nine or ten by then. Sometimes he'd try to get us together as a 'family,' but my wife wasn't interested in being with me anymore. 'You go with your father,' she'd say." He uttered a bitter sound. "And I had little idea what to do with him when we were together. I got expensive tickets to football games and learned later that he liked hockey. I took him camping once as a surprise and it wasn't until the second night when I found him in tears that I discovered he hated camping. And what did I do? I scolded him about it. I told him that camping would help to make him a man."

Jane winced inwardly.

"You get the idea. I blew it completely, all the while

telling myself what a good provider I was. That's what my own father was, a provider. My mother was the one I went to for everything that was important to me." He looked at Jane with tortured eyes. "You'd have thought, with my own experience, that I would have figured out that I hadn't liked or respected my father because he was so absent and distant. I was determined to be a 'good' husband and father and proceeded to imitate him. I didn't really know any other way to be, I suppose, since my own dad was the only role model I'd ever had." Regret seemed to fill the air around him. "By the time my wife left me, Mitch was fourteen. We asked him who he wanted to stay with and he laughed. 'Mom, of course. I'm too young to live alone.'"

Mr. Enrich sunk deeper into his chair looking dispirited. "But it gets worse. That business I slaved for? It went belly-up during the technology tumble. I lost everything I had, even the house."

"Where have you been living?" Jane murmured.

"In a one-bedroom efficiency apartment over the offices from which I used to run my business. It is a constant reminder of my failure."

"Where are they now?" Jane asked softly. "Where is your family?"

"Pittsburgh."

"Did you go to see them?"

He looked at her disconsolately. "I was in Pittsburgh for two days before I came here. I'm ashamed to say I never talked to them." He trailed a spoon through his tea. "The first day I was there, I was parked across the street from their house when I saw my wife drive up. I was about to jump out of my car to meet her when I realized that she wasn't alone. There was a good-looking guy, younger than I, with her."

"A friend?"

"I thought so at first. Then he kissed her before they went inside. After that, I kept coming back to the house and parking out of sight so I could watch the house. It was as if I were compelled to be there. People came in and out. She had a party. I could see people laughing and talking inside. Nothing like that happened when we were living together. Or if it did, I wasn't there to see it. When I was home, I wanted it to be quiet because I'd been working hard all day."

"And your son?"

"I didn't see him at first. I thought maybe I could catch him separately. I don't know what good I thought it would do. He hasn't shown much interest in talking to me for three years, why should he start now?"

"Did you talk with him?"

"The first time I saw him leave the house, I followed him."

This was as truly pathetic a story as Jane could imagine—a man who didn't know how to communicate with his wife or son, a man who skulked around to spy on them instead.

"He went to the library," Mr. Enrich continued. "I thought that was perfect. I could find him there, and we'd have some privacy in which to talk." He took a deep breath. "But he wasn't alone there. He'd met several of his friends. I overheard them say they were working on a project together."

He looked at Jane. "Yes, I spied on him too."

"Did you talk to him anyway?"

"No. Not after what I overheard."

Jane tipped her head questioningly but didn't speak.

"I guess it serves me right for eavesdropping. They were all talking about going to a hockey game. One of the boys said to Mitch, 'You're going with us, aren't you?'

" 'Of course he's going with you,' one of his other friends retorted. 'Everyone knows how much he likes hockey.'

"Then Mitch said, 'Everyone but my father,' and went on to tell them about the football incident. I knew I couldn't seek Mitch out then—not in that group and probably not at all. I could hear in Mitch's voice that he had no interest in or feeling for me. I'd doused that like water douses a flame. So I slunk out of my place behind the wall of books and went back to my car."

He looked at Jane oddly. "And I came here." A disconcerting silence hung in the air between them. "To kill myself."

The bottom seemed to drop out of Jane's stomach. *Here? At the inn? A suicide? It was unthinkable.* She looked him in the eye and asked, "What stopped you?"

"Cowardice, at first. I didn't want to live, but I didn't want to die either. But I know I could have done it if it hadn't been for," he drew a breath, "that apple pie."

Jane's eyes widened.

"All the time I was working myself up to end my life, you and your sisters were being kind to me, acting as if I actually *mattered* to you."

"Of course you matter," Jane said softly, remembering how all three sisters had been nudged to pray for their cantankerous guest.

"I saw that. I didn't believe it at first. I was as cold and as self-pitying as a human could be, and you just kept on being kind." He looked at her intently. "I didn't plan to be here for more than a night or two. Then I planned to be . . . gone."

The thought sickened Jane.

"I tried to build myself up to it, but it was odd, I couldn't bear to turn my light off at night. The darkness terrified me. So I slept with every light in the room burning.

"And two days became three, and three turned into four." He spread his hands in helpless amazement. "Then you all began to treat me less like a guest and more like, I don't know, family. I haven't had much experience with 'family,' but I guessed perhaps that was how it felt."

He continued more quickly now, as if relieved to talk about it. "This might sound silly to you, but the cat would come up to me and wrap himself around my legs just when I was feeling my lowest. And he started sitting with me while I read, so I began taking all those books of your father's out of the library. They're amazing books, really. I've never read anything like them."

Jane was not surprised that Mr. Enrich had not taken the opportunity to read anything about biblical history or the Christian faith before.

"And you noticed that Belgian waffles are my favorite."

How simple the act, Jane thought, but how profound the effect.

"And that tea party. If you'd told me a week earlier that I'd be sitting at someone's table drinking tea with my pinkie finger in the air . . . well . . ."

Jane could have hugged Josie at that moment.

"The day I ran into you at the pond was one of my most difficult times. If you hadn't been there then, well, I just don't know.

"But it was when you agreed to let me sleep in the library . . ."

Jane drew a breath, afraid that they could have pushed him over the edge somehow.

". . . that I knew I didn't want to commit suicide. That's when I realized you thought of me as kin." A smile flashed on his features. What a difference that smile made.

"You could have kicked me out. You'd never promised me a room during the reunion. I had no reason to anticipate you'd let me stay. I'm ashamed to say it now, but I was testing you, expecting that I already knew the answer—that your concern hadn't been sincere. And then you said 'yes.' I couldn't believe my ears. You didn't brush me off. Instead, you accommodated me as best you could."

What a small thing to bring about such an enormous result.

"Crazy as it sounds, everything you and your sisters did after that seemed to snowball. You even let me help you with some chores for the reunion." He peered at her. "Do you know how long it's been since I've felt useful to anyone?

"And the vase . . ." His tone changed. "You saw that it mattered to me and you gave it to me," he snapped his fingers, "just like that."

He grew pensive. "My wife came back before our divorce and cleaned out our house." His voice was soft. "She took everything. *Everything*. Including a vase similar to yours that my mother had given to me. It had been my grandmother's. It was the one family memento that meant something to me." He shrugged. "I've never really blamed my ex-wife for that. If I didn't seem to care about anything but my work, I suppose she thought I wouldn't even remember something as insignificant as a cheap vase."

"I am so, so sorry," Jane said.

"It's okay, because that's when I was really sure that things were different here."

"Have you figured out what that difference is?" Jane asked.

"At first I thought maybe you three, being pastor's

daughters and all, just didn't know any better."

Jane, somber as she felt, couldn't help but smile. "Like we were too dumb to figure it out?"

Mr. Enrich reddened. "Something like that."

"I see."

"But it became obvious that none of you was 'dumb.' You're the savviest group I've ever met—professional, wise, realistic and unerringly kind. After a while I guess I decided to 'hang around' to see what you'd do next."

Hang around? *Live.*

"And?"

"It's like you're in partnership with God, or something." His brow furrowed. "I've seen you all praying at one time or another when you thought no one was watching. I've seen people pray in church, but alone? Just because they want to? And when no one's looking? What good is that, I asked myself, unless there really is Somebody up there to talk to?"

Suddenly he looked ashamed. "I'm sorry. I sound like all I do is spy on people."

"No apology necessary. I'm happy to be caught praying."

"Then the reunion rolled around, and it was as if I couldn't help myself. Joe invited me to go with him to some of the activities so he wouldn't be alone. I understand more than anyone how hard that can be, so I said 'yes.' "

He appeared pensive. "I'd forgotten about parties and music. I'd forgotten about fun."

Now he blushed outright. "I even volunteered to help with the ANGELs' car wash."

"Alice never told me."

"She doesn't know. Pastor Thompson was there."

"So how was it?"

Mr. Enrich looked puzzled again. "Odd. Very odd. Hymns were playing and all those young people were talking among themselves about why they believed in Jesus. Yet, at other times they laughed and joked and acted so normal."

"Christians can be normal," Jane commented wryly. "I know several who are."

"Pastor Thompson was watching me, and he came up to ask me if I wanted to talk to him."

Good for you, Ken. God works in mysterious ways.

"He said he'd been compelled to pray for me for days and that when that happens, he always liked to . . . how'd he say it? 'Follow through and see what God was up to now.' "

So God had the entire Acorn Hill team praying for Mr. Enrich, not just Grace Chapel Inn? Jane thought.

"I don't know what came over me, but I spilled it all, just like I did now."

"And what did he say?" Jane asked.

" 'God loves you.' Then he gave me the little Bible out of his pocket and some pamphlets. He said, 'I have a sense that you need time to read this and formulate some questions.' We've set up a time to meet tomorrow."

"Ahh."

"And then I decided to cook a meal for you and your family to show you how grateful I am. I believe you saved my life."

"We may have been instruments in the process," Jane said, "but we were guided by Someone much greater than ourselves. Someone who loves us all equally."

"Mind-boggling," Mr. Enrich muttered. "I've been reading that material Pastor Thompson gave me. I have lots of questions."

"I'll bet you do," Jane said with a smile. "But first I have one for you. Mr. Enrich, what is your first name?"

He smiled, really smiled, and a softness settled over him. "Warren. My name is Warren."

"Warren, would you pray with me?"

"I've been trying that on my own, but I'm not very good at it. I'm not sure I'm getting through."

"I know you are," Jane assured him. "God is always listening. It's we who don't pay proper attention."

After Mr. Enrich thanked Jane for any- and everything he could think of and said good night, he went upstairs to the bedroom he had reclaimed after the other guests had left. Before Jane put out the lights, she went into her father's library. What she wanted to do most was to scream for joy. Instead, out of courtesy for her sleeping sisters, she hugged her arms around herself in delight.

Oh, there was surely a party in heaven tonight.

Chapter 🍇 Thirteen

When you finish changing,
you're finished.
—Benjamin Franklin

"I've never seen such a big fuss in my life," Clarissa raised her voice to be heard over the hammering and sawing behind her bakery wall. "I've had to come in early to get my bread and cakes done before these workmen arrive. I can't bake anything but cookies during the day because they're already flat and there's no danger of them caving in."

A rat-a-tat-tat shook the building.

"Plumbers," she said sorrowfully. "Digging holes all over the place. This noise has been going on for weeks."

"Zack showed me the plans your architect drew up." Jane had a giant molasses cookie with white frosting on her plate and a bag of Good Apple pecan sticky buns at her side. "The restaurant and the kitchen will be wonderful."

"That Zack has some fine ideas. He's spent a lot of time thinking about this and he's got his opinions, all right."

"Most chefs do. I didn't settle down at the inn until I could rearrange everything in the cupboards. That put Louise and Alice in a spin for a few days."

"I'll bet."

"And, since we're on the topic of families, how is Livvy handling this new life of yours?"

Someone dropped something very heavy on the far side of the bakery and started yelling. Both women jumped, then laughed.

"It's taking her awhile to switch gears. She was so convinced that there was a certain birthday at which one becomes 'old' that letting go of the idea is difficult. Realizing that 'old' can also be an attitude is an eye-opener for my daughter. Frankly, it's been good for Livvy. She's had tunnel vision all her life, believing her way is the best way. Now she's working hard to release some of the control she thought she had to have over her family and her life."

Clarissa smiled mischievously and that endearing web of wrinkles creased her face. Jane thought of them as wisdom-wrinkles now. "My son-in-law called to say it was a welcome change. Oh, and I almost forgot, I have something to show you." Clarissa rose and bent to dig underneath the counter beneath the cash register. "Here it is."

She gave Jane a small square box made of recycled cardboard wrapped in a raffia bow. "Livvy said I should surprise you with this. It's something she had made up when she got home from Acorn Hill."

Carefully Jane untied the bow. "Is this for me?"

"And there's lots more where that came from."

Curious, Jane lifted the lid from the box and gave a tiny gasp. "Oh, Clarissa, how beautiful."

"There's more than one, so keep looking." Clarissa

251

leaned over Jane's shoulder and beamed. "They turned out pretty well, don't you think?"

Gently Jane laid her new gifts on the table. Note cards. Each made from one of Clarissa's sketches at Fairy Pond.

"Even the people who printed them asked if they could buy some, according to Livvy. She's been stopping at gift stores and little boutiques and says several people have already placed orders and asked for a wider selection." Clarissa looked baffled by the very idea. "Now what do you think of that?"

"I think it is fabulous. Is Livvy sending more?"

"Soon, I think."

"Then I'd like to buy two dozen boxes to sell at the inn. No, make that three."

"You don't have to baby me, Jane. I'll understand if you don't want any. They're just little old sketches of a puddle and some imaginary pixies."

"Just a puddle and some pixies? Don't sell yourself short. These are truly remarkable. What is your next subject?"

Her friend brightened. "I've decided to do a few more drawings of Ed. You do remember Ed, don't you?"

Jane recalled the elegant frog Clarissa had first sketched at the pond. "Of course. How could I forget such a handsome fellow?"

"Something you said that day at the pond put an idea in my head," Clarissa confessed. "You said that my pictures of Ed were as good as the illustrations in some children's books."

"I did, and they are."

"Well, I've been thinking about Ed a lot lately. I've decided I want to leave something special for my grandchildren, something they know I made especially for them. So," and Clarissa grinned broadly, "I'm going to start writing and illustrating books for them about Ed and Fairy Pond."

Jane clapped her hands together in delight. "Oh, what a wonderful idea. I hope you'll share them with more than your grandchildren."

"I guess that depends on how the stories turn out. I'm thinking that Ed is the mayor of a little town called Lily Pad Landing, which is populated by not only frogs and fairies but also by gossipy birds and talking flowers. Maybe there will even be a little girl in my story, a girl with golden curls and cornflower blue eyes. I'll call her Cornflower. She and Ed will have adventures together and learn so many things, all the things I want my grandchildren to know about growing up. Maybe Ed will go to school with Cornflower one day. . . ."

Jane burst out laughing. "Why are you in here when you could be sitting in the sun making sketches for your books?"

"Come to think about it, I don't know. Nancy has already learned every trick about baking that I ever had. I'm just waiting for the cake decorating area to be done so I can feel useful around here again. And," Clarissa said, waggling her eyebrows playfully, "I'd like to report that our young couple is getting along much better now. Why, they're so sweet to each other, I've thought about not ordering sugar anymore."

At that moment, Zack appeared in the front door covered with sawdust. "Hi, Jane. Boy, am I glad to see you. I wanted to ask you what length counters you'd recommend for . . ."

Jane and Zack, heads together, went in the back for a consultation, and Clarissa happily leaned back in her chair to watch Nancy package the buns the Coffee Shop had ordered.

In the kitchen, or what would be a kitchen when it was finished, Jane gasped at the progress that had been made. The bakery equipment had been set up temporarily in what had been Clarissa's storage room, so that the bakery could remain open while construction was being done. In what would be the expanded kitchen, the walls and ceiling were in, the floor had been tiled, and overhead lighting had been installed.

Through the window, Jane could see a large tarp covering a mound of something outside. "What's that?" she asked pointing at the tarp.

"Oh, Clarissa didn't tell you? That's all the kitchen equipment we bought. We had an incredible stroke of luck, thanks to June Carter," Zack replied. "She has an acquaintance who owned a small restaurant and decided to close it. Her partner wanted out of the business, and she didn't want to try to run it herself. So, she was selling everything. June told her about us, and she gave us first shot at buying her stuff."

"Wow, that *is* good luck. I know from the inn that equipment always costs more than you estimate."

"Yeah, in fact, if June hadn't been so thoughtful, we might have been in trouble. Nancy and I had put away a fair amount of money, but it was starting to look as if it wouldn't be enough for all the kitchen stuff, not to mention the furniture and dinnerware for the dining room."

"So what did you buy?"

"Nearly everything we needed. The restaurant hadn't been in business all that long so the ovens, refrigerators, freezers and all were in good shape. The pots and pans aren't all shiny and new, but they're serviceable and the china is simple but modern and fits into my plans for the dining-room décor. We're a little short on glassware, but I'm sure we can get some more that matches or comes close to what we bought."

Jane smiled and shook her head slowly. "When you and Nancy first came here, it seemed that your dreams would never materialize, and now. . ." She gave him a one-armed hug. "Now it seems that doors are being opened for you everywhere."

"Yep," he agreed with a smile. "I can't imagine all this happening in any other place than Acorn Hill. Though I am a city boy, the idea of going back to live in one has absolutely no appeal for me anymore."

"I'm glad to hear that, Zack. I know Nancy loves small-town life, but it's important that you are happy here as well."

Just then, near the doorway they heard a familiar

"Yoo hoo!" and saw the flash of scarlet that signaled Ethel's approach.

"Living in a small town can require some adjustment," Jane said with a chuckle, "and some patience."

Viola had taken on the cat rescue project with her typical vigor.

When Jane, who had just come out of the pharmacy, saw her toting an enormous bag of cat food out of the General Store, she ran down the street to Viola and offered to help her carry it to the shelter.

"Perhaps I should be buying smaller bags of food, but this is so much more economical," Viola panted.

"It is unless you give yourself a heart attack trying to get it home to the cats."

"Perhaps I could borrow Josie's wagon from now on. Oh dear, I do think I have to rest."

"Need some help, ladies?" Ned Arnold pulled up beside them on the corner of Chapel Road and Berry Lane. He jumped out, slung the enormous bag into the passenger seat of his car and drove it to Viola's door. The words *Cat Rescue Shelter* were printed on cardboard and thumbtacked to the siding.

"On your way home?" Viola wheezed as Ned carried the bag into the house and back to the kitchen.

"Until the Palmers' next vacation." He looked at her with concern. "Are you having difficulty catching your breath?"

"It's nothing. Nothing at all. It will pass." Viola walked with him to the front door. "Drive carefully."

Ned backed toward his car looking doubtful about leaving the woman gasping for breath. Jane, however, gave him a reassuring wave. She and Viola returned to the kitchen where they scooped the cat food into a large, clean, lidded garbage can to keep it dry. *There should not be any danger of rodents getting into it,* Jane thought. *No rodent in the world would be dumb enough to try to dine in a place like this one.*

Cats peered from every flat surface. A sleek ebony tom with huge golden eyes stared at her accusingly, as if she had tried to break and enter rather than to deliver dinner. Several tabbies, none of them as healthy as Wendell, were curled into fur puddles on the furniture. A dirty white cat with one blue eye and one brown nursed two equally dirty kittens.

"Pastor Ley brought in that poor mama cat. She's nearly starved to death and nursing her two kittens besides. I took the entire batch to the veterinarian in Potterston yesterday and made sure they were all healthy and gave them their shots. I have purchased vitamins for all." Viola looked pleased. "Now I have to begin the next level of my little project."

Jane glanced around the room. Though not fancy, it had soft, comfy-looking old furniture. It was nothing she would want at the inn, but it was perfect for cats. "And what is that?"

"Adopting them out, of course." Viola eyed her speculatively. "How do you think Wendell would react to a kitten in the house?"

"About as well as if I brought a Doberman home. Not well at all."

"He is rather spoiled," Viola agreed kindly. "My own cats aren't interested in having any more at my house either."

How, Jane wondered, *did she know? Had she asked them?*

Viola suddenly broke into an alarming fit of coughing.

"Are you coming down with something?"

"I certainly hope not. I don't have time to be sick. My cats need me. Here kitty, kitty." She picked up the nearest feline, buried her nose in its fur and came up coughing and wheezing so hard her eyes watered.

"If you hear of anyone who wants a cat, let me know, will you, Jane? In fact, let me know about people who don't have any pets. They might not realize that they want a cat. Let's see, I have a pen and paper around here somewhere. I think I'll start a list."

When Jane slipped out some moments later, she could hear Viola start hacking again. If she sounded the same tomorrow, Jane decided she would encourage Louise to insist that Viola see a doctor.

Ethel was at the inn when Jane arrived. She and Louise were looking over photos Lloyd had taken at the reunion.

"Come see these, dear," she greeted Jane. "I'm sending these to my children. There's a lovely photo of you in here." Ethel clucked like a broody hen. "I hadn't realized quite how thin you are, Jane. Perhaps you should join Lloyd and me at the Coffee Shop for blackberry pie later."

Jane grinned at Louise over Ethel's head. "Thanks, but I think I'll pass this time."

"Then I'll make you some of my peach tarts. They'll fatten you up in no time."

So I'm not the only one to blame for Lloyd's figure, Jane thought.

On her way up the stairs, she met Alice coming down with an armful of laundry. "Are things quieting down out there?" Alice inquired.

"It's actually rather boring. I'm like Josie, waiting for the next party to begin."

"I know what you mean." Alice leaned against the banister and looked pensive. "It was nice to have so much activity. But who knows what will turn up next around here?"

"Alice, is there something going around, a flu or cough?"

"Not much of anything that we've seen at the hospital. Why?"

"Because I just came from Viola's new shelter and she sounds terrible. Her throat gurgles and she coughs like she's going to detach her head from her body. I'm a little worried about her."

"Have you talked to Louise? She and Viola spend the most time together."

"Not yet. Aunt Ethel is here and I don't want the word to get around town that Viola is ill."

"I'm going to put this laundry in the washer, and

then I'll walk down to Nine Lives and see her for myself."

"Thanks, Alice. Now I can breathe a sigh of relief."

"Not so fast," Alice advised. "We don't know what's wrong with her yet."

After Jane had retrieved what she had wanted from her room, she came down the stairs and saw Lloyd coming up the front walk, Jane noticed that he looked a little hangdog as he walked up the sidewalk to the porch.

"Is Ethel here?" he inquired.

"Yes, she is. She's looking at the reunion photos in the parlor with Louise. Is there something wrong, Lloyd? You don't look very happy."

"Oh, it's nothing really. At least I don't think it is. I certainly hope it isn't. We don't need a problem or anything. I can't see that it would be much of a problem. Of course, but Ethel might have other ideas. . . ."

He would have kept on for a long time with this one-sided conversation if Jane hadn't broken in to ask, "What is this potential problem we're discussing?"

Lloyd looked alarmed. "Do you think it *will* be a problem?"

"Not yet. I have no idea what you're talking about."

Lloyd blushed all the way to his scalp. "It's just that I ran into Viola a few minutes ago . . . she's got a nasty cough, by the way . . . but somehow she managed to get me to agree to . . . Oh, I'll bet Ethel will be upset . . ."

"Let me guess. She got you to agree to adopt a cat."

Lloyd's shoulders slumped. "Yes. It happened so quickly that I hardly knew what hit me. First she was discussing my bachelor status and how quiet it must be in my house. The next thing you know, she had me agreeing that it was fairly quiet most of the time. Then, before I could tell her that sometimes I *liked* it that way, she got me to agree to take a cat home for company. When I think about it, I'm still not quite sure what happened. I must have been listening to that cough of hers and she caught me unawares."

Viola, Jane thought, could sell ice to an Eskimo.

"Do you like cats, Lloyd?"

"Yes. I suppose I do. I like Wendell very much."

"Would you mind taking care of one?"

"They can't be so hard, can they? Food, water, a warm dry bed and a litter box, I suppose. Not much to that."

"Would you pet a cat if you had one?"

Lloyd pondered that for a moment. "Yes. I certainly would. I think it would be calming to my nerves."

"Then it sounds like it's just fine that you agreed to adopt a cat."

"But Ethel . . ."

"It's your home, Lloyd. Shouldn't you get to decide whether you want a pet there or not?"

It appeared that that sort of independent thinking hadn't gone on for quite a while in Lloyd's head. He rolled the idea over in his mind. "Yes, yes, indeed." He squared his shoulders and raised his chin.

"Excuse me, Jane, I have to go in and tell your aunt that I adopted a cat."

A week later, Louise peeked into her sister's room and found Jane doing an uncomfortable looking calf-stretch. "Jane?"

"Yes?" She shook out her arms and legs and bounced a bit on her toes, ready to go for a run.

"Do you have a minute? I would like to discuss something with you."

"Sure. Come in."

"Alice is waiting downstairs. I would like the three of us to talk."

"Okay." Jane followed her sister downstairs. She could not remember the last time Louise had called for a "family conference."

Alice was sitting at the kitchen table looking every bit as somber as Louise.

"Alice and I have been visiting," Louise began, "and she's brought up something unsettling."

"Something to do with the inn?"

"No. It is to do with Viola. We feel that she may be quite ill."

"I know she has that cough, and it worried me too, but she's been running all over town convincing people they need a cat or two. She can't be too bad if she has the energy to do that."

"But have you *heard* her?"

"Well, not lately, but when I did she sounded like a baby with croup."

"It's been getting worse," Alice said. "I told Louise that I thought Viola should go to the hospital and have it checked out."

"And?"

"And she will not do it," Louise said. "The woman is stubborn. I am afraid she may have a lung infection or pneumonia and she keeps saying that it is 'nothing' and that 'it will pass.' She says she does not have time for doctors' appointments right now. She is all booked up with the vet."

"Ride with her on her next trip to Potterston and on the way home, convince her to stop at the urgent care center at the hospital," Jane suggested. "Obviously telling her to plan the appointment herself isn't working. Maybe she'll do it on impulse if you encourage her."

"It's a good idea," Alice added. "Especially if she starts coughing in front of the emergency room."

It was an uneasy day. Jane found herself looking at the clock every few minutes, wondering how things were going with Louise and Viola. They had gone together to deliver a kitten to its new family, and Louise left determined to have Viola see a doctor before they returned. None of this would have seemed so important if Alice had not reminded them that Viola's father had suffered from emphysema and died at a young age. Louise had not rested since.

Jane walked down to Sylvia's Buttons just to wear off a little energy. Sylvia was buried in new fabric.

"Fall fabrics are in, I see." Jane peered over a stack of bolts at her friend.

"It's amazing how quickly time passes. Seems like it was spring only yesterday."

"Are we getting old, Sylvia?"

A chuckle emanated from behind the heap. "I hope I get old the way Clarissa is. With Nancy and Zack there, it's like she's had a breath of fresh air. She's been getting more energy every day. Just knowing she doesn't *have* to do all the work makes her work harder."

It was true. Clarissa was blooming.

"You don't look very happy," Sylvia commented as she wedged a few more bolts of fabric onto her already over-stuffed shelves.

"Louise is going to try to get Viola to see the doctor in Potterston today about that cough."

"Good. I thought she was going to choke to death in church on Sunday. And she keeps saying 'oh, it's nothing,' like she just cleared her throat instead of turning her own face bright red."

"Alice thinks it might be serious. We've been praying for her."

"I think several have. As much as we might shake our heads and chuckle behind her back, Viola is an important part of this town. The way she's thrown herself into that rescue place is remarkable. They did an article about her in the *Acorn Nutshell*."

"She feels such affection for those animals and loves placing them in good homes. She's as determined to put a cat in every household as she is to keep best sellers out," Jane said.

Sylvia looked at Jane, compassion in her face. "Hang in there. Louise and Viola will be back soon. Sometimes waiting is the worst."

In this case, however, waiting was not the worst. The facts were.

Later that day Louise came into the inn leading a sobbing Viola by the arm. Jane leaped to her feet and pulled out a chair while Alice ran for iced tea. Viola's wails seemed to pierce the walls. They certainly pierced Jane's heart.

"Is it serious?" Alice ventured.

Viola increased the volume of her sobbing.

"Surely there's something that can be done about this. . . ."

Viola shook her head and wailed.

"Louise, what did the doctor say? You're frightening us."

Before Louise could convey the information, Viola hiccupped and imparted the doctor's awful diagnosis. "He thinks I'm allergic to cats."

"She has had cats around before this, of course," Louise told them later. "It is just that now she is around so many cats all at once. It seems a bit odd, but that is the only thing the doctor can imagine might be wrong with her. Otherwise, Viola is healthy as the proverbial horse."

"But the rescue center," Alice stammered.

"That's why she is so upset," Louise said. "She

loves what she is doing there. The doctor told her that she should either find someone to handle the cats for her or get rid of them. Viola is beside herself. What is she going to do?"

Chapter 🍇 Fourteen

Beware the hobby that eats.
—Benjamin Franklin

It was not only Viola who was upset by the turn of events, but also most of Acorn Hill.

"Who's going to take the rescue center over if Viola can't do it?" Lloyd fretted.

"And this happened just after that lovely article came out about the cat shelter in the *Acorn Nutshell* too," Ethel added in dismay.

"It was a great commentary on our little village," Lloyd said.

"That Viola may not be able to continue is a terrible shame."

"What are Lloyd and Ethel worried about?" Sylvia whispered to Jane as they sat in the Coffee Shop. They could not help overhearing the pair complaining to Hope as she waited on them in the next booth. "Viola's health or the city's reputation?"

"A little of both, I think. Now Viola may have to hire someone to take care of the cats, which could be costly. I'm not sure she can afford that. And," Jane added, "Louise thinks Viola is in denial over this whole thing. Viola still insists that she's not allergic to the cats. She goes to the shelter to care for them and comes out red-faced and sounding like she's coughing up a hairball herself."

"Ewww." Sylvia made a face.

"Louise also says that Viola has made appointments with other doctors and an allergist, hoping they'll tell her she's *not* allergic to cats. As if that's going to make a difference in how she feels."

"I feel sorry for her," Sylvia said. "She was so pleased with her idea. It seems a shame that she might have to close the place so soon."

"It 'casts a pall on our otherwise happy community,'" Jane intoned, quoting her sister Louise.

"Other than this, however, the entire county seems to be smiling since the reunion." Sylvia looked half pleased and half relieved. "It went well, didn't it?"

"Thanks to you and your committee. Everyone loved the idea of having community reunions plus a countywide gathering. So," Jane asked, "did you take notes for the next one?"

"There'll be no 'next one' as far as I'm concerned. Somebody else is going to have to throw the next big party."

"Someone already is."

"Really?" Sylvia perked up. "Who?"

"Nancy, Zack and Clarissa. They're having their grand opening soon. Clarissa said that they're waiting for the furniture to arrive. You'll read all about it in the *Acorn Nutshell*."

"That should be quite an event."

"Clarissa's children are returning for it. They told their mother that they wouldn't miss it for the world. She's shining with happiness. And," Jane took a deep breath, "Warren Enrich called last night."

Sylvia's eyebrow arched with surprise. Jane had told her Mr. Enrich's story. "No kidding? What did he have to say?"

"He wants to come back for the grand opening. He says he feels 'connected' here and wants to see his friends again."

"Remarkable. From a man who came here to end his life."

"He also said he was going to attempt to contact his son."

"I hope it works out for him," Sylvia said.

So do I, Jane thought. *More than you can imagine.*

Several weeks later, as she worked in the garden, Jane heard a voice call, "Look who's here." Wiping her hands on the back of her jeans—a habit Ethel called "deplorable"—Jane walked to the front porch where Clarissa and Livvy were standing. "Welcome, Livvy. How nice to see you." Jane gestured toward the wicker porch chairs. "Can you sit for a minute?"

"We've got nothing to do but sit," Clarissa said. "Nancy and Zack kicked me out of my own place of business. Said I needed to be home visiting with my daughter."

"What do you think of that, Livvy?" Jane asked.

"Music to my ears. I can't help worrying about Mom even if she insists she's fine, so knowing that those two are making sure she gets a break is a real relief for me." Livvy smiled tenderly at her mother. "And now that I'm not nagging her about it, she's actually taking time off."

"Are you saying that all of your stubbornness didn't come from your father's side of the family after all?" Jane asked.

Both Livvy and Clarissa burst out laughing.

"The child was doomed to be contrary from the start," Clarissa admitted.

Livvy took her mother's hand and gave it a squeeze—quite a difference from the first time Jane had seen them together during the reunion weekend.

"Are you ready for the grand opening this evening?"

"Ready as I'll ever be. Ray and Kent are down at Zachary's helping out. Livvy made me go to Nellie's and buy a new dress. I'll be gussied up like a Thanksgiving turkey tonight."

"Good. We only have one guest this evening and he'll be coming with us to the party. Warren Enrich said he'd be here before five."

"Pretty nice of him to travel all this way for us."

"He says he's happy to have such a special place to go."

"Well, we're all happy as ducks in water then, except, of course, poor Viola."

"Have you talked to her today?"

"She came in for doughnuts early this morning. Said

269

she was on her way to another doctor. She's still looking for someone who will tell her she's not allergic to cats. The woman is persistent, no doubt about that."

Well, Jane thought after the Cottrells had left, *at least* most *of the people at the party would be happy.*

"Are you coming or not?" Louise asked at five minutes to six.

"I'm just writing a note for Warren Enrich telling him to come to the restaurant when he gets here."

"I thought he said he would be here by now."

"Something must have held him up. I hope he didn't have car trouble."

"Well, he knows the way. We should get going."

When they arrived at the restaurant, Alice glanced wide-eyed around the room. "Oh my."

"Indeed," Louise intoned.

Even Jane was surprised. She had been here several times a week during the construction of the dining room, but this was the first time that she had seen it as it was supposed to be. The walls were painted a creamy white. On them hung original art that was illuminated by small halogen spotlights. Many of the works were Jane's, some were Sylvia's quilt art and the rest were done by Clarissa. In fact, several people, including Ethel, Lloyd, the Humberts and Rev. Thompson, were gathered at the head of the room beneath a large painting in an ornate frame.

"Look," Alice said happily, "Clarissa's fairies."

It had been quite a project to help Clarissa turn her

small sketch into a full-fledged painting, but size only made the picture more delightful. Jane noticed that people were beginning to discover the artwork within the artwork and were trying to count how many pixies Clarissa had hidden in the picture.

In the softly lit room, the crisp white linen contrasted with the thick wine-colored carpet and the brushed steel chairs upholstered in gray velour. Silver candles in crystal holders and exotic, brilliant-colored fresh flowers decorated every table. At each place was a brushed steel charger that held a service plate decorated with one of Clarissa's scenes from Fairy Pond. These had been a surprise gift to the restaurant from Livvy.

Waiters in white shirts, black ties and black trousers passed the first course. They offered petite chevre tarts, miniature lamb kabobs, tiny meatballs in brandied apricot sauce and flutes of bubbling champagne. According to Alice, competition to work at the new nightspot had been keen among the young men in the area. Zack and Nancy had put them through an intense training program. Clearly the program had been effective, for the waiters were moving expertly through the crowded room making sure everyone was served.

"I simply can't believe it," Vera whispered to Alice after being served by an impeccably groomed young waiter. "That was Billy Hull. I had him in fifth grade. He always had his shirttails out. He'd spill his lunch on himself nearly every day, and now look at him."

Alice smiled. She, too, remembered Billy as a sweet but clumsy boy. "Yes, he looks like a Hollywood version of a waiter."

Ray and Kent Cottrell were acting as hosts along with Nancy and Zack while Clarissa, looking lovely in her new dress, held Livvy's hand and greeted her friends as they came through the doors.

Jane walked across the room to give her a hug.

"It can't get much better than this, can it, Jane?" Clarissa beamed. "I'm a blessed woman. Frankly, I've spent most of the day just saying 'thanks, Lord' as the sweet, God-given gifts in my life come by. Livvy, Kent, Ray, Nancy, Zack, you . . . and of course there's new life for both me and the Good Apple."

"God is awesome," Jane agreed. "In fact . . ." her voice trailed away.

A good-looking dark-haired man in a navy blazer and gray slacks strode across the room to where Jane was standing. In his wake followed a younger man of similar coloring and a stocky build. Although the younger man was quite serious, the older wore a wide smile.

"Warren?" Jane was afraid her eyes might be deceiving her. "Mr. Enrich?"

"Hello, Jane. Sorry we're late. Hello, Clarissa. Congratulations on your new venture."

"Mighty nice of you to come," Clarissa said.

Before they could chat, Sylvia Songer and Craig Tracy walked up to Clarissa to greet her. Jane and Mr. Enrich stepped aside.

"It *is* you. You look so different, so happy."

Mr. Enrich's dark eyes twinkled and Jane observed that he looked ten years younger than when he had first stayed with them at the inn.

"I *am* happy." Mr. Enrich turned to the young man standing behind him. "Mitch, I'd like you to meet Jane. Jane, this is my son Mitchell."

Now it was Jane's turn to be surprised.

"Mitch and I have been getting together occasionally, just to talk. When I told him I was coming for the grand opening, he decided to ride along so we could get to know each other again. I called Zack and he told me that it was fine to bring him."

"Welcome to Acorn Hill." Jane extended her hand.

"Hi," Mitch said as he took her hand shyly.

Another man of few words, she thought.

"Jane, good things have started to happen to me. One of my former clients approached me with a job. You know, I always thought that working for myself was the only way to go, but I really like being an employee. Oh, I work hard, but when I leave the office, I leave my work there. Mitch has seen the change in me," Mr. Enrich said. "I told him that I learned a lot when I was here and that I'd like to introduce him to some of the people who made a difference in my life. I've been telling him a little about my new relationship with God, too."

Mr. Enrich, Jane could tell, was hopeful. It had taken a long time to ruin the connection with his son, but at least he was getting a chance to try to mend it.

Suddenly there was the sound of a Spanish-accented voice from behind them and Joe Morales greeted his friend with pleasure, pounding him heartily on the back. "Mr. Enrich, you've come back. How is my amigo? I'm working here part-time now. Mr. Fred says that if I don't quit accepting jobs I'm going to be the richest man in Acorn Hill." Joe's laughter was musical. "But I don't need more money. I'm already the happiest man here."

"I'm afraid that you will have to share that title with me," Mr. Enrich replied.

It was nice for a change, Jane thought, *to have that kind of contest going on.*

Soon the guests were asked to be seated and Rev. Thompson offered grace. The salad course—butter lettuce with slices of ripe pears, crumbled blue cheese and toasted pine nuts—was being served when Louise leaned toward Jane. "I am getting worried about Viola. It is not like her to be late."

"Sylvia told me she was going to another doctor today. Maybe she was delayed there."

"I wish she would just accept the fact that she cannot run the shelter. Apparently a cat or two is fine, but twenty . . ."

At that moment Viola appeared in the doorway. She was smiling widely and seemed to be full of energy.

Louise rose and went over to her. "We saved a spot for you. Come sit down. How are you feeling?"

"I have never in my life felt better. I am fit as a fiddle."

"You are?" Louise tried to hide her surprise. "Well, let us go over to our table so you can tell all of us about it. I thought you were going to see a doctor today. You must have had good news."

When they were seated Viola greeted the others, then announced, "I found a competent doctor, finally. One who didn't just tell me to get rid of my cats. It took some research, but I finally discovered a *brilliant* doctor."

"But your allergy . . . it cannot have disappeared just like that," Louise said.

"Oh, no, my allergy is fully present and accounted for," Viola said with satisfaction.

"Then what are you so happy about?" Jane asked.

"Because my new doctor found out what I am really allergic to . . . *kitty litter.*"

Every head at the table swiveled to look at her.

"But you have always used kitty litter for your own cats, Viola," Alice said.

"Yes, of course, but at home I use unscented, dust free, top-of-the-line kitty litter. For the shelter, I've been buying whatever is cheapest on the shelves to save money. I'm not allergic to cats at all. I'm allergic to dusty scented litter. Isn't that wonderful?"

"So you don't have to get rid of the cats? Just change the brand of litter?" Jane made sure she was hearing this correctly.

"That's all there is to it. In fact, my new allergist is a cat lover himself. He liked my idea of a rescue shelter so much that he volunteered to donate two hundred pounds of scent-free, dust-free litter to the cause. Now what do you think about that?"

Jane could not remember when she had been so happy to discuss kitty litter.

Conversation ebbed as everyone concentrated on the entreé. Zack had poached wild salmon, topped it with *duxelles* and then wrapped it in puff pastry. The result was a golden flaky mound that sat on each plate surrounded by a creamy mushroom sauce. Accompanying the salmon were thin French green beans tied into bundles with strips of cooked red pepper.

As the waiters cleared the tables for dessert, Zack rapped a spoon against a crystal goblet to get the room's attention. Nancy stood at his side and Clarissa next to her.

Zack, who had been so bold and confident about this restaurant suddenly looked shy. "The three of us have so many people here to thank, that it might take all evening and, if you'll bear with us, we would like to do it individually. But Clarissa told me I had to get my priorities straight and do first things first."

He grinned boyishly. "So before I tell you how much it means to us to be a part of this community and to be so welcomed into your lives and into the community of Acorn Hill and, of course, into Clarissa's own business, I have one small announcement to make."

"Very small," Nancy said. Her eyes glistened with happiness.

"Nancy and I want you, all of you, to be the first to

know—after Clarissa, of course—that there will be a new little Colwin apprenticing at Zachary's early next spring."

A rustle of excitement ran through the crowd.

"We are so very happy because we can't think of a better place to raise our new family."

Jane leaned back in her chair as the applause began. Zack was one hundred percent right. There really was no better place to live.

"God is good," Louise murmured.

"The very best," Jane said as she started clapping.

Jane's Apple Pie

Filling

1¼ cups sugar
3 tablespoons flour
1 teaspoon cinnamon
¼ teaspoon nutmeg
¼ teaspoon salt
6 cups peeled, cored and thinly sliced tart cooking
  apples (about 2 pounds)
2 tablespoons butter
1 tablespoon lemon juice
Milk
Additional sugar

Prepare crust and line nine-inch pie plate with pastry.
Combine sugar, flour, cinnamon, nutmeg and salt.
Carefully mix into apples to coat fruit. Arrange apple
slices in prepared pie shell, mounding them slightly in
center. Dot with butter and sprinkle with lemon juice.
Top with crust and flute edges. Brush top lightly with
milk and sprinkle with a small amount of sugar. Bake
in four hundred-degree oven for sixty minutes; cover
edges of crust with foil if they brown too quickly.
Cool on rack. Serve warm or cold, plain or with
vanilla ice cream.

Pastry for 9-inch
Double Crust Pie

2 cups flour
1 teaspoon salt
¾ cup butter at room temperature
5 to 6 tablespoons very cold water

Sift flour and salt into bowl. Cut in butter with pastry blender or two knives until mixture resembles coarse cornmeal. Sprinkle water gradually over dry ingredients, mixing at the same time with fork until dough holds together and leaves sides of the bowl. Divide in half and shape into balls. Wrap in plastic wrap or waxed paper, and let stand at room temperature for five minutes.

On a lightly floured cloth or board, roll out one ball into circle 10¼ inches in diameter and ⅛ inch thick. Fit pastry into pie pan. Pour filling into shell.

Roll out the remaining dough into circle ten inches in diameter and ½ inch thick. Cut steam vents in center. Moisten the edges of the lower crust, cover with top crust and press edges together. Fold edges under and flute.

Center Point Publishing
600 Brooks Road ● PO Box 1
Thorndike ME 04986-0001 USA

(207) 568-3717

US & Canada:
1 800 929-9108
www.centerpointlargeprint.com